SCANDAL AT THE BELMONT

BOOK 2

THE GILDED SECRETS SERIES

DAN WALSH

BAINBRIDGE PRESS

COPYRIGHT INFO

Scandal At The Belmont

Bainbridge Press

Editor - Cindi Walsh

ISBN: 979-8-218-77639-8

Cover design by Bainbridge Press

Cover photo Design: Dan Walsh

Using Edited AI Image from MS Bing Free Image Creator

Printed in the United States of America

1

July 31st, 1914
Gramercy Park, New York City

Years later, when Charles Bennington looked back on this moment, he had the oddest thought: Given the fact that nothing in life ever goes as planned, why do we go on planning out our lives as if it matters? As if we had the slightest control of the present or the future?

What began as the most routine of Saturdays—breakfast together with Lily's parents and Cedric at the family manse—would, by the end of the day, unleash a series of events that reset the direction of all their lives in a most disturbing way.

But there was absolutely no indication of this as Charles turned off Fifth Avenue into the first blocks of Gramercy Park. It was a bright and beautiful summer morning. Flowers in the gardens were blooming. Birds were singing in the trees. Charles was sitting next to the great love of his life. His ice-making business was booming.

For these brief shining moments, he hadn't a care in the world.

The only downside to their Saturday morning routine was the dress code. The Whitakers still honored the tradition of the elite to "dress for breakfast." True, it wasn't as elegant and refined as the dress code for dinner, but still, Charles found their outfits far too uncomfortable and confining, especially for a warm summer morning.

Nevertheless, now parked outside the Whitaker home, as he opened the car door for Lily he had no complaints. She looked absolutely stunning. Of course, gazing on her beauty had a similar effect on Charles regardless of what she wore.

"I'm so looking forward to this," she said, as he led her to the sidewalk. "Mother told me on the telephone yesterday she'd asked the chef to fix Eggs Benedict and pancakes with fresh maple syrup. It's been over a month since we've had that for breakfast."

Charles laughed. Lily did so enjoy a good breakfast. Oddly, it never seemed to show up on her waistline. For his part, Charles would be more content with just a cup of coffee, cream, and a little sugar. But he knew he'd be expected to at least make some effort with the Eggs Benedict, if he wanted to stay in the good graces of his mother-in-law, Millicent.

They made it up the steps as the front door opened. "Welcome, Mr. and Mrs. Bennington," Quentin, the family butler said. "Everyone is already seated out on the veranda."

"Thanks Quentin." Charles handed him his hat and walking stick. "No need to lead us. We know the way. Go and enjoy your breakfast. If anyone needs anything, Lily or I will fetch it for them."

He smiled. "Thank you, sir. I might do just that."

Charles and Lily headed toward the veranda. Charles releasing Quentin from serving the family at breakfast had become a common practice on Saturday mornings, as well. In the months after their marriage two years ago, Charles had observed Quentin standing in the corner during the family breakfast. He just stood there while they ate and talked, paying him no mind. Unless someone needed a refill on their coffee, and he would quickly respond. Then back to the corner.

Finally, on one occasion Charles had asked Lily about this. He was somewhat surprised she hadn't really noticed. Apparently, that's what she'd always experienced. Fortunately, when Charles explained how much it bothered him, she quickly relented and agreed...either one of them were quite up to the task of refilling the family's empty coffee cups.

It was almost comical the following week, observing

the looks on Lily's mother's face when Charles first intervened. He saw Lily's father's coffee cup was empty, stood up, and said, "That's all right, Quentin. I'll take care of it. Why don't you go downstairs and enjoy your own breakfast." He walked over to the silver coffee pot and brought it back to the table. Quentin thanked him and headed for the hallway. As Charles refilled the cup, he noticed both her father and Cedric smiling widely, and both staring at her mother. Millicent's face almost fuming at the indignity of the moment.

But she held her peace, inhaled deeply, and looked away. Before Charles went back to his seat, he'd asked, "Anyone else care for a refill?"

"Yes, Charles," Cedric said. "While you're up, I could use a bit more."

When he'd gotten back to his seat, Lily had rewarded him with a firm but gentle hand squeeze under the table.

A small but significant victory.

Just now, when Charles and Lily walked into the veranda, he saw a silver dome over their plates to keep the food warm. He walked right over to the coffee service tray and picked up the pot. Lily had already taken her seat. He filled both their cups and was about to ask her father and Cedric if they'd like a refill. But he'd have to interrupt a fairly lively conversation they were engaged in about the goings-on in Europe.

Nigel Whitaker was holding up the morning edition of the newspaper, showing it to Cedric. Charles could see the headline in big bold letters:

GERMANY IN STATE OF WAR
(in Slightly Smaller Letters)
OUTLOOK IS HOPELESS; ALL EUROPE
MASSING FOR CONFLICT

CHARLES COULD ALSO SEE a large photograph of soldiers gathering together in a street and a second photograph of an officer sitting on a horse.

"I knew this would happen," Nigel said. "The fools, I can't believe they've gone and done it."

Charles had been paying attention to these events in the newspapers, too. It was hard not to. The growing conflict in Europe dominated the headlines for the past month.

"It's all the chaps at school are talking about," Cedric said. "They're convinced America will be forced to choose sides. And when that happens, we'll all be called into the fight."

Lily had just uncovered her food and took hold of her knife and fork. "Father, you don't think that's going to happen, do you?"

"Oh, Nigel," her mother said, "tell us it isn't so."

Still holding the newspaper, he set it down on the table. "No, of course not." He looked at Cedric. "President Wilson would never allow that and the Congress would never support it. Please don't bring up such a matter again, Cedric. At least not at the table. If you want to discuss it further, wait till we are in the study." He looked at his wife and Lily. "Don't upset yourselves about this. I've been following this closely, and I assure you, this is strictly a European matter. The US will not be drawn into such a war. I guarantee it."

"If you say so, Father," Cedric said.

Charles had just finished adding cream and sugar to his coffee. "For what it's worth, I agree with you, sir. I've also been reading the newspapers for the last month. Whenever we meet, all my clients are talking about it, too. It's the general consensus this is a European matter, and that the president would never get us involved. But some have concerns about how it will affect our economy. If it grows to be as large as it's promising to be."

"I agree with your clients on that," Nigel said. "Judging by these headlines, this could be the biggest war any of us have seen in our lifetimes. It's bound to have an impact on our economy here, given we're a port city."

With that, Cedric took the napkin from his lap, wiped his mouth, and stood. "I have to run. Please excuse me. I'm meeting Reggie down at the hotel gym for a morning workout. The basketball coach at NYU is getting us together next week. We decided we better start getting in shape."

"I thought basketball season didn't start until September," Charles said.

"You're right," Cedric said. "But last year, three of our starting team graduated. He wants to start evaluating us in August, see who'll be worthy to take their spots."

"You didn't finish your breakfast," his mother said.

"I had enough. Really, I've got to go. I'll be back in a few hours."

After he left, the breakfast chatter continued, always in between fresh bites, chewing, and the swallowing of food. Of course, no one dared utter a word with so much as a morsel of food in their mouths. Charles and Nigel discussed all the possible scenarios that might unfold, given the horrendous headlines in the newspaper. Lily and her mother chatted about the details surrounding their upcoming move. She and Charles would still be living at The Dakota but moving into one of the larger apartments two floors up.

THIS WENT on for about forty-five minutes until the telephone rang. The nearest one was on a side table in the foyer. A few moments later, Quentin appeared in the doorway, his face showing grave concern. "Sorry to disturb you, Mr. Whitaker, but it's Cedric on the phone. It must be something serious. He seemed quite upset and pleaded with me to get you right away."

Nigel stood, then Charles, then Lily. All three headed for the foyer, Nigel leading the way. He picked up the receiver. "Cedric, I'm here. What's the matter, son?"

Charles and Lily stood close enough to hear him yelling on the other end. Sounded like he was crying.

"Father, I don't know what to do. I don't know what happened, but when I got to the gym, as I came into the locker room, I heard some men yelling. Then I heard a strange noise, followed by a loud thump. I ran inside calling out Reggie's name, but he didn't answer. I just now found him. Lying on the floor. Father, it's awful. I'm certain he's dead. There's a pool of blood gathering under his head. And his eyes, they're wide open but he's not blinking, and he isn't moving. I don't know what to do."

2

The look on Nigel's face probably matched the shock on both Charles's and Lily's faces. He quickly glanced at them.

"We heard," Charles said. Lily nodded.

"Are you alone?" Nigel said. "You said you heard men arguing. Are they still there? Can you tell?"

"I think they've gone," Cedric said.

"So, you're safe."

"I think so. As I came upon Reggie, I thought I heard the back door slam shut. And I don't hear any other sounds besides me talking to you. But Father, whoever they are, they must be the ones who killed him. There's nobody else here. That's why we wanted to come first thing this morning, before other people started showing up."

"Where are you now?"

"I'm using the telephone by the sign-up desk. Just a

few aisles away from Reggie's body. I can see his legs from here."

Charles watched Nigel pull his pocket watch from his vest. "So, Singleton, the gym manager, he's not there, either? He should be."

"No, he's not. But you're right. He's usually here when we come in. Should I call the police?"

"Well, yes, I suppose so. We'll have to. But maybe you should find Mr. Keller first, the hotel security chief. He should be somewhere in the lobby area. Tell him what happened and bring him down to where the body is. Then call the police. Or better yet, have him do it."

"Okay, I will. But Father, there's something I don't understand. About Reggie. I didn't hear a gunshot. I'm sure if I did, half the people in the lobby would have, too. But there's a very clear hole in his forehead."

Nigel paused. "I don't know what to tell you, son."

Charles had a thought. He gestured to his father-in-law, "May I?" pointing to the receiver.

"Certainly." Nigel handed it to Charles.

"Cedric, this is Charles. Listen, you need to move quickly when fetching the security chief. Do you have any way of locking the gym door?"

"No, I don't have a key. Singleton takes care of that, usually."

"I understand. Then perhaps get one of the bellhops in the lobby to stand by the stairway door. Don't tell him why, but insist he not let anyone through that door until you return with the security chief. The police would be very upset if people start trampling through the crime scene."

"Okay, I can do that," Cedric said. "Are you and Father coming?"

"Yes, soon as we can. Make sure you don't touch anything, either. That's important."

Charles handed the receiver back to Nigel. He knew these things about the police after they'd handled some break-ins at his ice company last year.

"Cedric, it's Father again. Do the things Charles said. Then sit in one of the benches in the locker room until we arrive."

"I will. But please hurry. What if the police get here before you do?"

"They won't. Just sit tight."

NIGEL HUNG UP THE PHONE. By then his wife had joined them in the foyer, a look of horror on her face. "What's happened? What's going on? Is Cedric all right? Is he safe?"

Nigel walked past Charles and Lily and put his arm around her shoulder. "I believe Cedric's safe. At least it seems that way. I don't know if you heard the first part. Something terrible has happened. When Cedric got to the hotel gym to meet his friend, he heard some men arguing. A few moments later, he found his friend Reggie dead on the locker room floor. Apparently, from a gunshot wound."

"Oh, my Lord," she said, almost stumbling backwards.

"You must go down there right away and bring him home. Bring my little boy home."

Nigel looked at Quentin standing by the doorway. "Have the driver bring the car around immediately."

"Certainly, sir."

"Mr. Whitaker," Charles said, "may I suggest you and I drive there in my car. It's right out there by the curb. We can get there in no time."

"Yes, let's do that."

"Right." He leaned over and gave Lily a kiss. "We'll be back soon, love."

"Call me as soon as you know something."

"I will."

The two men hurried toward the front door.

Charles and Nigel rushed down the front steps and stopped at Charles's car. For a moment, Charles wasn't sure what to do. Nigel was used to the chauffeur holding open the back door until he got in. Should he do that? How odd would that be, driving on the road with his father-in-law in the backseat?

Nigel seemed to pick up on Charles's dilemma. "Charles, get in the driver's seat. I'm fine sitting next to you."

"Of course, sir."

"And would you mind not calling me *sir*? I've been meaning to talk to about this. Now's as good a time as any."

Charles got in and turned on the car, as Nigel sat beside him.

"You may call me Nigel, if you prefer. But *sir* or *Mr. Whitaker*, by this time, I think should be out of the question."

Which brought up something Charles never had the nerve to consider discussing. "How would you feel about me calling you...*Father*? Lily keeps wanting me to do that. Somehow, it never felt quite—"

"I'd be honored, Charles. I already think of you as a son regardless of what you call me."

Charles smiled as he drove the car away from the curb. Hearing this touched him deeply. "Thank you, sir. I mean, Father." The words felt utterly strange as they left his lips.

"See, that wasn't so hard," Nigel said. He looked around, noticed the speed Charles was driving. "I don't suppose you'd mind breaking the speed limit this morning? I'd like to get to the hotel as soon as possible."

Charles instantly pressed the gas pedal. "I'd be happy to."

"If you get ticketed by the police, I'll happily pay the fine."

AFTER HANGING UP THE PHONE, Cedric was still trembling inside. The closest he'd ever felt to feeling this afraid was right after the car accident two years ago that put him in the hospital. He stopped and listened again to make sure he really was still alone in the gym. Not hearing a sound, he inched closer to his friend Reggie's body.

This time when he saw it, he was more aware of the sudden reality of losing a close friend. How could this happen? Why would anyone want to kill Reggie? Of all the friends he'd met attending NYU the past two years, Reggie was by far the nicest guy. Well-liked by everyone. Great sense of humor. He never seemed to resent Cedric when the coach picked him over Reggie as the first-string point guard for the team. Every game, he'd sit happily on the bench cheering him on, yelling out encouragement whenever Cedric scored a point or made a great play.

Reggie was the one who introduced Cedric to Amelia, the young reddish haired girl Cedric was sure he was falling in love with. He stood now, looking down at his body as a wave of sorrow swept over him. "Reggie," he whispered. Then he sighed. "This is so awful. I can't believe you're gone."

Then he remembered the urgency in his father's voice. He needed to get a move on it. *Don't touch anything,* Charles had said. He needed to go get Mr. Keller, the security chief. Then Cedric noticed something. Both his and Reggie's locker doors were open. He understood why Reggie's was open, but why was his? Then he saw how the metal around the latch was all bent outward. Like it had been pried open.

Is that what happened here? Had Reggie walked in on two thieves trying to steal things from their lockers? And paid for it with his life? If so, what a waste. Neither one of them kept any valuables in their locker. He stepped around Reggie's body to get closer to his locker. Looked again at the door, then inside. Yes, things inside his locker had been moved around and messed with.

The zipper to his gym bag was undone. He always zipped it closed before he left. But really, they'd be sorely disappointed if they rummaged through it. All he had in it were some fresh socks and underwear. Wait, he did keep a small money clip in a side pocket, in case he wanted to grab something to eat after working out. But it was never more than a few dollars.

He picked it up and reached inside, searching for the side pocket, when he felt something hard, made of metal. He picked it up and was shocked to find it was a pistol. He smelled the end. It had definitely been fired very recently.

Just then, down the aisle, the stairway door that led down from the lobby opened. Two young men, a few years older than he and Reggie, walked in. Suddenly, they stopped and stared. They looked down at Reggie's body lying at Cedric's feet. Then at Cedric, standing there, a gym bag in one hand, a pistol in the other.

Their faces. Cedric instantly knew what they were thinking. They looked at each other then turned and headed back through the doorway, running toward the stairs.

"Wait," he yelled. "Come back. This isn't what it looks like. Come back. Let me explain."

3

Charles and Lily's father hurried down Park Avenue toward 42nd St. where the Belmont Hotel was located. He checked his speedometer, just over 22 miles an hour. The car could easily handle double that. The real challenge was not killing anyone on the way there. New York residents were used to vehicles traveling much slower, the pace of carriages, and they'd simply cross the road at any point that struck their fancy. Charles had two close calls already in the first five blocks.

"This is such a bizarre thing," he said. Nigel appeared deep in thought.

"What's that?" He looked at Charles.

"Cedric's phone call. Seems like such a bizarre thing. Who would shoot a young college student in a luxury hotel gym on a Saturday morning?"

"Or at any time," Nigel said. "Or any day of the week for that matter. "You're right, it doesn't make any sense.

Cedric could've interrupted our breakfast, called about a thousand different things, and I'd have never guessed it to be this."

"I can't remember the last time a murder was committed," Charles said, "in this part of town where the...uh, guess you could say—"

"Wealthier people live?" said Nigel. "No, you're right. People in mid and upper Manhattan never even think about being physically harmed or attacked. We can walk the streets in total safety, even at night. The last time something similar happened was over a year ago, but even that wasn't some random attack. It was that banker fellow, what was his name? Edey, or something."

"I remember," Charles said. "Shot his wife for being unfaithful, then turned the gun on himself."

"That's right. A nasty business," Nigel said. "But once again, nothing like this. Not some bright young college student shot by a stranger. In my hotel, nonetheless. We haven't even had a pickpocketing incident for longer than I can remember, let alone someone being killed." He released a deep sigh.

"Didn't Reggie come from a prominent political family?" Charles said. "Thought I remember Cedric saying something about his father being some kind of city councilman."

"In New York we call them Aldermen," Nigel said. "And yes, Reggie's father is an Alderman. But not just an alderman, he's the *Chief* Alderman for all the boroughs of New York City. I've never met him, but I've read about him in the newspapers a number of times. He is perhaps the most influential voice on the zoning commission, gets involved in all these high-rise construction projects going up all over town." He sighed again.

Charles understood why. Apart from a terrible tragedy for this young man's family, this would obviously become a major news story. Not the kind of publicity his father-in-law would want for his hotel. "Are you concerned about how this might affect your plans for expanding the hotel?"

"Very much so. Something like this could sink our plans altogether. Our investors won't like a story like this. Of course, I'm far more concerned with Cedric, finding his closest friend dead like that. In such a violent manner." He looked down the road again. "I wonder how he's doing?"

Charles wondered the same thing. Had Cedric ever seen a dead body before, let alone one who'd been shot? The poor kid. "We're only a few blocks away now."

"I'm not sure what we'll find when we get there," Nigel said. "Keller's a good man, got a good head on his shoulders. I'm sure he'll get the scene secured. Might even have the police on their way. I'm sure they'll want to interview Cedric at length. Not just about what happened today, but anything he can tell them about Reggie. And someone will have to call his family. The police may want to do that themselves, I don't know. I'm very concerned about our hotel guests. We're over half-filled. I'm going to try to see if I can keep all the activity confined to the basement floor."

"If you want," Charles said, "I can go be with Cedric and let you handle the details about the guests and the staff, and controlling the publicity."

"Thank you, Charles. That'll be a big help. Of course, I want to see him first—to make sure he's all right—before I handle the other things. But I know how much he cares about you. You being there for him will mean as much as me being there, if not more."

"Certainly not more, sir. I mean, Father. Cedric thinks the world of you."

"I know. You're right." He sighed again. "This is all just so awful."

When Charles pulled up to the front of the hotel, nothing seemed amiss. There was a mixture of cars and horse carriages, dropping people off and picking people up. He could see well-dressed people coming in and out of the front doors. Not many, but some. He didn't know what he'd expected to see, perhaps evidence that word of the crime had gotten out.

He pulled up to the front door to let Nigel out and said he'd park the car and be right in.

The scene inside was just about the opposite of the calm exterior. Charles had been in the hotel numerous times and knew well the layout of the ground floor. Like most of the newer uptown hotels, the lobby of the Belmont was exquisitely decorated with fine furniture and plush carpeting in the seated areas. On the left side, was the check-in desk. Just beyond that, the stairway door that led down to the basement area. He instantly saw Nigel arguing with two uniformed officers and the man Charles assumed to be Keller, the hotel chief of security.

All the guests in the lobby had stopped whatever they were doing to turn and pay attention to the scene. While the hotel staff did their best to ignore it and re-direct the guests' attention back to the business at hand.

As Charles drew closer, he listened to the conversation.

"Would someone please tell me, where is my son? Right now. Where is Cedric right now?"

The bigger of the two uniformed officers responded. "Please calm down, Mr. Whitaker. I know who you are. Mr. Keller here informed us this is your hotel. We can't let you go downstairs to the gym. The gym is now a crime scene. Our finest detectives are on their way here. They'll take charge of the investigation. They're the ones who instructed us to keep the gym off-limits to everyone, which I'm afraid, includes you, sir."

"I understand a crime has been committed," Nigel said. "A very serious one. My son called me about it no more than fifteen minutes ago. And he also reported it to Mr. Keller here, my chief of security for the hotel." He looked at Keller. "Didn't he?"

"Yes, Mr. Whitaker, he did. I have spoken with Cedric. Unfortunately, he wasn't the first person to tell me about what happened. Two hotel guests did. They came running up the stairs, yelling at me about seeing a young man in the gym downstairs, standing over a body holding a gun. Made quite a ruckus."

"What?" Nigel said. "A young man standing over a body, holding a gun?"

"Yes, sir. I'm afraid so," Keller said. "Of course, hearing

this, I didn't know what to think. So, I ran downstairs with my gun drawn, not knowing what to expect once I opened the gym door."

"And what did you see?" Nigel said. "Was the young man my son? Was it Cedric?"

"Yes, sir. It was Cedric."

"But he wasn't holding a gun, now was he?" Nigel said.

"No, Mr. Whitaker, he wasn't. When I first saw him, he was sitting down on a locker room bench, holding his head in his hands. And, of course, lying there right next to him, I could see the body of his friend, Reggie. They've both been here together a number of times before. I knew Reggie a little. As I came up on the scene, I could tell he was dead. There was a lot of blood around his head."

Charles's stomach began to churn and tighten. He glanced across the lobby, saw another uniformed cop talking to two men seated on a sofa, dressed in exercise clothes.

Charles refocused on the conversation before him.

"Mr. Keller," Nigel said, "where is my son? Where is Cedric? Is he down there still, in the gym?"

"No, sir, he's not," the cop said.

"Then where is he?"

"See, that's the thing," Keller continued. "When I came right up to him, to Cedric, I could see the pistol. It was sitting in the gym bag next to him."

"I can't believe this," Nigel said. "You can't possibly believe he had anything to do with this. Did he tell you he heard men arguing as soon as he stepped inside?"

"Yes, sir, he did," Keller said. "He stood up, very upset.

Told me all about the men arguing, something about a strange sound, hearing Reggie's body hit the ground, men running off. Then he sat right back down, told me about these two men who walked in on him just as he found the gun in his gym bag." Keller pointed to the two men across the lobby.

"So, where is my son?" Nigel said.

"He's being detained for questioning," the officer said. "Because of everything Mr. Keller just said. We had no other choice. But because of Mr. Keller vouching for him, we've allowed him to be detained in your office. He's there now with some other officers."

Nigel looked down to the floor, rubbed his forehead, then looked up at Charles. His face full of anguish and worry.

4

Charles had never seen Nigel like this. He genuinely didn't know what to do next. Charles stepped closer and said quietly, "I think we should go see Cedric. The rest of this can wait till later."

Nigel inhaled slowly. "Yes, of course, you're right. Let's go there now." He looked around the lobby. Almost all of the hotel staff were looking at him. "Cedric comes first."

Charles headed for the elevators. Nigel followed. So did Keller.

Nigel stepped inside.

Keller said, "What would you have me do, sir?"

Charles looked at Keller and said quietly, "Just handle it, Mr. Keller. Think of anything Mr. Whitaker would do to try to protect the hotel's reputation and get things back to normal for the guests. We won't be long." Charles stepped in next to Nigel, the doors closed behind him. For the moment, they were alone.

"Lord, give me wisdom," Charles heard Nigel mutter softly.

"This is definitely not what we were expecting," Charles said as the elevator rumbled. "But God knew. And he knows, and we know, that Cedric has done nothing wrong. That's the most important thing."

"But what will I say to him?"

"If you don't mind me suggesting, sir, just be his father. That's what he needs most. He's probably scared out of his mind. First with the shooting itself, then suddenly everyone's acting like he did it."

"Good, thanks. You're right. That's what he needs." He shook his head. "It was so hard leaving the hotel lobby with all that chaos in the air."

"But you did it, sir. And it will all get sorted out. First things first."

The elevator opened to the very familiar floor where the hotel offices were located. Fortunately, being a Saturday, there was hardly anyone there. As they walked to the far end where Nigel's office was, the few people they encountered seemed oblivious to what had taken place downstairs.

As they got closer to Nigel's office, the interior blinds were lifted high enough, so they could see Cedric through the glass panels, seated on a sofa by the front door. Two uniformed police officers were standing on each end. It didn't appear he was handcuffed. At least there was that.

As soon as Nigel walked through the front doorway, Cedric jumped up and rushed to hug him. Charles had never seen that before, either. Usually, they greeted each other with a warm handshake, Nigel occasionally a pat on the shoulder.

Nigel squeezed back. "There, there, son. It'll be all right."

Still in the hug. "But Father, they think I did it. They think I shot Reggie."

"I know. It seems they do." Nigel looked up at the two officers with a disapproving glare.

"So, you're the lad's father," one of them said, a slight Irish brogue. "He really needs to sit back down on the sofa, sir."

Cedric pulled back, started to comply.

"Officer, do you know who I am?"

"I believe I do. Someone said the lad's father owned the hotel. I assume that's you."

"Yes, and you men have made a serious error here, a rush to judgment, to put it bluntly. The very idea that my son would be involved in such a horrendous crime is preposterous. Why would he shoot Reggie?"

"Reggie would be the young man in the cellar?"

"Yes, the young man who was just killed. He and my son were the best of friends. They're star players on the NYU basketball team."

"That well may be, sir. But none of that matters to me. I'm told to detain him here until the detectives arrive to question him. They're on their way. They may have a bit to do downstairs before they come up here, but it's a kindness, believe me, that the lad's not in the paddy wagon outside."

"That's where he should be, you ask me," the other

officer said. "Shouldn't be giving special treatment to the rich. Haven't you been reading the papers? That's what that whole Curran Commission is about. Exposing police corruption, ending all the bribes and special favors you folks have been getting far too long."

Charles knew all about this. He'd been reading about it almost every day. He was pretty sure Nigel did, too.

Nigel stepped away from Cedric and walked right up to the police officer who'd just insulted him. "Listen, young man, I'll have you know I've never, and would never, offer a policeman a bribe, be he a low-level beat cop such as yourself or the Chief of Police. I've been reading all about this corruption scandal you speak of, and I wholeheartedly agree with the direction that Commission is taking. It's high time we root out all the corruption wherever it is found, in law enforcement and in politics."

The policeman took a step back, seeming somewhat intimidated.

The other officer spoke up. "I hear you, sir. Harry and me are among those who are happy to see the shakeup going on. But you know, you say you've never offered a bribe, but then again, the very first thing you said to us was letting us know who you are...the rich owner of this fancy hotel. What was your point in that, if not to try and influence us to treat you different? Or your son?"

Charles held back a slight smile. The man had a point.

Nigel shook his head. "You're right, officer. And I apologize. I was hoping to be treated differently. But not in the way you might think. I cited who I am, because I wanted you to know that I'm someone you can trust. I wasn't born rich. I've worked hard every day to get where I am. Nothing was handed to me. I never cheated anyone, always obeyed every law. I respect the police, always have. We are a law-abiding family. A church going family."

"I don't doubt it, sir," the first policeman said. "And our sergeant must think well of you enough, which is why your son's been allowed to wait here and not in the paddy wagon, as my partner pointed out. But still, from what I gather from the chatter downstairs, there's good reason to detain him. I don't know if you came up here expecting us to release him into your care. If so, I assure you that will not be happening."

Charles decided to step in. "Gentlemen, if I may. My name is Charles Bennington. I am Mr. Whitaker's son-in-law, and the owner of Bennington's Ice Factory."

"I've heard of it, sir. Seen your trucks driving about."

"I realize you are just doing your job. But you have to understand. We are utterly shocked by the events downstairs. Less than an hour ago, we were all eating breakfast together when Cedric had to leave to meet Reggie at the gym downstairs for a workout. And Mr. Whitaker is telling the truth, Cedric and Reggie are best friends. Regardless of the chatter downstairs, we know with certainty that Cedric could not have done this. It's a terrible misunderstanding, and I know things will have to be sorted out the right way. But could you give us just a few minutes to talk with Cedric alone before the detectives get here?"

Both men looked instantly concerned at this request.

"You could just step outside for a few moments. Look

around. This office only has the one door, and you'd both be standing in front of it."

One of the officers looked at the windows.

"Sir," Charles said, "we're on the third floor. If Cedric went out the window it would be to his death, not his escape."

"I suppose that would be all right," the Irish-sounding officer said. "Come on Harry, let's give 'em a moment."

Nigel and Charles stepped aside to allow the officers to walk around him. Once they were outside, Charles closed the office door. Cedric was already back on the sofa. Charles and Nigel pulled the upholstered chairs in front of Nigel's desk over near Cedric and sat.

Cedric was looking down by his feet. He looked up at his father. "Father, you know I had nothing to do with shooting Reggie, right? You believe me, right?"

"Of course, we believe you son."

He looked up at Charles. "You believe me, too, don't you Charles?"

"Cedric, you must be forgetting who you're talking to. Don't you remember two years ago when everyone thought I was a killer. But you never did. And you went out of your way to prove everyone wrong. Well, everyone downstairs is wrong about you, wrong about this. There's no way you'd ever hurt Reggie, let alone shoot him. But you need to tell us everything that happened downstairs, from the moment we hung up the phone. Don't leave out a single detail."

5

"Take a deep breath, son, and just tell us what happened," Nigel said.

Cedric looked up toward the corner, shook his head, a glazed look on his face. "I can't believe this is happening."

"That's all right, Cedric," Charles said. "We'll get to the bottom of this. Just start talking."

"Well, after I hung up, I walked back to our lockers. I knew you told me not to touch anything. How I wish I'd have listened. I don't know why I did what I did. I was thinking I needed to get to the stairs to do what you said about making the crime scene secure. But then I looked down and noticed how both our locker doors had been forced open, the way the latches were bent. I figured maybe that's what happened. They were thieves, and Reggie walked in on them. Maybe he confronted them, and that's what the arguing that I heard was about. So, they shot him so he couldn't identify them."

"I thought you said you didn't hear a gunshot," Nigel said.

"You're right, I did say that. Because I didn't hear one. I heard something, a strange sound, and then the sound of Reggie's body hitting the floor, and the men running off. When I got to Reggie, that's when I noticed the wound in his forehead. Looked like a gunshot wound. Anyway, as I stood there looking down at the broken lockers, I noticed my gym bag there. Looked like someone had gone through it."

"You didn't bring it with you?" Charles said.

"No, I forgot it the last time I was there. Anyway, I remembered how I had this money clip in there, so I reached in to see if it was missing. That's when my hand felt something hard, something metal. Not thinking, I picked it up. It was a gun. Again, without even thinking, I smelled the end of it and could definitely tell it had been fired."

Both Charles and Nigel had the same disgusted reaction. Why would you pick it up? How could you not know it was a gun? Neither said anything.

Cedric continued. "I was just about to put it back in my bag when the door to the gym opened, and in walks these two guys. They look right at me, their faces in total shock. I realize what they're seeing, and what they must think. They turned to run back upstairs toward the lobby. I start yelling at them to please come back and let me explain."

Tears welled up in his eyes, reliving that moment.

"But it was too late. They were gone. I tried to put everything back in the locker just the way I found it, but I knew how bad it looked. Them seeing me standing there holding the gun, with Reggie lying dead at my feet." He looked up at Charles. "Now, I know why you said it was important not to touch anything."

"You're right, son," Nigel said. "If they had just come down and saw you standing there...without the gun..." He didn't finish his thought.

But what Cedric had said deeply concerned Charles. Not just because of the appearance issue, that is, the young men seeing Cedric like that and assuming the worst. But he knew from a fairly recent break-in at the factory, police had begun using a person's fingerprints when investigating a crime. He had watched as detectives applied a fine powder around the various points of entry the thief might have used, as well as the various things he may have touched.

When Charles had asked what that was about, they explained all about how this new science regarding fingerprints worked, and how this new tool was beginning to spread throughout police departments. It was now being widely used even as evidence in court, considered an even more valuable piece of evidence than eyewitness testimony.

Charles knew from what Cedric had explained that his fingerprints were now all over that gun. He was pretty sure Cedric had never heard of such a thing. Nigel may not have grasped the seriousness of this matter, either. He wanted to say something, but it didn't seem like the right time.

"So, what happened next?" Nigel said. "Is that when Mr. Keller came down from upstairs?"

Cedric sighed. "Yes. He walked in with one of the two men. Father, he had his gun out, like I was some kind of criminal."

"Did he point it at you?"

"No. As soon as he saw it was me, he put his gun back in his holster. I was just sitting there on the locker bench by then, trying not to cry. He asked me where the gun was, so I told him, then tried to explain how this was all a big misunderstanding."

"You think he believed you?" Charles said.

"I'm not sure," Cedric said. "I think he did. But the guy was standing right there, saying I was the one he saw holding the gun, standing over Reggie's body. He had this panicked look on his face. Mr. Keller tried to calm him down, told him who I was. I don't know if it helped. Eventually, he told the guy to go back up in the lobby and join his friend. Said they needed to wait there until the police came. Then he looks down at me and apologizes, says he has to call the police now. Because of the witnesses, he had no other choice."

Cedric buried his face in his hands.

"Well, I'm sure Keller believed you," his father said. "He's known you since you were a child, and he can vouch that you and Reggie were good friends before...all this."

Cedric looked up. "Do you think the police will arrest me?"

Nigel didn't answer. As if he knew but couldn't say the words out loud.

"They might," Charles said. "They might not have any other choice, either. But listen, Cedric. These witnesses didn't see you shoot Reggie."

"Because I didn't. I didn't shoot him."

"I know that. We know that," Charles said. "I just meant, they can only testify they saw you holding the gun. You weren't pointing it at Reggie's body."

"No, not even close. I had just finished smelling the end of it."

"But the fact that they saw you right next to the body, holding the gun," Charles said, "even though they didn't see you shooting—"

"— would be enough to make them have to arrest me," Cedric said.

Charles nodded. "I think so. Think you need to prepare for that."

"But listen, son," Nigel said. "Our hotel has one of the finest law firms on retainer. As soon as we're done, I'm going to call them and have them send their best man down to meet you at the station."

"Does that mean they'll have to put me in jail? Like spending the night there?"

"I will make sure that's not what happens," his father said.

"But listen, Cedric," Charles said, "this is very important. I know you're going to want to explain to them everything you explained to us. But don't. You need to resist the urge to make people believe you're innocent."

"But I am innocent."

"That's not the point, Cedric. Not right now. Not in front of the police. You have a right to have your attorney present when they question you, so don't volunteer anything. Don't answer any of their questions. Not until your father's attorney is sitting right next to you."

Cedric didn't reply.

"Cedric," Nigel said, "tell me you'll do what we ask this time. What Charles is talking about."

"I will. This time, I'll listen and do what you say."

6

About twenty minutes later, two homicide detectives stepped out of the elevator and walked toward Nigel's office. The uniformed police officers instantly recognized them. The taller one with the Irish brogue talked to them first. Charles saw him turn and point to Nigel's office. He seemed to be pointing out the different individuals and, no doubt, giving his version of the events.

One of the detectives raised his hand, and the cop immediately stopped talking. Charles figured he must be the one in charge. Both men walked straight toward them. Charles decided to intercept him, see if he could get a sense of what they planned to do.

"Hello, my name is Charles Bennington. I'm the brother-in-law of the young man involved in the events downstairs. His name is Cedric. He's the one sitting on the sofa. Across from him is my father-in-law, Nigel Whitaker, Cedric's father and the owner of this hotel."

The lead detective extended his hand. "Lieutenant Rafferty. This here's my partner, Sergeant Shipley. Officer Donegan did his best to explain things, though he didn't know your names. I'll be in charge of this murder investigation. We've already been down to the crime scene in the basement, talked to the two witnesses and your security chief. What was his name?" He asked his partner.

"Keller, Lieutenant."

"Right, Keller. He went out of his way to make sure we knew the young man was innocent of the crime. Of course, seeing the father in there pays Keller's wages, wouldn't expect any less."

"Well, Lieutenant, it's not just that. Mr. Keller knows Cedric quite well, as well as the young man who was killed. He knows they are best friends and have come down to that gym quite often to work out. They're getting in shape for basketball tryouts at NYU."

"Okay, I get your point. You believe he's innocent too. That's fine. We're not here to bang the gavel on anyone. Just getting our hands around the facts. But looking at the scene downstairs, talking with the witnesses and the officers first on the scene, you have to know the young man in there is our prime suspect. And we'll need to be speaking to him, so if you'll excuse me."

Both men walked past Charles and into the office. Charles followed. Cedric stood up and faced them. Nigel started to introduce himself but was interrupted.

"We know who you are, sir. And that this is your son, Cedric, right?"

"Yes, sir. Cedric Whitaker."

"And you're the one involved in the shooting?" Rafferty said.

"Not involved," Cedric said. "I came into the gym right after it happened. I was meeting Reggie. We were supposed to work out together. He must've gotten there before me. I heard men arguing as I opened the door. Then some kind of strange noise, then these two men running away."

"Did anyone else see these two men you say you saw?"

"No. They must've run out through the back door. I called out for my friend, but there was no—"

"But you were the one the two men downstairs saw holding the gun?" Rafferty's partner, Shipley said.

"I was, but I didn't shoot him," Cedric said. "I can explain about the gun."

"Cedric," Nigel said sternly. "That's enough."

Cedric instantly stopped talking, looked down toward the carpet.

Charles inserted himself between the men. "I know you two men have a job to do. But I also know that young Cedric here has a right to have an attorney present when being questioned."

"That's right," Rafferty said. "But this isn't a formal interview, like the kind we have at the precinct downtown. Right now, we're just trying to understand what happened. Does the young man have something to hide?"

Charles could see the tactic. "Absolutely not. And if

that's all you're interested in, then let me explain to you Cedric's side."

"Cedric won't be saying anything more to you," Nigel said, "until his attorney is sitting beside him."

"So, that's the way it's going to be?" Rafferty said.

"Yes, Lieutenant," Charles said. "That's how it's going to be. You still want to hear Cedric's version of the story?"

"Yeah, sure. Go ahead."

Both men took out notepads and pencils. Charles spent the next ten minutes sharing everything Cedric had said. Several times as he did, one or the other detectives tried asking Cedric direct questions to follow up on what Charles said. But either Charles or Nigel would shut them down. Charles knew they risked getting on these detectives' bad side, but it couldn't be helped. If they got the chance, they would intimidate Cedric into saying whatever they wanted him to say.

When they finished, the two men stepped closer to Cedric. Sergeant Shipley pulled out a pair of handcuffs, asked Cedric to please turn around.

"Come on, gentlemen," Nigel said. "Clearly, this is unnecessary. Cedric isn't the sort to take off running. We are a very prominent family in Manhattan, this kind of thing could ruin his reputation, treating him as though he were guilty, when we've already explained to you what happened."

Shipley continued as though Nigel hadn't said a thing. "With all due respect, Mr. Whitaker...I don't doubt you're a prominent family, and all. Unfortunately, the young man your son will undoubtedly be charged with shooting is the Head Alderman's son. You folks are small potatoes compared to him. We don't do this by the book, our chief will have our heads."

Cedric looked at his father, a pleading look in his eyes.

"It's all right, son. Do as he asks."

"Are they taking me to jail now? Even though I explained what happened? I didn't do anything wrong. I would never shoot Reggie. He was my best friend." Tears started welling up in his eyes.

"We've got no choice, sonny," Shipley said. "It were up to me, I'd let your dad and your brother-in-law, here, drive you downtown. No handcuffs, no drama. But you know yourself — if this kid Reggie is your best friend, as you say — who his father is in this town. I'm sure by now, he's already been told his boy's dead. And for all we know, whoever informed him probably said you were the one who shot him."

"We don't know that," Charles said.

"It's a good bet," Lieutenant Rafferty said. "And with all the commotion going on downstairs in the lobby, "I'm sure the reporters are already on their way here. Some might already be downstairs looking for a scoop."

"There's a commotion going on downstairs?" Nigel said.

"Oh, yeah," Shipley said. "All the people in the lobby? You know how people are in this town. Word got out quick, especially when folks heard it was the alderman's son."

They put the handcuffs on Cedric and began walking

him toward the elevator. Charles and Nigel were right behind them.

"I'll be in the car right behind you," Nigel said.

"Sir," Charles said quietly. "I mean, Father, why don't you let me do that? You should stay here and contact your attorney, make sure they have someone get down to the police station right away."

"Oh, yes. You're right. And I better give Keller instructions on how to handle the crowds in the lobby. Especially the press."

They reached the elevator. Shipley pressed the down button.

"You heard what Charles said, Cedric? He'll go down to the station now, and I'll come down just as soon as I get those two things done."

Cedric glanced back at them, as he stepped into the elevator. "Okay, Father. And I won't say a word until your attorney comes."

7

When Charles got to the lobby, he followed behind the detectives and officers leading Cedric in handcuffs toward the front doors. At least twice as many people were now in the lobby as when they had gone upstairs, including a row of reporters. They were easy enough to spot with their fedoras and press cards sticking out of their hatbands. They were also the only ones holding notepads and pencils.

And they yelled the loudest as the police escort walked by. "No comment, fellas," was the only reply from the police.

Before Cedric's entourage reached the front doors, they had to stand aside to let the coroner and his crew through, pushing an empty gurney. Charles could guess which of the men was the actual coroner by his dress, age, and demeanor. When they saw this man, the two detectives, Rafferty and Shipley, changed course and stopped to talk with him.

Charles moved a little closer to pick up what he could from their conversation. It was clear he expected the two detectives to go with him downstairs as he evaluated the crime scene and the deceased. He watched as the rest of the police escorting Cedric continued through the doors and outside. He could see they were headed for what they called the paddy wagon.

This gave him an opportunity to do something he knew must be done. He figured the detectives would be detained downstairs for at least ten minutes. He hurried over to the hotel front desk then quickly decided he'd be better off talking to the concierge, who operated from a different desk nearby.

The impeccably dressed young man, named Jeffrey Hunter, stood staring at the spectacle before him, dread all over his face. He glanced at Charles heading toward him. "Mr. Bennington, this is so awful. I can't believe what I'm seeing. Even worse, what I'm hearing people say."

"What are they saying, Jeffrey?"

"That Master Cedric shot the Head Alderman's son in the gym downstairs. Now I see him being led off in handcuffs."

"Jeffrey, look at me." Charles paused until he did. "Cedric could not shoot Reggie. It's a terrible misunderstanding. Do you understand?"

"Yes, sir. I do. I'm glad to hear you say it. I could never believe such a thing about Cedric. He and Reggie were such good friends."

"Did you by any chance see them together, earlier in the lobby?"

"No, I didn't. Not together. Reggie came in first about ten minutes before Master Cedric and headed straight for the door leading down to the gym. Cedric came in a little later, even stopped by my desk for a moment to ask whether Reggie had already arrived."

"How did he seem?"

"Who, Cedric? I don't know. He was smiling, and clearly happy to hear Reggie was already downstairs."

Charles was glad to hear it. This could prove helpful later on. "Jeffrey, remember what you just told me. Maybe you should even write it down, exactly as you remember it, in case you get called to testify at some point."

"Testify? Me? Do you think it will come to that?"

Charles nodded. "I do. Sadly, I do." He was just about to ask Jeffrey if he could use his phone to call Lily and her mother and ask if Jeffrey would also give him some privacy but thought better of it. "Jeffrey, I need to use your phone to call my wife and Cedric's mother."

"Certainly, Mr. Bennington. I'll step outside for a—"

"That won't be necessary. In fact, since I'll be explaining to them what happened, I think you should stay close by, so you can hear it too. I need you to do your best to put out any fires, as it were, with the staff. They need to know that Cedric is innocent and what really happened."

"Okay, Mr. Bennington. If that's what you prefer." He stepped aside to allow Charles to get behind the desk closest to the telephone.

He picked up the receiver. "Yes, Operator. This is Charles Bennington."

"Yes, Mr. Bennington, go ahead."

"Could you put me through the direct line for the Whitaker residence?"

"Certainly, sir. Right away."

A few clicking sounds, and he heard the telephone ringing.

"Hello?" It was Lily.

"Hi, Love. It's me."

"Charles? What's going on? We've been so worried. It's been almost an hour."

"I'm so sorry, my love. But it couldn't be helped. When I explain, you'll understand why."

"So, this isn't you calling to say you're bringing Cedric home? Mother's been so worried. She was certain that's why you called."

Charles sighed. How could he say this? Where should he begin?

WHEN LILY HUNG up the phone back in the foyer at home, she was still in tears. Her mother — who had been standing right there when she'd first answered the call — had left when she figured out the gist of what was being said. She couldn't take it anymore.

Lily found a linen napkin in the entrance table drawer and brought it with her as she searched the house for Mother. She found her in the living room in the chair where she normally sat whenever she embroidered or read a book. But now she found her sobbing, her face buried in her hands. Lily realized she didn't have anything to wipe away her tears, so she quickly went back for another linen cloth and handed it to her. Then she took a seat in the closest chair.

She still hadn't been able to process the news. It was all just too much. To think, at this very moment, poor Cedric was sitting all alone in a paddy wagon, handcuffed like a common criminal. She thought back to the happy look on his face a short time ago, as he wolfed down the last few bites of his breakfast, so he could hurry out the door to meet his friend.

Now his friend was dead, and her dear brother was being wrongly accused of the crime. Such things didn't seem possible.

It took several more minutes before Mother was sufficiently able to compose herself to engage in conversation. When she did, Lily said, "Mother, I know you didn't hear the whole conversation, even during the time you were standing beside me in the foyer. I don't know which would be less painful for you. Should I summarize everything Charles said, or would you rather ask me questions?"

Mother took a deep breath. "I don't think I could bear to hear the whole thing retold. So, Cedric, our Cedric is definitely under arrest? They think he shot Reggie?"

"I'm afraid so." Lily didn't want to mention the part about the handcuffs or the paddy wagon. She went on to explain how the two men saw Cedric standing over the body holding the gun and what they thought it meant.

"But why was he holding a gun? He doesn't own a gun.

We don't even own any guns. I don't think he's ever fired a gun in his life."

Lily explained about Cedric thinking the men who shot Reggie had broken into their lockers, and the part about finding the gun in his gym bag."

"But why would he touch it? Why would he pick the gun up? I don't understand it."

"Neither does he, Mother. Charles thinks it happened so fast. He didn't take the time to think things through."

Mother looked down toward her lap, shook her head. When she looked up at Lily, the tears started to fall again. "I don't understand him. Both your father and Charles told him not to touch anything."

"I know, I know. I'm sure now he regrets it with all his heart. But nothing more can be done. Charles said Father is sending down his best attorney to meet them at the police station. He'll get things sorted out. Charles said Father felt confident his attorney would be able to get Cedric home tonight."

She wiped her eyes. "That's what matters most now, getting him home." She took another deep breath, looked up at Lily. "Could we pray for that? Now?"

"Sure," Lily said, "I think we should."

For a moment, no one said anything. Then Lily realized, her mom was expecting her to pray. So, she did.

"Lord, please comfort Cedric right now as he sits in the paddy wagon..."

"Cedric's in a paddy wagon?" Out came the linen napkin as the sobs began all over again.

8

The sound of the carriage wheels rattling over the bumpy road had a rhythmic finality to it — like the ticking of a clock marking the end of several things Cedric Whitaker had taken for granted his entire life.

Like freedom. Trust. Certainty.

He sat on one end of a splintered bench in the back of the paddy wagon, the metal cuffs around his wrists biting into his skin. They hadn't even asked him if he was comfortable, hadn't offered a blanket or a coat. Treated him like he was already guilty. At the other end, sat a disheveled soul, his clothes hung like rags, shoes torn, hair tossed about his head, scraggly beard. The man looked down as though lost in thought, hadn't even acknowledged Cedric's presence.

The wagon turned a sharp corner. Cedric's heart thudded against his ribs, the beat fast and uneven. He tried to steady his breathing. But every inhale came jagged, interrupted by memories playing on a cruel loop. All of them Reggie. Lying motionless on the floor of the gym. The blood. The eyes staring back without seeing.

Cedric turned his face away from the barred window and tried not to be sick. It had all happened so fast. Just over an hour ago, he'd been seated at breakfast with his family — cheerful, confident, making plans about basketball tryouts, thinking of Amelia's pretty smile and Reggie's fun sense of humor.

And now...now he was a suspect in Reggie's murder.

He leaned his head back against the wooden wall and closed his eyes. It didn't help. The images were still there.

The locker door, bent and pried open. His gym bag, rummaged through. The gun — cold, foreign, feeling so wrong in his hand.

I should never have picked it up.

He'd been told not to touch anything. Charles had said it. His father said it. But in that frantic moment, his instincts had taken over. He wasn't thinking like someone under suspicion. He'd been thinking like someone who'd just lost a friend, his closest friend — the one person he'd met at school who hadn't cared that Cedric came from money or a distinguished family, because Reggie came from both. Cedric had begun to view Reggie as someone who could easily become a lifelong friend.

But now... now he was gone.

The wagon lurched suddenly, throwing Cedric forward. He braced himself on the bench, grimacing as the cuffs dug even deeper into his wrists. Rain began to fall, tapping softly against the roof above. He glanced through the bars at the street rolling behind them. Somewhere back there, his family must be frantic. His father, probably on the telephone with their attorney, trying to pull strings on his behalf. Charles hopping into his car, hoping to beat the detectives to the police station. Lily and his mother, what were they doing? Did they even know that he'd been arrested?

Poor Father. Cedric felt especially bad for him. How hard he'd worked to build the Hotel Belmont's reputation over the years. It was now one of the top picks for celebrities and political dignitaries visiting the city. What would this mean once word had gotten out? How would it affect their business?

Cedric exhaled, slow and shaky. His thoughts drifted back to Lily. His sister had always been so kind and supportive. She'd be crying right now, or pacing. Maybe both. He hated being the cause of her distress.

And Mother...sitting in her favorite chair by the fireplace, eyes wide in disbelief, one hand pressed over her mouth. She'd be devastated. The scandal such a thing might create. Although that would surely play a part, he knew her anxiety would mostly be rooted in him, what her boy must be enduring.

He blinked hard, refusing any tears, angry with himself for letting his emotions rise. He had to stay strong, had to think. The truth is what mattered, the only thing that mattered. That had been the lesson Charles had taught him. And the truth would come out, if you held fast and didn't panic.

The wagon turned sharply again, and the street noises shifted. Voices now. Footsteps. The echo of an iron gate creaking open.

They had arrived.

The horses neighed as the wagon slowed to a stop. Then came the scrape of boots on wet stone, muffled orders, and the clang of the latch being released. The rear doors opened with a groan, letting in the faint scent of coal smoke. Cedric squinted, rain misting down into the open compartment.

Two officers stood at the back, one holding an umbrella, the other already reaching in.

"Let's go," said the taller one, his tone clipped and void of warmth. "On your feet, Mr. Whitaker."

Cedric stood slowly, hands still behind his back, every muscle stiff. The officer grabbed his arm, guiding him down the step, into the open yard beyond. The jail loomed ahead — a squat, imposing structure of stone and iron. A place built to hold men guilty of doing terrible things.

The other officer grabbed the vagrant from the back of the wagon, cursing at him for taking too long to get out.

They walked in silence, boots echoing across the cobbled path leading to the side entrance. No reporters, thank God. Not yet. He saw some in the lobby, knew it was only a matter of time before they'd make it here. The rain had likely kept them away for now.

Inside, the station was dim and institutional. Gaslights buzzed faintly above them. The air was heavy with ink, smoke, and the distant metallic tang of disinfectant. Cedric was led through a maze of corridors, each lined with doors bearing frosted glass panes etched with titles: *Detective Bureau*, *Homicide Division*, *Rogues' Gallery*.

They entered a room illuminated by a single overhead bulb. A wooden bench sat against one wall, beside a tall cabinet filled with files. A camera on a tripod stood in the corner, its lens trained on a marked spot on the floor.

"Stand there," the officer instructed, pointing to the spot. Cedric complied, the flash of the camera momentarily blinding him. The photographer adjusted the equipment and took a second shot from the side.

Next Cedric was guided to a table where an ink pad and a large ledger awaited. The officer pressed each of Cedric's fingers onto the pad, then rolled them onto the paper, leaving distinct black impressions. The process was meticulous, the officer ensuring each print was clear and legible. He handed Cedric a wrinkled cloth. "Wipe your fingers off with this."

"What is this you're doing?" Cedric said quietly. "If you don't mind me asking?"

"We're taking your fingerprints. It's the newest tool in our toolbox for catching bad guys. Ask your lawyer to explain it. I'm sure he knows all about it. Now, stand up."

Cedric was led down a corridor, past a long row of cells. They stopped at a small office. One of the officers unlocked the cuffs and gestured toward a chair.

"Sit," he said, and Cedric did.

He didn't know what had become of the vagrant who'd ridden in the wagon with him. Another officer entered moments later, a clipboard in hand. He was older, with a mustache stained from years of tobacco and eyes that scanned Cedric like a butcher measuring a slab of meat.

"Name?"

"Cedric Whitaker."

"Age?"

"Twenty."

"Occupation?"

"Student. NYU."

"Relation to the deceased?"

"He was my friend. A very good friend."

The man paused, looking up for the first time.

"Your friend, huh? Well...let's see how that story holds up."

Cedric felt the urge to respond but said nothing. Not yet. Not until Lawrence Beaumont arrived, Father's attorney. He was determined not to say a thing until then. The officer wrote some things down on the clipboard. He then measured Cedric's height against a wall chart and noted it down.

"Any distinguishing marks or scars?"

Cedric shook his head. "I don't think so."

The officer nodded, put the clipboard under his arm. "That's all for now. You'll be held in a cell until further notice."

Cedric was escorted back down a corridor to the row of holding cells. The officer pointed with a head nod. He wanted Cedric inside. The iron bars clanged shut behind him. He looked around, sat on the edge of a narrow cot, the thin mattress offering little comfort. The cell was dimly lit, the only illumination came from a small, barred window high on the wall.

"You sit tight," the officer said. "When the detectives get here, we'll move you to another room. They'll want to question you then."

He sat back in the chair and closed his eyes. The hum of the gaslight overhead was steady. He looked around, tried to suppress the growing sense of feeling completely overwhelmed by it all. He uttered a quick, silent prayer. A few moments later, from somewhere either inside or around him, a quiet resolve was settling in, almost a sense of peace. He would not panic. He would not plead. He would just wait.

At some point, Charles would be here. Then the attorney, and his father. And at some point, when the time was right, Cedric would tell the truth.

He leaned back against the stone wall and prayed it would be enough.

9

Back at the house, Lily and her mother waited anxiously in the living room. Very little was said. How much time had passed? Twenty minutes? A half hour? How long would they have to wait till Charles or her father called with more news?

Several times Quentin or one of the staff came in to check on them, see if anything was needed. They obviously knew something was wrong, very wrong, but dared not ask. They'd have to be told the truth, at some point. But Lily couldn't bear to face them now.

The silence that had followed since Charles's telephone call was not comfortable. It was heavy, dense, and full of unspoken fears. Mother finally stood a few feet away but didn't move. "Well, I've decided I need to hear more. I know more was said between you and Charles, and that you're holding things back to spare my feelings.

Your father would probably approve. But I want you to tell me everything else that's happened."

Lily turned slowly, looked up at her. "They're taking Cedric to the city jail. The police are calling it a murder investigation. Homicide detectives have already talked with him at the hotel."

Her mother's hand flew to her chest. She turned and walked toward the foyer in a daze. "Oh, my God in heaven." She spun around and came back.

"Charles is with Father," Lily continued. "They're doing everything they can. As I said, Father's probably already contacted Mr. Beaumont, our attorney. Charles is probably already driving to the station, to be with Cedric. Father will be going there as soon as he's spoken with the attorney and settled things at the hotel."

Mother sank back into her chair and reached for the armrest, like a woman twice her age. What little composure she had left seemed to be eroding by the second. "A murder investigation?" she whispered. "With Cedric? They think he killed Reggie? That sweet, respectful boy Cedric played basketball with? How could they even imagine such a thing?"

Lily went on to explain the rest of what she understood had happened, in as quiet and calm a tone as she could manage.

The whole while Mother's eyes were fixed on a spot on the floor, unblinking. She reached absently for the linen cloth Lily had handed her earlier and dabbed the corners of her eyes, careful not to smudge her makeup. "Obviously, our Cedric didn't shoot his friend, but why would anyone want to harm that boy? Who were these men who did this? What were they doing in our hotel?"

"I don't know, Mother," Lily said firmly. "Whatever those two witnesses think they saw...made the police arrest him...no one but Cedric heard or saw the culprits who fled after killing Reggie."

Her mother looked up sharply. "What will happen when the press gets hold of this? We'll be ruined. All the work your father has done over the years to establish his good name, and that of the Belmont."

Lily sat down on the sofa opposite her.

Mother buried her face in the cloth again. "And my poor boy. Oh, Cedric."

Neither spoke for a long moment.

Finally, Mother said, "Your father will be beside himself. You know how hard he's tried to provide for and protect Cedric's future. All his plans for NYU. That position in the hotel he was going to arrange for Cedric after graduation. All the expectations—shattered in a single morning."

Lily looked over. "I don't think Father's worried about those plans right now. I think he just wants his son back."

Mother lowered the cloth and met her daughter's eyes. "Of course, you're right."

Lily leaned forward. "We need to trust the Lord for this. And Father. And Charles. They won't let Cedric face this alone."

"Trust," her mother echoed. "What we need is a miracle."

They sat in silence again. Outside the window, the rain

had eased to a steady mist. Lily watched droplets bead on the glass, tracing lines down the pane like quiet tears.

"I keep seeing his face," Lily said softly. "The way he looked at breakfast this morning. So full of life. He was joking about beating Reggie in a footrace. Said they would most certainly impress the NYU coach at tryouts next month."

Her voice faltered. "But now...Reggie is dead, and...I don't even know what kind of cell they've put Cedric in."

Mother's hand went to her heart again. "I pray they're not treating him like a criminal."

"I think that's the part hurting Charles the most. Seeing Cedric like that... after everything they went through together two years ago. Back then, Cedric stood by him when no one else would. Now it's Charles's turn."

Mother nodded faintly then said, "Could we pray again?"

Lily blinked, looking almost startled. "Yes...yes, we should."

Lily reached for her mother's hand. For a moment, neither spoke. Then Lily began. "Lord," her voice trembling, "we come with heavy hearts. We don't understand what has happened today, but you do. You see Cedric, even now, sitting in that cell. You know he's innocent. Please, Father, protect him. Strengthen him. And send your truth like a river to wash away every lie and false accusation."

Her voice cracked. "Give Father and Charles wisdom. And Mr. Beaumont. Let the truth come out quickly. And please...please comfort Reggie's family. Their grief must be unbearable."

Mother added softly, "And help us be strong for Cedric, Lord. Like Lily said, keep him safe from harm. And especially, Lord...let him come home tonight. Don't make him have to spend even a single night in that jail cell."

When they finished praying, Lily noticed their butler Quentin standing over behind the entrance to the living room. His eyes were closed. He mouthed the words, Amen. She saw tears roll down his cheeks.

10

Charles gripped the steering wheel as his motorcar shuddered over a rough patch of paving stones along Broadway. The sky had cleared since the morning drizzle, but the roads were still damp and the tires hissed lightly over the glistening surface. He glanced at the speedometer — 20 miles per hour. That was 5 mph over the legal limit in central Manhattan, and even that felt reckless. He resisted the urge to push harder. Getting arrested himself for speeding wouldn't help Cedric, and he needed to arrive at the jail clear-headed, not rattled from dodging constables and trolley carts.

Still, every block between him and the precinct stretched his nerves. The city bustled as it always did, carriages and motorcars weaving among slower delivery wagons, pedestrians crossing wherever they pleased. A milk cart jostled by on his left, its wheels shrieking in protest, while a newsboy stood on a corner hawking the latest edition.

Charles slowed but couldn't hear him clearly. Of course, it would be too soon for him to be saying anything about what happened. But Charles had seen two reporters he recognized in the lobby, one from the Times and another from the Herald. So, no doubt they'd be getting the story onto the presses as quickly as possible. He hoped they'd at least not make it in time for today's evening edition.

Not that it much mattered. At the very least—given who was involved—it would be in the papers tomorrow.

Charles's stomach twisted, remembering his own bouts with the press two years ago. The idea of Cedric's face and name smeared across every paper in the city before a proper investigation, filled him with a familiar kind of dread. He knew all too well what it felt like to be judged by whispers and headlines.

Back then suspicion, false accusations, and gossip had nearly stolen everything from him. If not for Lily's courage and Cedric's loyalty, he might have lost her forever, as well as his ice-making business.

Now, poor Cedric was the one in the fire.

The city flew past in bursts — uniformed officers at crosswalks, more newsboys shouting, horses trotting, steam rising from sewer grates. Somewhere beyond the rhythmic clatter of hooves and engines, a church bell struck the quarter hour. He calculated quickly — Cedric had been in custody for about thirty minutes now. That meant fingerprinting. Mug shots. Possibly even a jail cell.

Now he wished he'd had some reason to tell Cedric about the new use of fingerprinting in law enforcement. If he had, maybe it would've been enough to make Cedric think twice before picking up that stupid gun.

He released a sigh and turned onto Houston Street, braking slightly to avoid a reckless bicycle messenger. "Watch it!" Charles muttered, though the boy didn't hear. The poor kid could've ended up under his wheels.

He thought back to the scene he'd left at the hotel. The Belmont had quieted a little. Guests and rubberneckers were being shuffled out of the lobby by hotel staff with practiced grace, and Keller was doing his best to muzzle the press. That, Charles knew, would become an ongoing battle. Nigel had stayed upstairs to telephone his attorney.

It was up to Charles to get there as quickly as possible, hopefully ahead of the detectives.

That thought sank deeper than the rest. He'd read too many newspaper articles in the last year — about corruption hearings, beatings in back alleys, confessions "secured" with fists instead of honest interrogations. Spurred by other sensational cases of police and political corruption, The *Curran Commission* had launched only months ago. Already it was exposing the rot in the city's underbelly. Dozens of officers—even high-ranking ones—had been implicated in payoffs, false arrests, and planting evidence to protect the powerful or punish the unfortunate scapegoats caught in their nets.

But so far, the papers had pointed out, no arrests had

been made, and none of the guilty involved had even lost a day's pay.

How would they handle Cedric Whitaker — son of a wealthy hotelier, accused of killing the son of a powerful Alderman? Poor Cedric was sitting now like a mouse in a snake's cage, subject to that same system, vulnerable to the same cruelties.

Will they see him as a young man in shock, or just a rich boy trying to get away with murder? Charles shook his head, put his foot a little harder on the gas pedal. He had no illusions about how envy worked, having been on the receiving end too often. Some officers wouldn't care that Cedric was innocent. They'd see the suit, the last name, the family's address in Gramercy Park — and decide the boy was due for a lesson.

Lord, please let him keep his mouth shut until I get there, or at least until Beaumont arrives. Don't let him say anything that could be twisted.

A trolley clanged up ahead and Charles veered slightly, maneuvering around it. The jail was just a few blocks now. His shoulders were taut with tension, his collar damp with sweat beneath his coat.

He thought again of Lily — the way her voice cracked when he told her the news. And her mother, both obviously shaken, yet holding it together as best they could. They'd been totally blindsided, all of them had. But now came the part Charles knew best: the fight to uncover the truth and clear Cedric's name. Not with fists or loud voices but with careful words, clear thinking, patience, and the quiet power of persistent prayer.

He turned onto Mulberry Street and spotted the precinct up ahead, all of stone and tarnished brick. He rehearsed a plan that had been forming in his mind. Two immediate goals: Do what he could to protect Cedric from the circling vultures and do everything humanly possible to get him out of that place.

11

About the same time, Nigel Whitaker stood in the center of his office, the receiver pressed to his ear with one hand, the other clenched at his side. He paced slowly across the rug as the operator connected him to Lawrence Beaumont's private line. Every second that passed added weight to the dread in his chest.

Finally, the line clicked.

"Lawrence Beaumont," came the cool, stoic voice.

Nigel exhaled sharply. "Lawrence, it's Nigel Whitaker."

A pause. "Nigel. I assume this isn't a social call, given it's a Saturday and the tone of your voice."

"It's Cedric," Nigel said, turning back toward the window. "He's been arrested." That word *—arrested—* tasted bitter on his tongue.

"Arrested? Cedric? Good Lord. On what grounds?"

Nigel moved behind the desk and finally sat down, the

receiver cord stretching tight between his hand and the cradle. "It's…all a terrible misunderstanding. He was scheduled to meet his friend, Reginald Ashcroft, at the gym in the basement of the Belmont this morning. They call him Reggie."

"Ashcroft," Beaumont repeated. "As in the Head Alderman?"

"Yes, Reggie's his son."

"Right. Go on."

"When Cedric arrived," Nigel said, "he heard men arguing, then he said some strange sound, then two men running away. When he reached Reggie, he was lying on the gym floor. Shot. He called me at once—he was shaken to the core."

"Shot?" Lawrence repeated. "Reginald Ashcroft is dead? And by shot, I assume you're saying foul play was involved."

"Yes, Lawrence. He was shot, with a gun. But oddly, Cedric said there was no sound of gunfire. Nevertheless, when he got to Reggie's body, he saw a clear gunshot wound in his forehead, and Reggie was very obviously deceased.

"So, you're saying your son was found at the scene of a murder?"

"Yes, Lawrence. But it gets worse. But before I explain, you have to know…he didn't do it." Nigel spent the next several moments filling Lawrence in on the details. Lawrence had a way of trying his patience, constantly interrupting with follow-up questions, before Nigel could finish his points. He finally had to ask

Lawrence to please stop interrupting and listen till he was through.

After Nigel had finished, there was a pause. A long one.

"I understand your loyalty, Nigel," Lawrence said finally. "He's your son, and you love him. And I believe you believe him. But if he was found alone with the body...holding the murder weapon...and you've already said, no one else saw or heard the thieves he alleges were the real culprits, then how can you be absolutely sure—"

Nigel slammed his palm on the desk. "He didn't shoot Reggie, Lawrence! Cedric's never held a weapon in his life. He was in shock. He didn't think. He made a foolish mistake—yes. But he didn't kill that boy. Reggie was his closest friend."

"Then why in the world would the weapon be in his bag?" Lawrence asked.

"I don't know," Nigel admitted, the words grinding out of him. No one had asked that question yet. "He said the lockers had been forced open. Maybe someone planted it. Maybe Cedric interrupted the killers and they panicked."

"I can see such a scenario. But given that, wouldn't it have made more sense for them to take the gun with them? Why take the extra time to look for a hiding place?"

"I don't know, Lawrence. None of it makes any sense yet, but the one thing I am certain of, the Cedric I raised would never—*could never*—take another man's life. Let alone a dear friend."

Lawrence released a low sigh. "Okay, I hear you, Nigel. But please understand, my questions don't come from a place of doubt or mistrust in your judgment. But these are the kinds of questions the police will be asking. So, where is Cedric now?"

"At the city jail. They took him away in handcuffs. Charles said he's probably been booked and fingerprinted by now. Possibly in a cell with God knows who. You do know about fingerprints? Charles recently explained the process to me."

"I do know of them. But only from reading. Haven't dealt with them in a case just yet. But from what I gather... if they are present at the scene and on the weapon, and can be matched to your son...well...and you're certain they've charged him?"

"Not certain yet. They said he's being *detained*, but we both know how fast these things escalate. The press is already involved. They know Reggie's father is Alderman Ashcroft. That makes this even worse. They'll be wanting someone to blame."

"And quickly," Lawrence added. "Who were the arresting detectives?"

Nigel had to think a moment. "I believe the one in charge was named Lieutenant Rafferty. His partner was Sergeant Shipley."

Lawrence didn't immediately reply.

"Do you know them?" Nigel said.

"Give me a moment."

Then he came back. "I was just checking. Fortunately, their names have not come up yet in the Curran Commission's investigation. Doesn't mean they're clean, but at least one can hope."

Nigel remembered what the two detectives had said about being glad a shakeup was going on with the New York police. He hoped they meant it. "So, Lawrence. Can you help us? I know it's a Saturday—"

"I'll leave for the station immediately. But Nigel, you must understand, given the nature of the accusation... we're talking murder here—"

"I don't care," Nigel cut in. "You have to get Cedric out of there. He is innocent. I will not allow my son to spend the night locked in a cell with cutthroats and thieves."

"But Nigel, there are protocols," Lawrence said gently.

"Then circumvent them," Nigel said, quieter now but no less forceful. "Use your influence. Pull whatever strings you must. I will pay any amount—*any amount*. Cedric cannot spend the night in that place. Do you understand me?"

There was a silence on the other end. Nigel could hear Lawrence breathing, hear the shift in his tone before he even spoke.

"I believe I can get the magistrate to approve bail tonight," he said. "He owes me some favors. Although I may have to sweeten the pie, given the enormity of the task."

"As I said, Lawrence, I'm willing to pay any amount. And it's not just because he's my son. I know with all my heart he is innocent of this thing." Nigel leaned back, releasing the tight grip on the receiver only slightly.

Lawrence took a deep breath. "I will have to make a few quick calls. I'll have my driver ready my car. Then I'll be down at the station as soon as possible."

"I knew I could count on you, Lawrence," he said, voice raw. "Please...just get my boy out of there. Charles, my son-in-law, should be with him now. I think you've met Charles."

"I have at one of your get-togethers. Seemed like a very amiable and competent fellow."

"He is," Nigel said. "One of the finest men I know."

"Then your son is in good hands until I get there. He does know — Cedric, I mean — he is not to answer any questions from the police."

"Yes, he does. Both Charles and I stressed that to him numerous times."

"Good. Then I'll handle it from here. Go be with your family, Nigel. You've done what you can. Now let me do the rest."

"Well, since you and Charles will be with him. Maybe it's best I go home for a short time to comfort Millicent and Lily."

"That's a good idea. And please tell them — and you take heed of this yourself — do not grant any interviews with the press, under any circumstances."

"Okay, I'll make sure that message is understood. And when you see Cedric, tell him I'll be there shortly. Hopefully within the hour."

"That's fine, Nigel. Certainly, go and be with your son, as much as they'll let you. But you need to be careful here, my friend. I know you are a commanding man who runs a very large and successful hotel. Well over a hundred employees do whatever you tell them. But you can't be that person when you come to the jailhouse. You need to come just as Cedric's father. You start throwing your weight around down there, and it'll have the opposite effect you intend. They will only resent you and possibly even treat Cedric worse as a result. Do you understand what I'm saying?"

Nigel knew exactly what he meant. "Thank you, Lawrence. I'm sure I needed to hear that. Now, go. Be with my son as quickly as you can." Nigel hung up slowly, the receiver settling into its cradle with a soft *click*. He sat there, unmoving, the weight of the morning's events pressing into his shoulders like a millstone.

He had spent his entire life building order out of chaos, sometimes out of nothing. Creating master schedules, magnificent structures, a sterling reputation. But in a single morning, it was as if the devil himself had walked through the doors of his hotel, wearing the mask of death, and dragging his son off in chains.

As he always did in times of wonder, but especially in times of trouble, Nigel prayed, mostly for strength and peace...and the wisdom to know what to say as he faced Millicent and Lily, and the rest of the challenges this day had to offer.

12

Charles's motorcar came to a juddering halt along the east side of Mulberry Street, not far from the steps of the precinct house. He pulled in where he could, careful not to block the fire hydrant or the hitching post still used by mounted patrols. A beat cop gave him a quick glance but said nothing. Charles took that to mean where he'd parked was okay. Adjusting the brim of his fedora, he stepped over the curb and hurried up the worn granite steps.

The station loomed above him — a red brick monolith with soot-streaked columns and iron-rimmed windows. He walked under the high-arched entryway and through the front doors. Typewriters clicked in the distance, boots echoed on the tile floors. Somewhere from inside, a man was yelling but no one seemed to notice.

A patrolman walked by. "Who do I talk to if I'm looking for a suspect recently brought in?"

"Head over to the sergeant's desk." He pointed to a wide, high counter about twenty feet away, where a much older officer scribbled notes into a leather-bound logbook. A brass bell sat beside him.

"Thanks." Charles stepped up to the desk. "Good afternoon," he said, clearing his throat. "I'm here about Cedric Whitaker. A young man brought in this morning. I'm his brother-in-law, Charles Bennington."

The sergeant didn't look up immediately. He finished whatever he'd been writing, then turned with a short nod. "What they bring him in for? We got different places he might be taken to, depending on what he did."

Charles wanted to say he hadn't done anything. "He's being detained on suspicion of murder."

"Murder? Well, don't get too many of those in this precinct. Pretty sure I know who you mean. A young fella?"

"Yes, Cedric's a college student. Goes to NYU."

The Sergeant flipped a few pages. "Whitaker...yes. Came in just after ten. Homicide picked him up."

"I need to see him."

The sergeant eyed him cautiously. "You an attorney?"

"No. Family. As I said, I'm his brother-in-law. I understand his attorney is on the way."

The man chewed on that for a moment. His lips pressed together, then he said, "Wait here."

Charles stepped aside, glancing around the station house. It was bigger than he'd expected — open like a warehouse in the middle, a wide staircase off to the right. One hallway stretched toward the back, lit by bare bulbs and lined with heavy wooden doors. On the wall nearby was a mounted bulletin board littered with mugshots and wanted posters. Many curled at the edges, browned by time.

Involuntarily, he began to read the largest ones, then two men came walking around a corner. It was Lieutenant Rafferty and Sergeant Shipley, following behind. Rafferty spotted Charles first.

"Mr. Bennington?" he asked, approaching with long strides.

"Yes."

"Lieutenant Rafferty. This is Sergeant Shipley."

"I remember your names. I'd like to see Cedric."

"I'm afraid that's not possible just now," Rafferty said. "We're preparing to question him."

Charles frowned. "If you recall, his father gave instructions at the hotel for Cedric not to be interviewed without his attorney present. Mr. Whitaker asked if I'd come sit with Cedric until he arrives."

"We understand," Rafferty said, smoothing his mustache with a thumb. "But your father-in-law is not in charge here. This is a murder investigation, not some petty crime. We're handling everything by the book. Your brother-in-law has a right not to answer our questions. But we've got every right to ask them... without family interference. Don't want you intimidating him when we talk."

"Me? Intimidate Cedric?" Charles raised his voice. "We both know if he feels intimidated during your interview, where it'll be coming from."

Rafferty made a face. "You can see your brother-in-law when we're done. If you wanna wait, wait over there." He gestured toward a row of stiff-backed chairs lining the corridor wall.

Sergeant Shipley said nothing, only watched Charles, as if sizing him up.

Charles hesitated. Then, with a curt nod, he walked toward the chairs. The moment the officers moved down the hallway and around the corner, Charles followed at a distance. He stopped just short of the corner. From there, he could hear them plainly just a few feet away.

"Why'd you tell him he couldn't see the kid?" Shipley asked, his voice lowered. "That's not in the book."

"Because this is likely our last shot," Rafferty muttered. "Once that lawyer walks through the door, the kid'll clam up. You saw how shaken he looked when they brought him in — there's a chance he might talk if we get in there first."

"You think he'll confess?"

Rafferty shrugged. "He might say something useful. I don't need a full confession. Just something that sticks."

Charles's jaw tightened.

The two men continued walking, moving further away from him. Charles peeked around the corner, saw them at the end of the hallway talking to another cop. Rafferty's voice got loud and annoyed.

"What do you mean, he's not here?"

"Still in holding, sir," the cop said.

"Well, get him," Rafferty snapped. "Now."

That officer turned left and disappeared. Footsteps

echoed down the corridor. Charles leaned back against the wall, heart pounding. It was just as he suspected. These men weren't looking for truth. They were looking for leverage, some way to make their trumped-up accusations against Cedric stick.

He hurried out the front door, hoping to see any sign of his father-in-law's attorney pulling up in his car.

CEDRIC SAT HUNCHED in the holding cell on a narrow wooden bench, his jacket rumpled, his collar open. He couldn't stop shivering. Heavy footsteps echoed in the corridor outside. A moment later, the key rattled in the lock. The iron door scraped open.

"On your feet, Whitaker," barked the same officer who'd stuck him in the cell. "You've got company."

Cedric stood slowly. The officer didn't wait for Cedric to collect himself. Instead, he reached in, grabbed his arm just above the elbow, and yanked him out into the corridor. "You're headed to the interview room," the cop said, walking briskly as he steered Cedric down the corridor. "Lieutenant Rafferty and Sergeant Shipley want another word."

Cedric didn't say anything.

The officer sneered. "Word of advice, kid. You'd better open up and talk to them. You don't want to get on their bad side."

"I already told them all I'm gonna say until my attorney gets here," Cedric muttered.

The officer laughed. "That's not what they think. And let me tell you — they don't take kindly to rich boys who think they're smarter than the law."

They turned a corner, passing another cell. A man inside with dead eyes watched them walk by.

"You talk now, things'll with go much better for you," the officer went on. "Keep playing the innocent choirboy, and they'll throw the book at you. Or worse. Rafferty, he's not one to be kept waiting. You hear me?"

Cedric gave no reply.

They reached the interview room, and the officer opened the door with a grunt. Rafferty and Shipley were seated at the same side of the table.

"Well, look who decided to join us," Rafferty said. "Come in, Cedric. Have a seat."

Cedric hesitated, then stepped inside. The officer shut the door behind him. The room was narrow, windowless, and hot. A single lamp buzzed above the table.

Shipley gestured toward the empty chair. "We just want to follow up. You understand."

"I told you everything I have to say at the hotel," Cedric said, his voice strained. "I've got nothing new to add."

Rafferty leaned back in his chair, arms crossed. "You sure about that? No new details come to mind? Nothing you might've remembered after sitting in that cell the past hour?"

Cedric looked down at his hands. "Not until my attorney gets here."

Shipley chuckled. "You really think your lawyer's gonna fix this? He's not going to bring Reggie back, son."

Cedric's jaw clenched. "But I didn't kill Reggie."

Rafferty leaned in closer. "Then you've got nothing to hide. So why the need for a lawyer? Innocent men don't need lawyers, do they?"

"I—" Cedric stopped. His heart pounding.

"C'mon," Rafferty said as he stood, began to pace. "You walk into the gym. Your friend's already there. Maybe you two argued. Things got heated. Somebody said something they shouldn't say. The situation escalated. It happens."

"There was no argument," Cedric said through gritted teeth. "Not between us. And I didn't shoot him."

Shipley said in a softer tone. "Son, listen. We know what those two guests said they saw. You with the gun. Standing over the body. And you haven't disputed what they said, so we're treating it as fact. Nobody else saw anybody else in that basement. Nobody but you. You come clean now, maybe we can get the DA to go easy on you. Right now, it's your word against all the facts at the scene."

"And facts don't lie, kid," Rafferty said. "The way things stack up now, I'd say you're looking at a seat in the electric chair...and not too many weeks from now. Sing Sing, ever heard of the place? That's where you're headed. This thing is almost open and shut...unless you can tell us something we're not seeing so far."

Cedric shuddered inside at these things but suppressed the almost aching desire to defend himself. He imagined screaming at them, "I didn't do it." Instead, he looked down at the table, said, "I want my attorney. I'm not saying anything more."

Rafferty's face darkened. "We're trying to help you, boy. You think this Ashcroft situation's going to just blow over? You know who his father is. He's one of the most powerful men in this town."

"I know," Cedric said. "That's why I need a lawyer."

The room went quiet for a beat.

The door burst open.

"Enough," Charles said. His voice cut through the tension like a blade. "That's enough."

Rafferty turned. "You have no authority in here, Mr. Bennington."

"Maybe not," Charles said, "but according to the Constitution, neither do you. You were told an attorney was on his way. So, this stops now. If you've any interest in actual justice, you'll respect his father's wishes and wait until Cedric is properly represented."

Shipley glanced at Rafferty. Rafferty said nothing.

Charles stepped farther into the room, stood beside Cedric's chair. "I suggest," he said coldly, "you find something else to do with your time until Mr. Lawrence Beaumont arrives."

"Beaumont." Rafferty scowled.

"So, you've heard of him," Charles said.

Rafferty said nothing and stormed from the room.

Sergeant Shipley lingered a moment longer, then followed.

Cedric let out a breath he didn't know he was holding.

Charles sat down beside him. “They didn’t lay hands on you, did they?”

“No,” Cedric said. “Not yet.”

Charles nodded. “Good. Mr. Beaumont will be here any minute.

Cedric nodded. And for the first time in over an hour, felt something that resembled a feeling of safety.

13

Charles stood near the far end of the corridor outside the interview room, his arms crossed, eyes on the wall clock, hoping to see the attorney arrive. Every ticking minute felt soaked with tension. He'd kept his distance since interrupting the detectives, staying where the desk sergeant could see him but not interfering further. He wasn't family, not legally anyway, and the officers made it known that he had no standing.

But Charles wasn't going anywhere.

They had taken a short break to escort Cedric to the bathroom.

The weight of it all—Cedric's arrest, the hostile detectives, the looming shadow of Reggie Ashcroft's powerful father—pressed down on him. The police clearly had no interest in justice, only in resolving the case quickly, efficiently, and with someone adequate to blame. Charles feared that Cedric, in all his youthful idealism, was the perfect scapegoat.

A few minutes later, now just past noon, the double doors at the front precinct opened, and in stepped a tall, silver-haired man in a tailored gray suit. His dark eyes scanned the station like a general entering a battlefield. The desk sergeant — who'd obviously recognized the man — gestured toward Charles.

"Mr. Bennington?" the man said. "Lawrence Beaumont."

Charles stepped forward and extended his hand. "Thank you for coming so quickly."

"Nigel Whitaker rarely calls in a favor, and when he does, it's never trivial."

"They're taking a short break," Charles said, "to let Cedric use the bathroom."

"Okay, tell me everything you can in less than five minutes. I don't want to leave Cedric alone with them any longer."

Charles walked him quickly through the morning's events: the discovery of Reggie's body, Cedric's arrest, the rushed and aggressive nature of the investigation, and the heated exchanges with Lieutenant Rafferty. "They've got nothing conclusive," Charles said. "Only that Cedric was found with the gun in his hand and was alone with the body. But they're clearly trying to box him in as the murderer. You should have heard how this Lieutenant went after Cedric a few moments ago."

A glimmer of restrained anger passed through Beaumont's eyes. "Let's make sure that doesn't happen. Take me to him."

Charles led him down the corridor. As they approached the interview room, Rafferty and Shipley were just bringing Cedric back in. Rafferty spotted them and stepped forward.

"Listen, Mr. Bowman. You can't come barging in and derail our investigation—"

"Beaumont," the attorney corrected. "Counsel for Cedric Whitaker. And I most certainly can. We're done here unless you wish to proceed in violation of the Constitution and the State of New York."

Shipley opened his mouth, then closed it again. Rafferty muttered something under his breath and pushed the door open.

Inside, Cedric took a seat at the table, still visibly shaken. His shoulders sagged with exhaustion, but seeing and hearing Beaumont, something in his posture lifted.

Beaumont crossed to him, set down his briefcase, and placed a steadying hand on Cedric's shoulder.

"From this moment on, say nothing unless I instruct you to. Understood?"

Cedric nodded.

"Can I stay?" Charles said. "Just to support Cedric? His father should be arriving soon."

"Yeah, but he ain't here yet," Rafferty said. "And you ain't exactly family, so no, you can't stay." He looked at Beaumont, almost for approval.

Beaumont nodded to Charles then turned to the

detectives. "Gentlemen, if you have questions, I'm listening."

So, Charles was out in the hallway again.

CEDRIC HATED the way they talked to Charles and especially hated that he wasn't going to be there. But he did seem to be in good hands now with his father's attorney.

For the next fifteen minutes, Beaumont and the detectives danced around the same accusations. Shipley took a more active role than before, soft-voiced and conciliatory. He spoke of how much evidence they had stacked up, how silence sometimes worked against a suspect, how juries respected those who spoke truthfully and without fear.

Beaumont cut in every time Cedric tried to answer.

Finally, frustrated, Rafferty slammed his palm against the table. "Listen, Beaumont, all you're doing is being vague and evasive. It's obvious we're not going to get any further here. But the thing is, we already have enough to charge him."

Beaumont calmly rose. "Then I suggest you do so, if that is your intention. But know this—any premature move unsupported by evidence will be undone by the truth. And I will ensure it happens publicly."

Rafferty stared at him then pushed away from the table.

. . .

Outside in the corridor, Charles stood waiting nearby. The interview door opened and out walked Rafferty and Shipley.

"Don't get any ideas about going back in there. We won't be gone that long."

Just before the interview room door shut again, he glanced down the hallway and saw two familiar faces enter the precinct front doors—the two hotel guests who had seen Cedric with the gun. They were speaking with an officer and being guided into a separate room—no doubt to give formal statements.

His gut turned. He didn't despise these men. What other choice did they have? They saw what they saw, but he realized how bad things would go for Cedric when the statements were made on paper and notarized. Between them, the gun in Cedric's gym bag, with his fingerprints... things looked very bleak. He knew what their testimony might mean, especially when manipulated or misinterpreted.

An idea popped into his head as he thought again about the damaging fingerprint evidence. His thoughts turned to Keller, the hotel security chief. Charles needed to speak with him as soon as possible —Keller's background as a former cop might prove invaluable right now.

Back inside the interview room, Beaumont remained beside Cedric, completely composed. Cedric tried to match that stillness, but inside, a storm was turning in his gut. He leaned toward Beaumont. "They're going to charge me," he whispered, "aren't they?"

"Let them," Beaumont said. "If they do, it doesn't mean this is over. We've barely begun this fight. So far, all I've seen from them is posturing."

But it didn't feel like posturing to Cedric. It felt like the walls were closing in. Like every ounce of truth and decency in the world was being swallowed up by some dark, unseen hand.

The door creaked open again. Rafferty strode in with purpose, holding a manila folder. He opened it slowly. "Mr. Whitaker, you are hereby charged with the murder of Reginald Ashcroft. You will be arraigned later today."

Cedric said nothing. His throat was dry. Beaumont simply gave a curt nod. "Then we're done here."

Rafferty stared at Cedric for a beat longer, as if expecting a reaction, then turned and left.

Sergeant Shipley was there to lead Cedric back to the holding area. Beaumont leaned in and spoke low. "You will not be staying here tonight, son. I'll see to that personally."

Cedric glanced at him. "But how?"

"Night court," he said. "It's not that common, but with enough pressure—and a few promises—I believe I can convince a magistrate to set bail."

Cedric blinked, uncertain. "Even for murder?"

"Under normal circumstances, no," Beaumont said. "But you're not a flight risk. You're not some nameless vagrant. You come from a prominent, established family.

You attend one of our premier schools. And I intend to remind the magistrate of that—firmly."

A slight hope flickered inside Cedric. "Thank you."

Beaumont gave a faint smile. "You're welcome. And you did well in here today. Keeping your mouth closed when so many accusations are being flung about takes real courage."

Cedric smiled. They shook hands then he was escorted down a side hallway. The last thing he saw before they turned a corner was Charles and the attorney chatting about something. Whatever it was, Charles looked quite animated.

He paused, nodded to Cedric, and kept right on talking.

14

The afternoon light filtered softly through the lace curtains in the Whitakers' formal parlor, lending the room a fragile calm that felt completely at odds with the heaviness in Lily's chest. She sat beside her mother on the sofa, hands clasped tightly in her lap. Quentin stood a few respectful feet away, near the hearth.

Mother had always been a woman who carried herself with unshakable composure, but today, she looked smaller somehow—drained. Her hands clutched the linen napkin Lily had given her earlier, although the tears for both had temporarily abated.

They anxiously awaited Father's arrival. He'd called a short while ago, informing them he was coming home briefly to share how things had gone at the hotel.

After that call, Lily gently insisted that her mother inform the house staff. Mother had agreed, so they'd asked Quentin to join them. He'd been with the family longer than Lily had been alive, and he loved Cedric like one of his own. Quentin had come at once, his usual graceful poise touched by a grave expression on his face.

"I'm grateful you called me in, Mrs. Whitaker," he said softly. "I've been worried about the young master ever since that phone call this morning. Then the way Mr. Bennington and your husband hurried out the door in such haste."

Mother nodded once, looked to Lily. Lily felt it was her mother's place to say these things to Quentin, but she'd said she feared losing her composure halfway through in a flood of tears.

Lily took a breath, steadied her voice. "Quentin, there's no good way to begin this tale. Cedric has been arrested. They're saying he shot Reggie Ashcroft."

The color drained from Quentin's face. "Shot him, Miss Lily? That can't be right."

Quentin still called her that, even though now — by rights — he should refer to her as Mrs. Bennington. But Lily couldn't bring herself to correct him.

Mother cleared her throat delicately, keeping her emotions in check. Lily continued. "It appears shortly after it happened, two witnesses found him with the weapon in hand standing over the body. But Charles and Father are convinced — after hearing Cedric's explanation —it's all a terrible mistake."

Quentin took a measured step closer, his voice lower now. "This is so awful. Does the young master have an advocate at the station? A solicitor?"

"Yes," Mother said. "Nigel sent for Mr. Beaumont. He's likely arrived at the precinct by now."

There was a long pause. Lily noticed Quentin's lips part slightly as if he meant to speak, but he pressed them together again.

"You can say it, Quentin," Lily said gently. "Whatever you were going to say."

He bowed his head. "Only that I know the kind of man Master Cedric is. He would never—never—do such a thing. He's kind and honest, and he always stands up for others, especially when they're being treated unfairly. And as best I can tell, he and master Reggie are the closest of friends. I've never even heard a cross word between them. Whatever happened at the hotel, it must undoubtedly be a misunderstanding of some grievous kind."

Mother nodded, but her eyes were glassy now. She raised the handkerchief to dab them.

"Forgive me," Quentin said quickly. "I don't mean to upset you, Ma'am. It's just...I've known him since he was in swaddling clothes. I can't even imagine what he must be going through right now, being falsely accused of something so terrible."

His voice broke slightly at the end. Lily swallowed hard. She looked over at her mother, whose composure was starting to fade. Lily quickly rose to her feet, stepped to the drawer in the nearby sideboard where her mother kept extra linens, and returned with three folded napkins.

She handed one to Quentin, who took it with a quiet nod of thanks. Then one to her mother, who accepted it without a word. She kept the last one for herself. For a long moment, the room was still but for the heavy sighs of shared grief.

"Would you be willing," Lily said, "to gather the household staff in the servant's dining room and explain what's happened?"

Quentin nodded solemnly. "At once, Miss Lily."

As he turned and left the room, he stopped briefly. "And we will all spend a few moments in prayer for you all. And for us. I know everyone will be utterly distressed by this news."

Lily resumed her seat beside her mother, offering quiet comfort with her presence. The clock on the mantel chimed the half-hour. The seconds dragged by.

THE FRONT DOOR opened a short time later. Father stepped into the parlor, removed his hat, and exhaled. His wife rose immediately. Lily stood beside her.

He crossed the room and wrapped Mother in his arms. She clung to him more tightly than she had in years.

"He's all right," Nigel said softly. "Shaken a good bit, but all right."

Lily touched her father's arm. "They didn't hurt him, did they?"

"No," he said. "At least not physically. But the situation is very serious."

They sat again on the sofa, Lily on one side, Mother on the other. Nigel placed his hat on the tea table and rubbed his forehead, preferring to stand.

"Likely by now, Cedric has been formally charged," he said.

Mother gasped. To Lily, it felt like a punch in the stomach.

"Given the nature of things, it seems," Nigel said quickly. "But I'm sure Mr. Beaumont is with him now. He will have stopped the detectives from pressing Cedric any further and advised him not to say another word. By what Cedric said as they led him out the front doors of the hotel —" His voice broke saying that. He cleared his throat and continued. "I'm sure Cedric is now doing exactly what we need him to."

He briefly summarized the rest of what he knew: the failed attempt by Rafferty and Shipley to get Cedric to confess, the arrival of the witnesses from the hotel, the chaos in the lobby. He neglected to mention whether the press had shown up yet, but Lily knew, if they had he wouldn't have said so, for her mother's sake.

"Mr. Beaumont says he's going to petition for Cedric to be released on bail," Nigel added. "He's going to try to get it done tonight through night court."

Mother looked alarmed. "Night court? But will a judge even hear such a thing for a murder charge?"

"Normally, no," Nigel said. "But Beaumont knows the system. He believes with the right arguments—and with a name like Whitaker attached to the case—he can make a compelling plea."

Lily leaned forward. "Do you think it's possible they will let Cedric come home?"

"If the magistrate grants it," Nigel said, "he could be

home before midnight. But we must be patient. Beaumont may need to make arrangements behind the scenes."

Mother's hands trembled slightly as she reached for her tea. Lily moved to steady the cup.

"That's really all there is to say at the moment. I only came home to check on the both of you," he said. "I can't stay. I'm going back now to wait with Charles and Mr. Beaumont until we see this thing through."

Mother stood and hugged him. "Go, Nigel. Don't you worry about us. You just do whatever you must to bring our boy home."

Nigel released her from the hug and immediately embraced Lily.

"We're proud of you, Father," Lily said. "We're praying God gives you and Mr. Beaumont supernatural wisdom and favor with these people."

"Thanks." He smiled faintly, gathered his hat, and moved toward the front door.

"And don't forget to tell Charles I love him," she said. He smiled again before he left, and she realized how awkward it would be for him to say something like that to Charles.

15

Still at the police station, Charles found a couple of pay phones in a recessed alcove of the police station lobby. Neither were occupied. He stepped into the wood-paneled booth, dialed the operator, and gave her the number for the Hotel Belmont. After a moment, the operator patched him through to Mr. Keller's office.

"Keller speaking," came the steady voice of the security chief.

"Mr. Keller. It's Charles Bennington. Thank you for taking the call. So glad you haven't left yet."

"Well, actually I live here at the hotel. After my wife left me a couple of years ago, well, Mr. Whitaker found out about it and offered me a room here. Hardly charges me anything for it, said it would be good to have someone like me on the premises. Well, sorry, you didn't call to hear my tale of woe. How are things going there? How's everyone holding up?"

Charles took a few minutes to bring Keller up to speed. "Listen, I need to ask you something, and it's important. Has the gym at the hotel remained closed off since this morning?"

"Yes, sir," Keller said. "Mr. Whitaker instructed me personally to keep it sealed. No staff, no guests, in or out."

Charles breathed a sigh of relief. "Good. That's really good. Keller, back when you were a cop, did you work with fingerprints at all?"

"Fingerprints? A bit, yes. I wasn't in homicide, but I worked burglary cases during my final year. We'd started using fingerprints to identify suspects. It was becoming a pretty common thing."

"Then you'll know exactly why I'm calling," Charles said. "The police will no doubt present Cedric's fingerprints on the murder weapon as key evidence."

"I thought about that as soon as I heard he handled the gun."

"Right, and we already know they'll find them— Cedric already admitted to holding it. But if Cedric is telling the truth — and I believe he is — then at least two other men were in that gym this morning. They forced open the lockers, likely handled the bag, and used the rear exit."

Keller was silent for a moment. "I follow you. If we can get hold of those prints, it'll prove what Cedric said."

"Exactly. I want someone to dust the lockers, the gym bag, and especially the rear door and knob. But it must be done quietly. The police aren't going to help us, not with who Reggie's father is."

"Understood," Keller said. "But Mr. Bennington, without having those two culprits in custody, we won't have any way to connect any prints we might find to them."

"That's true. But we need to preserve those fingerprint samples at all cost, just in case we find out who they are down the road."

"Gotcha, but you know, I don't have the kit anymore. My old partner might. He left the force when I did—same reason. Sick of the corruption. I got the job here at the hotel. He became a private detective. I'm certain he'd help."

"Can we trust him?" Charles asked. "Truly?"

"I trusted him with my life...many times. He's one of the good ones."

"Then make this your top priority, Keller. I'll pay whatever he charges, no questions asked. Just stress the need for total discretion. Not a word to anyone."

"You have my word, Mr. Bennington. I'll get right on it."

"Thanks, and Mr. Keller. If we're going to be working together, just call me Charles."

"Right, sir. And you can call me Bill...if you're okay with that."

"All right, Bill." Charles was about to hang up but remembered something. "Bill, I've been meaning to ask you...I know you carry a gun at the hotel. But how about the other men who work for you? Do they carry guns also?"

"No. There's only four of us. But I'm the only one with a gun. I gave them nightsticks. But they're purely for looks, to maybe intimidate someone who might think of causing trouble. But, I gotta tell you. They've never even swung those sticks at anyone. You know the kind of people who stay at this hotel. I've never even pulled my gun out of the holster before this."

"Thanks, Bill. We'll be in touch." Charles hung up and said a quick prayer of thanks for this small glimmer of hope.

After the call, Charles returned briefly to the holding area, where he learned Cedric had been placed back in his cell to await his arraignment. With nothing more to be done at the station, Charles, Nigel, and Beaumont left for the Belmont Hotel dining room to get a meal and regroup. And it gave Nigel a few moments to get with his department heads and give them a quick update and fresh instructions.

During dinner, Charles shared his fingerprint idea with the others. Beaumont clearly liked it, said it was a solid plan, and could potentially make a big difference in the case.

Most of the rest of the meal was spent preparing for what lay ahead in night court. Beaumont gave a careful rundown of what he expected to happen, including some hints at the conversations he'd already had with the magistrate, as well as the strings he'd pulled. He said a few things in code, particularly to Nigel, that seemed to indicate some money might have changed hands.

Nigel nodded and didn't seem the least bit disturbed by this news.

NOW, back at the courthouse that evening, night court was just getting underway. The room was small, less formal than the daytime proceedings, but it was surprisingly crowded. The magistrate sat atop a raised platform, gavel in hand, robe slightly askew, as if hastily dressed.

Cedric stood near the front, flanked by two officers, his wrists no longer cuffed. Beaumont stood beside him, composed and confident. Charles and Nigel took seats behind them in the gallery.

More than two dozen newspaper reporters filled the rear benches of the courtroom, some scribbling furiously, others whispering to one another about the case. Charles recognized several that had been at the Hotel Belmont earlier that day. Now they were back, their editors clearly sensing this story was gaining traction fast.

To the left, seated a few rows back, were two unfamiliar but imposing men—one older, with a finely trimmed beard wearing an expensive waistcoat, the other younger, looked all around, taking in the scene. Both had bowler hats sitting on their laps. They had entered quietly, drawing little attention. Charles hadn't even noticed them at first.

The magistrate cleared his throat. "Bring forward the case of the People vs. Cedric Whitaker."

Rafferty and Shipley stepped forward to offer the charge. Rafferty spoke, "The defendant is formally accused of the murder of Reginald Ashcroft, your honor. All of the reasons given for this action are listed there in the report."

Murmurs rippled through the courtroom. Reporters leaned forward, pens poised.

Beaumont stepped forward immediately. "Your Honor, the defense requests immediate release of the accused into the custody of his father, Nigel Whitaker, pending trial. My client is a lifelong resident of New York, comes from a well-established and reputable family, is enrolled in one of our prestigious universities, has absolutely no criminal record, and poses no flight risk."

The magistrate looked down at him, expression unreadable. "Mr. Beaumont, you and I spoke earlier today. I understand the circumstances."

There was a pause.

Just as the magistrate began to speak again, the older man from the gallery stood.

"Pardon the interruption, Your Honor. I am Franklin Dorlan, representing Head Alderman Ashcroft and his family. The Alderman is not present due to the profound grief at the loss of his son. But he strongly opposes the release of the accused."

A quiet gasp ran through the room. Beaumont turned slowly, studying Dorlan with interest.

"The court is well aware of who you are, Mr. Dorlan,"

the magistrate said. "On what basis do you raise this opposition? The points raised by Mr. Beaumont on behalf of the accused are factually true."

"On the basis of the overwhelming evidence already presented against the accused. I have read the reports submitted to you by the detectives. My clients are concerned that allowing this defendant to walk free—even under supervision—poses both a flight risk and a danger to public confidence. Not to mention adding greatly to the grief being experienced by the Head Alderman and his family."

Beaumont stepped forward. "Your Honor, with all due respect, Mr. Dorlan represents neither the district attorney's office nor the state. He has no standing in these proceedings."

The magistrate hesitated.

"If the court pleases," Beaumont added calmly, "I request a brief recess to discuss this matter in chambers."

The magistrate agreed, and both men exited the courtroom.

Charles leaned forward. "Who is that man?"

Nigel whispered back, "A political viper. Ashcroft's attack dog."

IN CHAMBERS, Beaumont closed the door behind them and faced the magistrate. "I understand your hesitation," he said. "Truly. But you gave me your word."

"That was before the Alderman's office got involved."

"And now I ask you to remember what else we

discussed," Beaumont said, lowering his voice. "The Curran Commission is watching everyone these days. Have I mentioned that they've asked me to serve on their advisory panel?"

The magistrate paled.

Beaumont leaned in. "You've already accepted a favor in this case. If you reverse course now, I'm afraid you won't just have me to answer to."

There was a long pause. Then the magistrate gave a slow nod. "Let's get back in there."

They returned to the courtroom. The gallery quieted.

THE MAGISTRATE CLEARED HIS THROAT. "The defendant, Cedric Whitaker, shall be released into the custody of his father, Mr. Nigel Whitaker, under condition that he remain within the city limits and report to the court weekly. Bail is set at one thousand dollars."

Gasps broke out again—this time from Dorlan, who rose in protest.

"Your Honor, I must insist—"

"Sit down, Mr. Dorlan," the magistrate said curtly. "You are out of order."

The gavel struck wood.

Cedric turned to Charles and Nigel, a mix of disbelief and relief on his face. Beaumont leaned over.

"We've bought you some time, young man. Let's use it well. Remember, we are by no means out of the woods here."

As the courtroom began to empty, the reporters surged forward like a breaking wave.

"*Mr. Whitaker!*" "*Cedric, did you do it?*" "*Mr. Bennington, what happened in there?*" "*Was bail arranged ahead of time*?"

Beaumont raised a hand and spoke firmly. "No comment, gentlemen."

The four of them moved swiftly through the crowd, ignoring the flashing bulbs and shouted questions. Behind them, Rafferty, Shipley, and Dorlan remained near the magistrate's bench.

Dorlan lingered, eyeing the press with calculating interest, as though deciding whether he might soon offer a statement of his own.

16

When Charles awoke, his first thoughts were about the dramatic scene at the front door last night when Cedric first arrived. Prior to this, he had never seen Millicent display a single emotion that wasn't held tightly under wraps. But she was simply undone seeing him walking through the door. Shrieks of laughter mixed with tears, bear hugs, and a face full of kisses. She was so happy.

A pleasant memory.

Charles rolled over and looked out the window. The morning light seeped in through the sheer curtains of Lily's childhood bedroom, casting long lines across the embroidered bedspread. It had been two years since she'd lived in this room. It felt very strange for Charles to wake up in the same bed where she'd spent her youth. Only now, they were together as a married couple. He smiled as he recalled, he hadn't even been allowed up here in this room for the entirety of their engagement.

Charles, already dressed in a crisp, dark suit, was fastening his cufflinks near the tall mirror, as Lily smoothed down the sleeves of her modest breakfast gown. She caught his reflection watching her.

"I really appreciate you being willing to do this. To sleep here, I mean." Lily offered a faint smile. "I know it's not ideal. Did you hate it?"

"No, I could never hate being with you, regardless of where. It was just...I don't know..."

"Awkward?" she said.

"That's the word."

"Well, you needn't worry about whether my parents even gave the two of us a thought, being in here I mean. I'm sure they were both totally overwhelmed by what happened yesterday."

"I'm sure you're right," he said.

"I just didn't want to be away from them—not after everything that happened. I think it will help, at least some, having us here as soon as we all get up, rather than them having to wait on us to get down here from our apartment." She moved to stand beside him, adjusted his collar. "This house...it's where Cedric needs us to be right now. Maybe my parents, too. I still can't believe we got him home."

Charles nodded. "Of course. I understand." He glanced toward the hallway. "I just hope they got some rest." He actually felt quite rested.

Lily took his hand, and they walked downstairs. "I'm not sure I'll have much of an appetite," he said.

"Me, either. But I think it's just being here that matters."

The faint clinking of china and the scent of coffee met them as they approached the dining room. The scene was so familiar it might have been comforting, if not for the undercurrent of grief and worry hanging in the air. It was hard to believe they were here just twenty-four hours ago, facing a similar breakfast scene. The one where Cedric had excused himself early to drive over to the hotel gym to meet Reggie for a workout.

Charles pondered, how differently everything might have gone had Cedric simply stayed at the table and finished his breakfast. If he and Reggie had scheduled their workout for later that morning. Of course, it did no good to dwell on things like this. They had to face the hand they'd all been dealt and trust God to guide them through this odd maze that had now become their lives.

Nigel sat at the head of the table, Cedric to his right, both hunched and hollow-eyed. Millicent sat upright at the other end, her posture immaculate despite the strain visible on her face. Cedric's hands were wrapped around a steaming cup of coffee, just staring at his plate of food. Even the staff moved more quietly than usual, as if in mourning.

Charles pulled out a chair for Lily before sitting beside her. Quentin stepped forward and began to pour everyone's coffee with the same ceremonial grace he'd perfected over the years.

But Nigel barely acknowledged the gesture, frowned. "Quentin, where is my morning paper? You always bring it with the coffee."

Quentin hesitated, still holding the silver carafe. "Forgive me, sir. I…wasn't sure if you'd want to see it at the table this morning."

Nigel's brows rose. "Why wouldn't I?"

Quentin's voice lowered. "Given the subject matter, sir. The headline. It's quite…startling. You know, given yesterday's events. I thought maybe you'd want to read it privately in your study, afterward."

"Maybe he's right, Nigel." Millicent said, "It might ruin what little appetite I have left."

Nigel shook his head. "No. We've all lived through this together. Let's not pretend it didn't happen." He looked at Cedric. "Unless you'd be too upset, son."

Cedric looked up. "What? No, I'm okay, Father. I saw the reporters in the lobby and we all saw them yelling at us last night as we left the station. Given who Reggie's father is, I knew they'd have to say something about it in the papers."

Quentin continued standing in place. "It's quite a bit more than *something*," he said.

Nigel looked up at him. "Thank you for your concern, Quentin. But please bring it here."

He hesitated a bit longer then gave a small bow. "Very good, sir."

He returned moments later, newspaper neatly folded. With some reluctance, he handed it to Nigel, who unfurled the front page with practiced precision.

The bold headline screamed across the top in thick black ink. Charles could see it from where he sat:

SCANDAL AT THE BELMONT
Son of Head Alderman Found Dead in Gymnasium
Young Man Arrested

A sharp silence fell over the table. All the color seemed to drain from Nigel's face. He read it over and over, his eyes darting back and forth.

"Nigel, what does it say?" Millicent said. "Let us see."

Nigel held it up.

Millicent gasped, her eyes wide as saucers. Cedric looked horrified. Nigel exhaled heavily, eyes narrowing as he continued reading.

"Are you just going to read it to yourself?" Millicent said.

"Yes, dear. Just give me a minute." He kept reading, the lines in his face seemed to grow deeper with every paragraph.

When he looked up, Lily said. "Please, Father. Can Charles and I see it?"

He passed the paper across the table toward Lily. She laid it down between her and Charles so they could read it together. Her mother and Cedric got up and both came behind them, and read it over their shoulders.

In a startling development that has sent ripples through Manhattan's upper circles, Reginald Ashcroft, son of the powerful Head Alderman Herbert Ashcroft, was found murdered yesterday morning in the private gymnasium of the prestigious Hotel Belmont. The victim, aged 21, was discovered in the locker room with a single gunshot wound to the forehead. A pistol, believed to be the murder weapon, was recovered at the scene.

Cedric Whitaker, son of hotel proprietor Nigel Whitaker and a promising athlete at NYU, was arrested shortly after the body was discovered. Mr. Whitaker, 20, was reportedly the first to find the body and was seen holding the gun when two guests entered the gymnasium and fled in alarm. Mr. Whitaker was immediately detained by hotel security and, shortly after, handed over to the authorities.

The case, already drawing significant public interest due to the standing of both families involved, took a dramatic turn late last night during an unusual session of night court. Appearing before Magistrate Townsend, Whitaker was formally charged with murder but was then released on bail.

This sparked outrage in the courtroom gallery. Attorney Franklin Dorlan, representing Alderman Ashcroft and his family, stood to oppose the bail motion, citing public safety and the gravity of the evidence pointing to the young Whitaker's guilt. Attorney Beaumont, representing the Whitaker family, was able to secure bail for the young Whitaker.

Sources suggest that Attorney Beaumont plays some role in the ongoing Curran Commission investigation into municipal corruption.

As the gavel struck to conclude proceedings, a flurry of questions rained down upon the Whitaker family and Attorney Beaumont, as they exited the courthouse. All declined to comment.

Lieutenant James Rafferty and Sergeant Frank Shipley, the detectives assigned to the case, have promised a thorough investigation.

The funeral of Reginald Ashcroft is scheduled for early next week. Meanwhile, the Curran Commission continues its probe into corruption within City Hall and the police force. Whether this case becomes a turning point in that effort remains to be seen.

— Submitted by Harold S. Wainwright,
Staff Reporter

"Wainwright from *The Times* wasted no time getting this thing out," Charles said. "Look at all the speculation and innuendos." He was sure he'd seen him at both the hotel lobby and the precinct last night.

"Whatever happened to innocent until proven guilty?" Lily said.

"I didn't catch anything like that from the police yesterday," Cedric said. "They talk like they're certain I did it."

"The papers aren't interested in the truth," Charles said. "They only care about what sells more copies."

Just then the doorbell rang. Not once but several times. Followed by people banging on the front door.

Quentin hurried to answer it. They couldn't see him behind the foyer wall, but clearly he was arguing and raising his voice, and yelling at whoever was there. Sounded like several people, not just one.

Finally, he slammed the door shut and appeared in the dining room doorway.

"Who is it, Quentin?" Millicent asked. "Who are those people? What are they yelling about?"

"I'm sorry, Ma'am. But it was reporters, looking for a comment from Master Cedric, or from you, sir." He nodded at Nigel. "Of course, I sent them away. Or at least, told them to leave. I don't know if they'll take heed."

"So, it's begun," Nigel said. "We're not just living it now. Soon, the entire city will be, too."

17

Late Sunday Morning, District Attorney's Office
Criminal Courts Building on Center Street,
Lower Manhattan

It was unusual for District Attorney Gerald Tilford to be in his office on a Sunday morning, but an hour ago the newsboy's cry on the corner had summoned him there. "*Extra, Extra... Read All about It! Head Alderman's Son Murdered at The Belmont! Extra, Extra*!"

Tilford had been on his way home from a walking trip at a nearby bakery to fetch his wife some of her favorite Italian pastries. A little thing he liked to do every Sunday morning. Ignoring the fact that he'd have a copy of *The Times* waiting on his doorstep, he paid the newsboy, took a copy, and sat down on a nearby bench. As soon as he'd read the first few paragraphs, he knew everything on his calendar was about to change.

For this week and, likely, many more to come.

He'd stayed on the bench until he'd read the whole thing, then walked the four blocks home as fast as his middle-aged legs could take him. He handed the pastries to his wife, apologizing after a quick peck on the cheek, said he was sorry but he'd have to quickly leave and drive down to the office. Something urgent had come up. Before he'd even gotten out the door, the telephone rang. He'd spent the next twenty minutes navigating an unsettling phone call with Herbert Ashcroft, the Head Alderman himself, the very man whose son Reginald had just been murdered at The Belmont. The consequence of that phone call forced him to call Police Commissioner Albert Mallory, also at home, telling him to meet Tilford at his office immediately.

Commissioner Mallory had apparently read the same article and offered no hesitation. "I'll be right there."

Twenty-five minutes later, Tilford was unlocking his office on Center Street. He sat on his chair, and re-read the article in *The Times*. He wasn't alone for long. A knock on the frosted glass of his door announced the arrival of Commissioner Mallory, his homburg hat tucked under one arm, his jowled face set in a grim line.

"Gerald," Mallory said by way of greeting, lowering himself into the chair opposite the desk. "So, you've seen it?"

Tilford gave a wry smile and lifted the folded front

page from his desk. "Hard to miss, Albert. Half the city probably had their breakfast ruined over this."

"I know Alderman Ashcroft didn't miss it. Called me not more than an hour ago. Said he was going to call you, too. Demanded I give you his home telephone number. Hope you understand."

Tilford nodded. "He called just before I called you. The man's not subtle."

Mallory grunted. "No, he's not. And he sounded a tad more angry than grieving, you ask me. Told me straight up—this thing needs to be wrapped up clean and fast. Said his wife's on the verge of a breakdown, and the last thing she needs is weeks of courtroom drama dragging their son's name through the mud."

Tilford raised an eyebrow. "Told me the same thing. Word for word."

"Makes you wonder," Mallory muttered.

The DA steepled his fingers. "Well, what's our move?"

"Simple," said the Commissioner. "We've already got our man. This young NYU student, Whitaker, was found holding the murder weapon. The witnesses saw him standing over the body right after. His prints are sure to be all over the gun. Ashcroft wants us to stop wasting time looking for anyone else."

Tilford tapped the paper. "But we've got to make it look proper, or they'll be screaming rush to judgment on our part. Don't want anyone on the Curran Commission looking our way. We've got to seat a grand jury, first thing. Ashcroft wants it convened no later than Tuesday. Is that even possible?"

"Anything's possible," Mallory said. "Ashcroft said the same thing to me. I'll get my team assembling the witness list, right away."

"You mean first thing in the morning?"

"No, I mean right away. Otherwise, we can't possibly get it together by Tuesday. You make sure Rafferty and Shipley are ready to testify."

Mallory nodded. "Done. And I'll tell them to sit tight on other leads, should any arise. No need to confuse the grand jury with...unnecessary information."

"Careful how you word that, Albert."

"I hear you."

They sat in silence a moment, both men knowing full well what wasn't being said aloud. Ashcroft's pressure wasn't just the grief of a bereaved father. It was quid-pro-quo. Favors owed, backs scratched. Still, neither man relished the appearance of being controlled by someone else.

Tilford straightened his shoulders. "Look, it's not just about Ashcroft. The longer this case stays in the papers, the worse it is for everyone. The public needs to see swift justice."

Mallory gave a slow nod. "Exactly. We're not bowing to pressure—we're preserving public trust."

Tilford almost smiled. "Exactly."

They both stood, exchanged a curt handshake, and parted with the mutual understanding of seasoned politicians: Men who could convey entire paragraphs with a certain look or glance.

Tilford paused before heading back to eat Italian

pastries with his wife, glanced at the front page one more time. He thought briefly of the Curran Commission hearings—still underway, according to a smaller article at the bottom right corner of the first page, still threatening to drag every misdeed into the public light.

ABOUT THE SAME TIME
Whitaker Mansion

THE VERANDA of the Whitaker mansion offered a surprising calm amid the storm brewing in the streets out front. Charles and Lily sat in wicker chairs, steam curling from the delicate porcelain cups resting on the glass-topped table between them.

After breakfast, Nigel had retreated to his study. He said he needed time alone to pray and consider his next moves. Charles thought he looked deeply troubled, understandably so. Millicent had claimed a headache and had taken to her room, requesting the charcoal powder she typically used from the housemaid. Cedric had vanished upstairs, seeking some distance from the clamoring crowd out front beyond the wrought-iron fence.

Lily stirred her coffee. "Do you think Cedric got any sleep at all last night?"

Charles shook his head. "I doubt it. Not with all he's carrying now."

She nodded slowly. "You said Mr. Beaumont explained

what happens next to you and Father. Can you walk me through it?"

Charles set down his cup and leaned forward. "Well, he shared quite a bit."

"I want to understand it all."

"Okay then. Let's see…now that Cedric's been formally charged, the next step is the grand jury. Normally, Beaumont said, that would take about a week to assemble. But given the political heat because of who Reggie's father is, he warned we might not get that long."

"What does a grand jury do exactly?"

"They decide whether there's enough evidence to indict Cedric—to formally put him on trial. It's not like a regular trial. Cedric won't be there. Neither will Mr. Beaumont. Just the district attorney who will present their evidence and witnesses. It only takes a majority of the jurors to return an indictment."

Lily looked alarmed. "That hardly seems fair. So, Cedric has no voice in that room, not even his attorney?"

"No, none. That's why it's so dangerous. It's totally one-sided. But the idea is, this isn't about whether he's guilty or innocent, just if there's enough evidence to move forward with a formal trial. Now, sometimes a defense attorney can challenge a grand jury's findings, but Beaumont said that is rarely ever done. He honestly didn't seem all that concerned. He said we could likely expect they will find reason enough to indict Cedric."

"What about the evidence they present? Is there no one there to challenge it, or show the jury the evidence on Cedric's side?"

"No. Grand juries often rely mostly on police testimony and summary evidence. There's no cross-examination. No opportunity for rebuttal. Even hearsay can be admitted."

She glanced away, sighed heavily. "And what if they do indict him?"

"Then we prepare for trial. We should have time to build Cedric's defense, and hopefully win an acquittal. That's what the main trial is about. And the jury they pick for that trial will be totally different people than the grand jury. People who shouldn't have any bias in either direction. But Lily...we've got to prepare ourselves...the indictment itself will be a blow—publicly, and personally for Cedric and the family.

"Does Cedric remain out on bail until then?"

"If nothing changes, then yes. He has to remain available to the court for any required appearances and isn't allowed to leave the city without approval."

"Will the judge be the same man from night court?"

"No. Once the indictment is filed, the case gets assigned to a trial judge. Likely one of the criminal court justices downtown."

Lily exhaled slowly. "Oh Charles, it feels so...overwhelming. And Father? This will ruin him, won't it? The hotel? *Scandal At the Belmont*...everyone in town will think of it like that, as some terrible place."

Charles reached over, covering her hand with his. "It's going to be hard, Lily. But your father's strong. And he's not alone."

She looked down. "Will you talk to him today? Please?

He needs someone he can trust. Mother...is just too fragile."

Charles gave her hand a gentle squeeze. "Of course. I will, Love. Think I should try him now, or give him some time?"

"I think you should go now. He may not want to talk just yet, but at least he'll know you're someone he can lean on for strength. I know he really respects you. Who knows? Maybe he'll start to open up to you."

Charles got up and kissed her on the forehead. He prayed quietly, if his father-in-law did confide in him, that he might have something useful to say in reply.

18

Late Morning
Nigel Whitaker's Study

A while ago, after excusing himself from the breakfast table, Nigel had walked through the carved double doors of the study, shut the doors behind him and was half-tempted to lock them. But he knew it was unnecessary. No one in this house would come in uninvited. But he needed some time alone.

He moved slowly toward the liquor tray, not to pour a drink—he hadn't touched a drop since yesterday—but simply to rest his hand on the familiar surface. He needed grounding. The study, with its thick Oriental rug, dark wooden shelves, and rich leather chairs, had always provided a sense of order and command, like a captain's cabin on an old sailing ship.

But not this morning.

He crossed to the heavy desk and sat, exhaling a long breath as he reached for the receiver of the telephone and turned the small crank. This had to be done. The hotel switchboard operator answered almost immediately, and at the sound of his voice, offered a warm, "Yes, Mr. Whitaker?"

"Please get me with Jeffrey, the concierge. If you can find him."

"Connecting you now to Mr. Hunter." Moments later, the line clicked again. He heard the Operator and Hunter talking. "Mr. Whitaker? I have Jeffrey Hunter on the line. Go ahead, sir."

"Mr. Whitaker," Hunter said, "thank goodness. I've been hoping you'd call. We've all been terribly concerned. All I've got about the situation since the police took Cedric away yesterday is this terrible newspaper article in *The Times*. And now copies from the other newspapers in town have arrived. They're no better. Some say even worse things. Do you have anything you can tell me that might... perhaps, improve my outlook? Can you give me something more positive I can say to the staff and guests? I'm sorry to talk this way, especially to you, sir. It's just that —"

"— Jeffrey, it's okay. You don't have to apologize. It's a very upsetting situation, for all of us. I do plan to come down there first thing tomorrow morning and have a meeting with all the department heads. You plan to be there, too. You have a very important role there in the lobby, and I want you to be equipped with the latest information. But I'll get to the point of my call. I need to assess the situation there at the hotel. What has the fallout been since the story broke? Not so much looking for the mood, which I'm sure is unpleasant. I'm talking specifically about things that might be affecting us financially, reservations and bookings, for example."

There was a pause. "It's not good, sir."

Nigel found himself gripping the arm of his chair. "How bad is not good?"

Hunter's voice lowered, as if reluctant to be overheard. "I'm trying to hold the team together, to project some sense of calm, but...well, the front desk reports that at least half of our guests have checked out already. And some of them had several days left on their stay. All of them cited the same reason—the scandal, the headlines, the murder."

Nigel shut his eyes. "I see."

"Of course, I didn't really need the front desk to tell me this. I can see it with my own eyes in the lobby. The bellhops are working nonstop. Cabs are lined up outside. Luggage moving every which way. It's chaos."

"And new reservations? I know Sunday is usually a big day for that."

"Not today it's not. We've had none," Hunter said. "From what I'm told from the lead operator at the switchboard, all the calls they are putting through, not a single reservation this morning. Only cancellations. She says it's been that way since shortly after the story broke. People all citing the same concern."

Each thing Hunter said landed like a body blow. Nigel reached for a handkerchief to blot his brow.

"There's more, I'm afraid," Hunter continued. "Mr. Sheffield, from our Commercial and Convention bookings office, has asked to speak with you directly, if you came in. I'm not sure of the exact matter, but I assume it's related."

Nigel nodded slowly. "Thanks, Jeffrey. Can you put me through to him?"

"Of course, sir. And—Mr. Whitaker—I'm terribly sorry. I want you to know, and I've talked with countless hotel staff this morning...none of them believe Cedric is guilty of this. We don't care what the newspapers say. We know him. It was good the way you had him working at every position in the hotel these past few years, sir. He never put on airs or treated anyone as though they were inferior to him in any way. We are all so upset by what's happened, but no one can even imagine he'd do what they're saying. Not to Reggie or anyone else."

"Thank you, Jeffrey. So relieved to hear you say this." He genuinely was. But it did little to offset the horrible news about all the guests leaving and cancelling their stays. "I'll speak to everyone first thing tomorrow morning. Please tell the senior staff for me, I'll be calling a leadership meeting in the Blue Room at nine sharp."

Hunter agreed. "I'll put you through to Mr. Sheffield now, sir."

Nigel sat motionless for several seconds, then heard ringing, then a click. A moment later, a man's voice came on. "Mr. Whitaker. I've been trying to reach you."

"Yes, Sheffield. I understand. What's happened?"

The young department head hesitated, clearly searching for the gentlest approach. He'd only had the job for six months. "It's the dentists, sir. The large convention booked for next month. Over one hundred rooms for an entire week. Full ballroom use. Daily meal service. They've...they've backed out, sir."

Nigel's stomach tightened. "They did this today? On a Sunday?"

"Yes, I'm afraid so."

"And they're backing out of the event? All of it?"

"Yes, sir. I did everything I could. Spoke to Dr. Wescott personally. He was adamant. Said his board agreed—under the circumstances—they needed to move their event."

"How could he have gotten together with his board already?"

"I don't know, Mr. Whitaker. I know their main offices are on Long Island. I guess they got the newspaper already somehow."

Nigel's hand gripped the phone. "How about the staff? Do any of them know?"

"Just the ones who are working today. But I'll have to tell all of them tomorrow. This was a very big deal for us, as you know."

"How did those who heard take it?"

"They're nervous, sir. Honestly, so am I. What if this is just the beginning? What about when copies of *The Times* gets delivered to places like Philly and New Jersey tomorrow? The bigger hotels in New England often get Sunday editions by Monday evening. There may be more cancellations coming by midweek."

Nigel couldn't restrain a pent-up sigh.

"I wanted to ask?" Sheffield said, "is there any messaging you'd like me to share with everyone? Any positive news? Something that could maybe reassure people?"

"For now, just keep assuring them Cedric did not do this. He is innocent. I know some of what the newspapers say looks very bad. But I'll address you and all the department heads tomorrow. In person. Please let your staff know. Blue Room, 9am."

"Yes, Mr. Whitaker. I will. Thank you."

They hung up.

Nigel remained seated, his eyes drifted up to the framed photo of Wilbur Wright above the mantle. He'd put the picture there because it served as such a symbol of triumph, discipline, and hard work. That had been a special day for The Belmont. One of the first big events where over a hundred rooms had been booked at the hotel. It had given them the idea that working hard to book the hotel for big commercial events and conventions could be a very lucrative venture.

But this morning, the picture seemed to mock him.

19

Charles knocked softly.

"Come in," Nigel said.

Charles stepped in quietly, closed the door behind him. "Sir...Father, I hope I'm not intruding."

"Not at all, Charles. Please." Nigel gestured toward the seat Charles usually sat in when he came.

No one said anything for a long moment. Charles could easily see, though, the toll the past twenty-four hours had etched deep into his features. He looked older, exhausted, all the light was gone from his eyes. "I thought I'd check on you," Charles said gently. "Lily's worried. So am I."

Nigel gave a tight nod. "It's kind of you to come." He glanced at the surface of his desk, then away. That's all he said. Felt like a minute went by. When he turned to look at Charles, tears had welled up in his eyes. "Everything's falling apart, Charles. Cedric... my name, our family's good name, and now the hotel? It's like some ungodly avalanche has been unleashed against us. Everything hitting all at once, and I can't get out of its way." He took a hanky sitting on his desk and wiped his eyes.

Charles walked around the desk, put his hand on his shoulder. "You're not alone. You know that, right? You don't have to carry this alone. We're all here, Lily and I, Cedric, your wife. Have you talked this over with the pastor yet? I know he'd be an amazing source of encouragement for you. The way he handled that crisis with me two years—"

"I know," Nigel said, "you're right. I need to call him. Tony's a good friend. Always knows just the right thing to say...when people go through times like this. I've seen it." Then more tears. "Just never thought I'd be the one needing...that kind of help from him." He quickly wiped the tears away again.

"Well, Father, I mean it. If there's anything—anything—I can do, just let me know."

Nigel's voice dropped. "I wish there were, son. But this isn't a problem we can fix with good leadership or clever strategy." He sighed.

Charles had an idea, hesitated, then said, "May I read something to you?"

Nigel looked up, startled. "Of course."

Charles reached for the Bible near the corner of the desk and opened it. "It's Psalm 46. I memorized it during that horrible patch I went through two years ago. It helped me then. He read slowly:

God is our refuge and strength, A very present help in trouble.

Therefore we will not fear, even though the earth be removed, and though the mountains be carried into the midst of the sea; though its waters roar and be troubled, though the mountains shake with its swelling.

There is a river whose streams shall make glad the city of God, the holy place of the tabernacle of the Most High. God is in the midst of her, she shall not be moved; God shall help her, just at the break of dawn.

The nations raged, the kingdoms were moved; He uttered His voice, the earth melted.

The Lord of hosts is with us; The God of Jacob is our refuge. Come, behold the works of the Lord, who has made desolations in the earth. He makes wars cease to the end of the earth; He breaks the bow and cuts the spear in two; He burns the chariot in the fire.

Be still, and know that I am God; I will be exalted among the nations, I will be exalted in the earth! The Lord of hosts is with us; The God of Jacob is our refuge."

When he finished, he set the Bible down and looked up.

"Thank you," Nigel whispered. "I really needed to hear that right now."

Charles patted his shoulder, said, "Can I pray for you? If that's all right."

Nigel nodded. "Yes, by all means."

Charles offered a prayer echoing the words from the Psalm: for refuge, for strength, for God's nearness in times of trouble.

When it ended, Nigel took a breath and looked up. "Thank you, Charles. Means more than I can say."

Just then, Charles got another idea. "There might actually be one thing I can do. Tomorrow. I'm going to go to *The Times* editorial office. See if I can speak with Wainwright. Maybe convince him to print a follow-up article. Tell him all the things on our side, things that might help him see the situation is not at all the way he described. Get him to write something more balanced."

Nigel managed a faint smile. "Well, I guess if anyone can sway a man like Wainwright, it might be you."

Charles returned quietly to Lily's bedroom, where he found her sitting, staring out the window with a book in her lap. She looked up the moment he entered.

"Good book?" he asked, smiling.

"I wouldn't know. I just keep reading the same paragraph over and over, then my mind drifts away. How is he?"

Charles came to sit beside her. "Worn thin, as you might expect." He didn't want to burden her with all the details about the dreadful situation at the hotel. "He's going through a lot, not just worrying about Cedric but also the hotel."

"I can't imagine what must be going on down there since the story came out."

"It's nothing good," Charles said, "but we had a good talk. I read to him from Psalm 46. One of the passages I read often back when I was going through our ordeal two years ago. It seemed to help."

Lily nodded, reached for his hand. He stepped closer, squeezed hers gently. "Thank you for going," she said. "What's he going to do?"

"I suggested he should talk with the pastor. He really helped me back then. He's also going to call a big meeting with his leadership team at the hotel tomorrow morning, try to reassure them as best he can."

"What about you? How are you doing?"

He gave a soft smile. "Okay I guess. It's just...I feel so helpless. Just watching all these terrible things unraveling all around us. I did think of two things I can do. Tomorrow morning, I've decided to drive down to the ice plant and talk to Abe. I'm going to ask him to hold down the fort for a while, so I can be more available to help around here. And I also told your father I was going to make a trip down to the editorial offices of *The Times* tomorrow, see if I could talk to this fellow Wainwright. The reporter who wrote the article."

"Think it would do any good?"

"Suppose it can't hurt." He leaned down to kiss her forehead. "Maybe you and I can go out and take a drive, or even a walk. It's so nice outside. Maybe a change of scenery would do us both some good."

"I'd like that. Oh, and I've been thinking. We can probably head back to our apartment tonight. I still want to spend a lot of time here the next few days, but I don't think we have to stay overnight any longer."

Charles smiled. "That would be nice."

20

The following morning, a Monday, after enjoying a quick breakfast with Lily at their place at The Dakota, Charles—dressed in his typical business attire—drove his Simplex Touring Car the twenty-five minute drive south from Upper Manhattan to Lower Manhattan, to his ice factory on Madison Street. Keeping to the 15mph speed limit the whole while. In the last few years, he'd found the best possible route that made for the least congested drive.

Still, sometimes it startled him as he made his way south, just how much the city had changed, as he made his way from the most affluent sections to the least. A contrast between the Haves and the Have-Nots every day. Majestic homes and luxury apartments giving way to almost tenement squalor. Clean, uncrowded streets traveled only by fine automobiles to roads clogged with horse-drawn carriages and wagons, peddlers hauling pushcarts, and the ever-unsettling presence of pedestrians darting in and out of traffic, with no regard for their safety. And, of course, this...bright, beautiful blue skies to a grey overcast scene, blighted by smoke from a hundred coal stacks belching factory exhaust into the air.

Including his own, the Bennington Ice Factory.

The steady drone of the big compressors was already humming as he got out of the car and walked across the gravel parking area to the stone steps, through the back door, then up the steel stairway leading to the upper office.

Inside, Abe Henry was seated at his desk, a pencil behind his ear, flipping through a stack of delivery forms. He looked up quickly.

"Charles. Didn't expect to see you today. Not after the weekend you've had."

Charles smiled and stepped forward to shake his hand. "Well, won't be staying for long, Abe. That's partly why I'm here. Felt like I should say what I need to say in person."

"Uh-oh." Abe gestured for him to sit. "Is it as bad as the papers make it sound?"

Charles sighed. "No, not quite. There's a lot that story in *The Times* left out. But still, it's bad enough. Cedric is innocent, for one thing. I know the whole story, and I totally believe him. But the public doesn't know any of it, and frankly, the police don't seem all that interested in finding out the truth."

Abe rubbed his chin. "They really think he did it? The paper almost makes it sound open and shut."

"They're sure he did it. Least that's how they talk. They've ignored his account entirely. Charles spent several minutes bringing Abe up to date."

Afterward, Abe leaned back. "That just ain't right."

"No, it isn't," Charles said. "Which is why I need to ask you a favor. I'm going to have to step away from the plant for a week. Maybe more. The Whitakers are in a real crisis, and someone has to keep pushing to find the truth. That someone, at least for now, is going to be me. It's the least I can do after all the Whitakers have done for me. Especially Cedric."

Abe nodded. He knew all about what had happened to Charles two years ago. "You do what you need to do, Charles. We'll hold things together here."

"Thank you. I knew I could count on you. And look, check my calendar, if you don't mind. I have a few lunches with clients. See if you can bump them to next week. I don't think there are any contracts to sign."

Abe said he'd do that, then hesitated for a moment. "If I may ask, Charles... can you try to keep things quiet? I mean, about your role in all this. None of our clients, so far, seem to have connected you to the Whitakers yet, or the Belmont. If your name winds up in the papers..."

Charles nodded. "I understand. I hate the thought of sneaking around, but I get it. I'll be careful."

Abe smiled then stood. "Before you go, there's one more thing. You think maybe you could say a few words to the men? They're working hard as ever, but I know they're rattled. That article hit everyone like a punch in the gut.

They all know who you're married to. And Cedric's been in here lots of times."

Charles stood. "You're right. It's better to say something now than let imaginations run wild."

Together, they stepped out onto the grated metal platform that overlooked the plant floor. Abe gave a few sharp whistles and waved. Within moments, the machines were silenced and workers began to gather below, looking up.

Charles rested his hands on the railing. "Men, I won't keep you long. You've all seen the article in yesterday's paper. I just want to say, not everything in it is true. It *is* true, that Cedric has been arrested for this murder. But you all know Cedric. He's a fine young man. He's not capable of doing something like this. And besides, the young man who was killed, he and Reggie were the best of friends. Cedric's told me what happened, and I believe him. I'm taking a short leave to do what I can to help clear his name. Abe will be in charge while I'm away, and I know things will run just as well under his leadership."

He paused, scanning their faces. "Please, don't believe everything you read in the papers. Or the rumor mill. Hopefully, we'll soon get this thing sorted out. Well, guess that's all I'll say for now. Thank you men."

They all nodded and murmured quietly as they dispersed, some tipping their caps in Charles's direction. Abe clapped Charles on the back. "You did good. That'll go a long way."

"I hope so."

"What do you think Cedric's chances are to beat this thing?"

Charles shook his head. "I'm not gonna water this down, Abe. Right now? Not good. It's definitely gonna be an uphill battle. But I know he's innocent. And I'm gonna prove it, one way or another...I'm gonna make them see." They shook hands. "I'll be in touch. And if you need to reach me on anything, leave word with Lily."

"Will do," Abe said.

Charles headed back down the steps, and out the door. Behind him, the sound of the ice-making machines grinding into motion once more.

21

Fifteen minutes after leaving his ice plant on Madison Street, Charles pulled alongside the curb just east of Times Square and climbed out. Despite the coal smoke lingering in the spring air, this part of Manhattan was much improved than the tenement neighborhoods downtown. The sidewalks here bustled with better-dressed pedestrians, and storefronts gleamed with enticing merchandise behind large plate-glass windows. Horse-drawn cabs and electric streetcars still rattled past at a steady clip, but motorcars made up at least half the vehicles in sight.

Rising above it all, the *Times Tower* loomed like a sentinel at the confluence of Broadway and Seventh Avenue, its narrow Gothic profile thrusting skyward. Though not the tallest building in the city, it certainly stood out around here. This was the first time he'd ever been here. It was a little intimidating thinking that this was the place where all the biggest stories, not just in New York but in the world, were created.

But he also found himself somewhat dismayed when he realized how badly the story about Cedric had been botched. How incomplete and lopsided toward the police's version. It tended to undermine his confidence, a little. Just how much could he trust other stories printed by *The Times* in the future? Stories where he didn't have inside information like he had here. Information that, if printed, would totally change the reader's perception about the story.

Inside, he was directed to the newsroom floor, which, according to the clerk, was up the stairs and "second on the left." There, Charles was met by a flurry of activity. Desks filled the open floor space, each stacked with paper, carbon copies, and metal ashtrays brimming with cigarette butts. Reporters typed furiously at their machines while others scribbled in notebooks or talked loudly over each other. Phones rang at random intervals, a chorus of unending noise.

He could never work in this atmosphere.

A harried young man in short sleeves intercepted him before he could step any farther. "You can't be back here, sir." He looked Charles up and down, likely at the way he was dressed. "Reporters only."

Charles kept his tone even. "My name is Charles Bennington. I'm a relative of the Whitaker family—Cedric Whitaker is my brother-in-law. I have information about the Belmont murder case — the story spread across the front page yesterday — information the reporter, Mr. Wainwright, would want to know."

The man seemed skeptical, gave Charles another once-over, pausing to notice his pocket watch chain and polished shoes. "Wait here," he said, disappearing through a narrow paneled door.

Moments later, he returned and motioned for Charles to follow. "This way."

Wainwright's office, if it could be called that, was a small room off the main floor. The glass pane in the door read: "*H. Wainwright, Staff Writer.*" The young man opened it. The room was barely large enough for a desk, two chairs, and a coat rack, though a window offered a partial view of the neighboring rooftop. The walls were yellowed by smoke, and a stack of newspapers rested precariously on a filing cabinet.

Wainwright, sleeves rolled and tie loosened, glanced up from a sheaf of notes.

"This is the guy I told you about," the young man said, then left without waiting for a reply.

Wainwright looked at Charles. "You've got five minutes. Wish I could give you more. But hey, not like you made an appointment."

Charles offered a polite nod. "I appreciate it. I know you're busy."

"I am. So, make it count."

Charles sat. "You wrote the article about the Belmont Hotel. You know, *Scandal at the Belmont*?"

Wainwright leaned back. "If you're here to complain—"

"I'm not, Mister —"

"Just call me Wainwright. Everyone else does."

"Okay... Wainwright... I'd like to know? Why you only shared half the story, why you didn't include any of the facts that might point away from Cedric Whitaker?"

Wainwright frowned. "Because there weren't any. At least none we could verify."

"Well, that's why I'm here. Let me offer a few," Charles said. "And yes, I'm close to Cedric. He's my wife's brother. But that doesn't make what I'm about to tell you any less true."

Wainwright hesitated. "Go on."

"First, Cedric's never had any trouble with the law. Not so much as a parking fine. His father—who happens to be a respected church deacon— said he's never owned a gun, never even fired one. Says there are no firearms in their home."

"Then how do you explain the shooting?"

"That's just it. No one knows where the gun came from. The hotel only has one registered weapon—that belongs to the chief of security, Mr. Keller. None of his men carry firearms, only nightsticks. Keller's available to interview, if you care to. He'll verify what I've said. So again, where did Cedric get hold of a gun?"

Wainwright scribbled something in a notebook.

Charles leaned forward. "Cedric says he heard two men arguing with Reggie Ashcroft when he entered the gym. Then he hears a scuffle, some kind of strange sound, then Reggie's body hitting the floor. Then sounds of the two men running toward the back door, slamming it open, then disappearing out of sight. When Cedric reached him, Reggie was already dead."

"Strange sound," Wainwright repeated. "What's that mean?"

"That's just it," Charles said, "no gunshot. Cedric didn't hear any. I talked with Keller. He said with the acoustics in that gym, everyone in the lobby would've heard a gunshot. But no one did."

Charles could tell this meant something to Wainwright. "Do you have any idea how that kid could have been shot but no one heard it? I don't know what to make of that."

"The police definitely said the kid had been shot," Wainwright said. "Kind of rings a bell. We did a story a couple years back about some guy who invented this thing you can stick on the end of a gun to muffle the sound. Think he called it a silencer. I didn't write the story, but I'm friends with the guy who did."

"Well then," Charles said. "There's a lead, isn't it? If whoever killed Reggie used a...silencer...there was no silencer gadget on the gun they found in Cedric's gym bag. Means the killer must have taken it with them. And if that's true, it proves Cedric wasn't the killer. What else could explain the lack of a gunshot?"

Wainwright's face showed skepticism again. "It's interesting, Mr. Bennington. I'll grant you that. But it's not proof. Not finding something isn't the same as finding evidence of something."

"What's that mean?" Charles said.

"It means it's not evidence. It's an idea. Something that

might explain a sound, a strange sound. But that's all it is. And from what I understand, no one else saw or heard these two intruders Cedric mentions, correct?"

"Yeah, but there's evidence they were there. The lockers," Charles said. "Two of them were forced open. The steel is twisted—clearly tampered with. Why would Cedric break into his own locker? If you want to see it, Keller can show you."

Wainwright wrote something down.

Charles continued. "I've hired a private detective. He's already begun searching the lockers and door handles for fingerprints—any prints that don't belong to Cedric would support his version of events."

Wainwright's eyes narrowed. "Police didn't mention anything about fingerprints."

"Because they're not looking. They seem convinced they already have their man. I'm sure they'll test the gun. And the gun will have Cedric's fingerprints on it. Stupidly, and he admits this, he picked it up when he found it in his gym bag. That was the moment the two hotel guests walked in."

Wainwright nodded slowly.

"But if you ask me," Charles said, "the biggest thing that vindicates Cedric is *motive*. Cedric had absolutely no motive to kill Reggie. Cedric and Reggie were best friends. Teammates. Reggie came to the hotel that morning looking forward to working out together. No tension. No threats. Ask the concierge. Ask Keller. Ask their basketball coach, ask their teammates. They'll all tell you the same thing. There was no animosity between them. Cedric had no reason to hurt Reggie."

Wainwright leaned back and folded his arms. "You know, police don't care that much about motive when they've got all the other boxes checked."

"Maybe, but you should, Wainwright. You're not a policeman. You're a journalist. Think about top-notch journalists like Lincoln Steffens ... He didn't get famous printing only what the authorities told him. Neither did Ida Tarbell or Ray Baker. They chased down the truth, even when it embarrassed powerful men."

Charles stepped closer to his desk. "Motive matters, Mr. Wainwright. It may not matter to the police when they think they've checked their boxes. But if you ignore motive, you ignore the heart of the crime. No one murders their best friend for no reason. Especially not someone like Cedric, who has no history of violence, no trace of rage. Isn't it your job to ask things the police won't?"

Wainwright now wore an almost pained expression. "Mr. Bennington, I'm not unsympathetic here, but I need more than a compelling narrative. My editors demand hard evidence, official sources, especially to go up against the powerful people involved in this case. Less than an hour ago, the DA and Police Commissioner have gone on record naming Cedric as the suspect, and announced they're convening a grand jury tomorrow to indict him. That's what's going to print in the evening edition."

Charles's shoulders sagged. "That's disappointing."

Wainwright sighed. "It's not personal, sir. It's pressure.

This city moves fast, and no one waits for the truth to catch up."

Charles stood, then paused. "But you should."

Wainwright stiffened, his eyes studying Charles.

Charles decided to plunge the blade in a little further. "You have a chance to be more than a reporter, Wainwright. You could be an investigator. Don't you want to be the one who uncovers what everyone else missed? Break the lead that shifts the entire narrative? The real murderer is still out there. This story has all the hallmarks of a rush to judgment, and you know it. But it also has the makings of something bigger—for someone who's willing to dig. And with everything I've told you, you don't even have to dig that deep."

Wainwright didn't reply. Finally, he leaned back and exhaled. "I'll tell you what. Get me that fingerprint evidence. If it holds up, if it proves there were others there in the room with your brother-in-law, I'll consider everything else you've said. Seriously."

Charles nodded. "Fair enough. I'll be in touch."

They shook hands and Charles left the room, but now with a small flicker of hope in his step.

22

Late Monday Afternoon
Whitaker Mansion, Gramercy Park

Charles had just come home from running a few errands and was sitting in the front parlor reviewing some notes when Lily entered and handed him a message. "It's from Mr. Keller at the hotel. He called for you just after lunch, said it was urgent."

"Did he say what it was about?"

"No, but he actually sounded a little upbeat."

"Thanks, Love." Charles wasted no time. He stepped into the hallway and dialed the hotel's operator. "Hello, this is Charles Bennington. Please connect me to Mr. Keller, head of security."

A moment later, Keller's familiar voice came through the line. "Mr. Bennington, thank you for calling me back."

"Of course. Lily said it sounded urgent."

"It is. My detective friend—his name's Wallace Kane, by the way—has worked nonstop on this fingerprint thing. He delivered some findings to me this morning. I think you'll want to hear this."

"I'm listening."

"Turns out, there *were* a pair of unknown fingerprints all over the lockers—particularly near the one that had been pried open. And another two sets of fingerprints were found around the rear exit door and jamb. And get this, none of them belonged to Cedric."

Charles sat up straighter. "Did one of the sets at the back door—did it match the ones on the locker?"

"It did," Keller said. "Wallace is convinced now—what Cedric said was true. He must have encountered someone in that gym, maybe two someone's, and they both got away."

"That's extraordinary," Charles said. "Please thank your friend for his diligence. Can you have him prepare a full report? Include his findings and copies of the prints. We'll need several."

"He's already on it."

Charles paused, thought about his talk earlier that day at *The Times*. "Keller, have you ever heard of something called a gun silencer?"

"Yes, actually. I've never seen one, but I've heard about them. Come to think of it, Wallace owns one. That's where I've heard about it. Some new invention. He says you stick it on the end of a pistol, and it does a pretty good job of muffling the shot. You can still hear something, but it's nothing like the sound of a gunshot."

"Well," Charles said, "that's got me wondering if that's not the sound Cedric described hearing. Remember he said there was no gunshot, just a strange noise before he found Reggie." Charles leaned forward. "Here's what I'm thinking. Could you get your friend Wallace to come to the gym—soon—and fire a round using the silencer while Cedric stands near the stairwell door, the same place he entered? We'll get Wallace to fire a round with that silencer over where they found Reggie's body, see if the sound matches what Cedric remembers."

"I like it," Keller said. "Okay, I'll ask him. Oh, by the way, something else I wanted to run past you."

"What's that?"

Keller hesitated. "Actually, it's about Singleton."

"That name rings a bell."

"He's the guy who manages the gym for us."

"So, what about him?"

"Well, he still hasn't shown back up. Not Saturday, not Sunday, not today. He hasn't called in, either, and he's not returning any messages. I've asked around—none of the staff have heard from him, either."

Charles's heart quickened. "This could be significant. Cedric said he was supposed to open the gym Saturday morning. Is that normal for him? To miss days of work and not even call in?"

"Not at all," Keller said. "Singleton is usually Johnny on the spot. He like, probably hasn't missed a day since we hired him a few years ago. I asked him once when he came in a little hung over, why he didn't just take the day off. He said he needed the paycheck."

"This can't be a coincidence," Charles said. "We need to find him."

"I agree. I was going to suggest we give Wallace that assignment."

"Please do," Charles said.

"But—" Keller hesitated again.

"What is it?"

"Well...Wallace gave me a bill for the fingerprint work. It's more than I can cover. I don't think he'll want to take on more without some kind of payment."

Charles should have thought of this. "I'll be down there within the hour. And I'll bring enough to settle things, including the new assignments."

"Thank you. That'll help a lot. By the way, which of the two tasks do you want him to do first? The silencer test or find Singleton."

Charles thought a moment. "Let's find Singleton first. That one might knock over a few more dominoes. But as soon as he finds him, let's set up the silencer thing at the gym."

"Got it. I'll contact him as soon as we hang up."

Charles put the receiver back on the hook and went looking for Lily to tell her the news.

23

Tuesday morning arrived in a haze of anxiety at the Whitaker mansion. Last night, just before dark, Attorney Beaumont had arrived at the house and briefed them all he'd just learned the grand jury would be convened first thing today. He did his best to brief them on what to expect. Cedric would not be required to attend the grand jury proceeding—New York law did not grant a defendant the right to appear in person or present a defense.

This morning, all the power would reside with the District Attorney, Gerald Tilford. Fortunately, Cedric had been permitted to remain at home on bail, but so far that day he hadn't left his room, didn't even come down for breakfast.

. . .

AT THE COURTHOUSE, a panel of 23 jurors had just been sworn in right at 9 o'clock. Presiding Judge Horace Billings, a man known for his no-nonsense demeanor and meticulously combed white mustache, addressed the jury in clear and formal tones. "Your responsibility," he said, "is not to determine guilt or innocence. Your sole duty is to decide whether there is enough evidence for this case to proceed to trial."

The grand jury room was modest but orderly. Jurors sat in a U-shaped configuration around a polished wooden table. The bailiff stood near the door. District Attorney Tilford entered and set his briefcase on the table, his demeanor calm and confident.

"Ladies and gentlemen," Tilford began, "you've been called today to examine the evidence in the matter of the People of the State of New York versus Cedric Whitaker. On Saturday morning, young Mr. Whitaker was discovered in the gymnasium of the Belmont Hotel, with a pistol in his hand, standing over the body of Reginald Ashcroft, son of Alderman Herbert Ashcroft. We believe the evidence will show that Mr. Whitaker acted alone and shot young Ashcroft with deadly intent."

He gestured to the door. "We'll begin with testimony from the hotel's head of security, Mr. Malcolm Keller."

Keller entered, removed his bowler hat, and took the stand. After swearing him in, Tilford asked him to recount what he witnessed that morning.

Keller's voice was measured. "I was approached by two guests who said they'd decided to go down to the gym for a workout. As soon as they'd opened the front door, they saw a young man standing over a body, holding a pistol. The body on the ground was another young man. A pool of blood was spreading out from around his head. One of them said it looked like a murder scene."

"Did they identify the man they saw?" Tilford asked.

"Yes, sir. One said he'd seen the man in the hotel a few times before. Shortly after, he identified him as Cedric Whitaker."

"And what did you do then?"

"I proceeded down to the gym with another member of my staff. As I said, we found Mr. Whitaker sitting on a bench near the body of Mr. Ashcroft. He seemed in shock."

"Did he attempt to flee?"

"No, sir. He just said Reggie had been shot. He claimed he'd heard other voices when he entered. Some men arguing loudly."

"Did you find any other persons in the gym?"

"No."

"Were there signs of a struggle?"

"A little, but not much. Cedric pointed out to me how it looked like the lockers had been messed with. But nothing that would actually confirm multiple people had been there. But later on —"

"Thank you, Mr. Keller. No further questions."

The next witness was a young patrolman named Strout. Once sworn in, he addressed the jury in a clipped, matter-of-fact tone.

"Officer, how did you come to be involved in the case?" Tilford asked.

"I was informed by two hotel guests that there had been a shooting in the gym. They described a young man standing over the victim with a gun. I spoke with Mr. Keller, who had also confirmed the scene. I arrived shortly thereafter."

"And what did you find?"

"The body of Reginald Ashcroft was found near the steel lockers, a fatal wound to his forehead. A pistol was found in Cedric Whitaker's gym bag, next to where he stood."

"Was the weapon tested for fingerprints?"

"Yes. Mr. Whitaker's fingerprints were found to be on the grip and trigger of the gun."

"Any other prints on the gun?"

"None. It appears to have been handled only by Mr. Whitaker."

"Was the fatal bullet recovered?"

"Yes. The coroner later confirmed the bullet matched the caliber of the pistol recovered at the scene."

"Was Mr. Whitaker arrested at that time?"

"Yes. He did not resist. He maintained that he heard voices arguing when he entered and found his friend already dead."

Tilford paused before continuing. "From the state of the crime scene and the absence of other suspects, did you find any evidence that contradicted Mr. Whitaker's account?"

"I guess you could put it like that. Certainly didn't find any evidence that anyone else but him had been down there."

Tilford nodded. "Thank you, Officer. No further questions."

He called two final witnesses: the hotel guests who had seen Cedric standing over the body. Each described the scene similarly—entering through the gym door. Seeing a young man—later identified as Cedric—holding a pistol and standing over the body, kind of with a shocked look on his face.

After each had testified, Tilford concluded, "Ladies and gentlemen, the facts are clear. Cedric Whitaker was at the scene. He was found with the murder weapon. His fingerprints were on the gun. The victim and accused were alone. I believe there is no doubt that this case warrants a trial. Thank you for your service."

The jurors were excused to deliberate. They returned just twenty minutes later with a true bill of indictment.

By noon, Judge Billings reconvened court. Tilford formally presented the grand jury's findings. "Your Honor, the People of New York hereby indict Cedric Whitaker on the charge of first-degree murder."

The judge nodded. "Very well. A trial date will be set. Given the public interest and gravity of the charge, I will consider a speedy trial."

Tilford raised a hand. "Your Honor, the People respectfully request the earliest possible date."

Judge Billings turned to his clerk. "Schedule the pre-trial hearing for two weeks hence. The trial is to begin shortly thereafter."

. . .

THAT AFTERNOON, Attorney Beaumont made his way to the Whitaker home. He found Cedric, Lily, and Charles in the sitting room. Nigel, weary from the day's tension, had retreated to his study. But upon Beaumont's arrival, he came back in with the others.

Beaumont spoke gently. "The indictment came down. As expected, the grand jury returned a true bill."

"What's that mean?" Lily asked.

"It means they found sufficient evidence to indict Cedric for first-degree murder."

Cedric closed his eyes, exhaled slowly. Lily squeezed his hand.

"But this changes nothing," Beaumont added. "It's a formality. We knew it would happen. What matters is what comes next. We now have time to build your defense."

Cedric looked up. "Okay, but...do you have a plan? I mean no disrespect, Mr. Beaumont, but so far I haven't heard anything."

Beaumont offered a measured nod. "We have several avenues to explore Cedric. Lots of witness statements to gather, from people who have things to say that would counter what the DA is saying. Then there's character testimony. Specifically, yours. You are a young man of fine, moral character. And I'm sure as we dissect how the police have handled this, we'll find all sorts of procedural gaps. We'll examine every angle."

It sounded polished. Rehearsed. But Cedric didn't seem very reassured.

Charles cleared his throat. "Actually, Cedric, Besides

what Mr. Beaumont just shared, I've been working with Mr. Keller at the hotel. There are some promising leads we're developing—some fingerprint evidence that I think backs your version, some things involving some hotel staff that seems suspicious, even an experiment that might explain that strange sound you heard. It's early on, but today for the first time I've felt a glimmer of hope about all this."

Beaumont brightened. "That's encouraging, Charles. By all means, please get me everything you have as soon as possible. Any pieces of evidence that casts doubt on the prosecution's case could make all the difference." He looked at Cedric again. "Remember, that's all we have to do, create sufficient doubt in the DA's case. We don't have to prove anything."

Lily looked at Charles, her eyes filled with hope.

For the first time that day, Cedric allowed himself a faint smile.

But even so, Charles knew...hope was not enough to turn things around, and he wouldn't feel secure about their chances in a jury trial unless he really could somehow prove Cedric's innocence.

24

Later that evening, as twilight settled over Gramercy Park, Charles sat in the front parlor with Lily and Millicent. The room was quiet, save for the occasional clink of teacups on saucers. Dinner would be served soon. Cedric had retreated to the veranda, still preferring solitude to company. It wasn't like him to be so withdrawn, but in light of recent events, no one questioned him about it.

Through the opening to the foyer, Charles noticed movement. Quentin, the butler, walked by toward the front door, returning with the freshly delivered evening edition of *The New York Times* tucked under his arm. Without a word, he made his way to Nigel's study.

Charles's curiosity stirred. He leaned toward Lily and whispered, "There's gotta be another article in there about the investigation. I think I'll go see what your father thinks about it."

Lily nodded, concerned. "Please come back after and let me know what it says."

"I will."

Charles waited a few minutes, knowing full well that Nigel would flip immediately to any article related to the case. Then he stood, crossed the hall, and tapped lightly on the study door. Hearing no objection, he stepped in.

Nigel sat behind his desk, the newspaper opened before him. His eyes scanned the print with intensity. He barely acknowledged Charles even when he took a seat across from him.

"So," Charles said softly, "what do you think? Does this new article seem any better than the first one?"

Nigel didn't look up, released a sigh. He simply slid the paper across the desk. "Read it. See for yourself."

Charles unfolded the page. The article was on the front again, but this time, relegated to the lower half. Above it, headlines from Europe hinted at more rumblings of war. He exhaled, already relieved.

SCANDAL AT THE BELMONT – NEW DETAILS EMERGE

By Franklin Wainwright

THE TRAGIC EVENTS that unfolded Saturday morning at the Belmont Hotel continue to reverberate throughout the city. With the indictment of Cedric Whitaker now secured by the grand jury, the District Attorney's office is moving swiftly to ensure that justice is served in the murder of Reginald Ashcroft, beloved son of Alderman Herbert Ashcroft.

According to statements issued by Police Commissioner Mallory and District Attorney Tilford, the evidence remains compelling and unequivocal. Mr. Whitaker was found at the scene, alone with the deceased, and a pistol bearing his fingerprints was recovered nearby. These facts, authorities contend, are sufficient to bring the matter to trial without delay.

Sources close to the investigation confirm that there were no signs of forced entry and no evidence of other individuals present at the time of the shooting. The accused has maintained his innocence, stating he heard raised voices and a struggle upon entering the gym. However, the police have yet to corroborate this version of events, and no alternate suspects have been identified.

Public reaction to the case has remained intense, with widespread sympathy for the Ashcroft family. Still, some observers—particularly those with connections to the Whitaker household—have questioned whether all avenues of investigation have been fully explored. Among the questions raised is the matter of motive. There would appear to be none, and the police have not revealed anything that would speak to a motive in the case. What reason, some will ask, would Mr. Whitaker have had to kill his longtime friend?

Indeed, several individuals familiar with both men—such as classmates and teammates at NYU—describe them as inseparable companions. They were often seen together even in the gym where young Ashcroft was killed, as well as at public events.

For now, authorities stand firm in their assertion that the case is strong and the path to conviction straightforward. A police detective assigned to the case used the phrase "nearly open and shut" in an interview.

CHARLES FOLDED the paper and looked up. "I'd say there's at least a slight shift our way," he said. "Don't you think? It's still quite slanted, but...he seems to be offering a little more restraint. And that last paragraph, the one about the lack of motive? I could tell that bothered Wainwright when we talked."

Nigel's expression remained pensive. "Perhaps. I guess it's a very slight improvement. But that first half, still seems quite biased. You think there's any way you can get him to stop referring to this as the "*Scandal at the Belmont*?" It's really hurting us. The hotel's occupancy is less than half. Guests are canceling daily. Our marketing director says it's only happening with us—every other hotel in central Manhattan is nearly full. Like you'd expect in the peak of summer."

Charles leaned forward. "I can try. I was going to go down there again tomorrow, now that the fingerprint evidence proves what Cedric said. It's all the more reason we keep pushing. If the press begins to entertain doubt, it could help turn the tide."

Nigel sighed and nodded. "Let's hope so."

"And I will specifically ask if he could start using another phrase to describe the Hotel."

. . .

AFTER CHARLES LEFT Nigel in the study, he went back to the parlor thinking to update Lily on the article and his chat with her father. But while he was gone, her mother had fallen asleep in her chair. Lily motioned that she would meet him in the foyer. But when he reached her, she said, "When you were in there with Father, I had to use the bathroom. On the way back, I happened to see Cedric alone out on the veranda. He just looked so sad. I thought maybe I'd go out there, try to cheer him up. But then I thought maybe he'd really more appreciate some time with you. Ever since this happened, I don't think he's talked about any of it with anyone. I know he really looks up to you. Would you mind going out there to talk with him?"

"Not at all," Charles said. He walked toward the back of the house and stepped through the open French doors. A wave of exhaustion swept over him. He paused a few moments to catch his breath, utter a quick prayer for strength. Cedric sat slouched in a wicker chair, arms folded, his gaze fixed on some distant corner of the twilight sky.

"Mind if I join you?" Charles asked.

Cedric didn't move. "Sure."

Charles took the seat beside him and waited a moment. "You've been out here a while," he said softly.

Cedric finally turned his head. "Just thinking."

"About the indictment news?"

Cedric gave a faint nod. "That...and everything else. I go back and forth about a bunch of different things. At times, I'm just trying to come to grips with what's happened, and how it's pretty much turned my life inside out."

"Like how," Charles said, though he could easily guess.

"For starters, my best friend is dead. I still can't believe it. Then there's other lesser things. For example, no chance I'll be on the basketball team again this season. Not that it's so important, but given what the newspapers have said, I doubt anyone on the team would even want to be seen with me. I know Amelia doesn't."

"That's your girlfriend, right?"

"I guess, we weren't official yet, but we were getting close. Now her father won't even let her talk to me. Then there's this...which is far more significant. I might not even be on the planet much longer, if the jury doesn't buy into the *shadow of doubt* that you and Mr. Beaumont are trying to create. But then this...I'm just deeply saddened I no longer have Reggie for a friend. He really is dead. Somebody really did kill him, and I can't begin to figure out why."

"I've thought a lot about that myself," Charles said.

"At first," Cedric continued, "I was thinking it was a robbery, but then, they didn't take anything. Not even the money clip in my gym bag. Instead, they left a gun. Why'd they do that? They seemed to be in such a hurry to get out of there once they heard me coming. Why take the time to stick that gun in my gym bag? None of it makes any sense."

Charles watched Cedric closely as he talked. He mostly wanted to comfort him, not try to figure everything out. Even though Cedric touched on many of the same things that bothered Charles. So, he decided to get Cedric talking about his friend. Maybe stir up some fond memories. "So Cedric, I met Reggie but never really got to know him. Tell me some things you really liked about him."

Cedric took a moment, then said, "Lately, all Reggie mostly wanted to talk about was how lousy he had it at home. He and his dad didn't get along at all. He was really envious about my relationship with Father, said he couldn't remember his father ever saying a kind word to him. He barely paid him any attention at all. And if he did have something to say, it was usually some kind of criticism."

"Actually, sounds a lot like the few memories I have about my Dad," Charles said. "Your father is really very different in that way."

Cedric didn't seem to hear what Charles said. He started talking some more about Reggie. "Reggie said he really appreciated how honest and decent my father was, and that his own was pretty much the exact opposite."

"Wonder what he meant by that?"

"Not sure. I got the impression he didn't approve of the way his father conducted his business dealings. You know, the Alderman stuff. He went on and on about what a hypocrite he was. The way he presented himself to people in public, compared with the kind of person he was behind the scenes. Reggie said he didn't want to be anything like him."

Then Cedric thought some more. "I don't know what it was, but that morning at the gym? Really, the night before on the telephone, Reggie told me he had something pretty serious he wanted my advice on."

"Any idea what it was?"

"No, I know he wasn't thinking of anything stupid like running away. He knew he was stuck there at home at least until he graduated. He talked about wanting to do something with his life that had nothing to do with politics. Maybe he wanted some advice about what to choose as his major in college. I really don't know. Of course, now I'll never get to find out what it was."

25

Shortly after breakfast on Wednesday morning, Charles pulled his car alongside the curb of the Whitaker mansion. Lily sat beside him, her gloved hands folded in her lap. She had wanted to spend another day with her family, continuing to offer emotional support. Charles had agreed and planned to use the time to keep pulling on the various threads of the case, following them wherever they led.

Earlier that morning back at The Dakota, Charles had taken a moment to glance at the latest edition of *The New York Times*, delivered to his door as always. Over breakfast, Lily had served coffee while Charles quickly opened the paper. He was relieved to see the coverage of the murder investigation had been further diminished—now relegated to a small article in the bottom left corner of the front page. The growing unrest in Europe had taken center stage once more, as war now seemed inevitable.

Multiple nations were beginning to line up on either side of the growing conflict. The article about the murder was brief and restrained, not even written by Wainwright. It was mostly announcing that the funeral of Reginald Ashcroft was to take place the following morning, Thursday at ten o'clock.

As they exited the car, Charles wondered whether Nigel had read the paper yet. Likely he had. The doorbell had barely rung when Quentin, ever punctual, greeted them at the front door and led them to the dining room. The family was still seated at the long table, their breakfast plates pushed aside, each person sipping coffee in subdued conversation. Nigel, as expected, held up *The Times* with one hand, a half-empty cup in the other.

"Good morning," Lily said, offering kisses to her parents before taking a seat.

Charles smiled warmly. "Morning, everyone."

Millicent turned to Quentin. "Would you please fetch coffee for Charles and Lily?"

Charles gently waved it off. "Thank you, Quentin, but I'll get it. Please, feel free to join the rest of the staff downstairs."

"Very good, sir."

As Charles filled two cups at the sideboard, Nigel lowered his paper. "I assume you've seen the article?"

"I did," Charles said as he returned to the table. "Short, and much better than it's been."

"Indeed," Nigel said, folding the paper on the table. "The most telling thing about it is what it *doesn't* say. No sensational headline. No '*Scandal at the Belmont.*' They mention the hotel only as the location of the crime."

Millicent nodded soberly. "That's progress, I suppose."

"They also listed some of the likely funeral attendees," Nigel added. "A parade of city officials like the mayor, the DA, the police commissioner, most of the other aldermen. No doubt all coming to curry favor with Alderman Ashcroft."

Cedric, who had been unusually quiet, finally spoke up, his tone with an edge. "Well, we know one person who *won't* be there—*me*."

Everyone turned toward him.

"One of Ashcroft's men called not long ago," Cedric said, "before the newspaper had even been delivered. Quentin took the message. Said the Alderman wished to make it clear, neither I nor anyone from this family would be welcome at the funeral."

Millicent's eyes widened with offense. "How dare he?"

"It's obvious what he meant," Cedric continued. "He still thinks I did it."

Charles and Lily exchanged glances.

"It's not just hurtful," Cedric said, softer now. "It's sad. I didn't do anything wrong. And now I'm shut out from properly saying goodbye to one of the best friends I've ever had. Probably ever will have."

"So sorry, Cedric," Charles said. "That's not right."

Everyone else said similar things.

Nigel leaned back in his chair, his mind on something. "Perhaps," he said slowly, "you two could attend?" He was looking at Charles and Lily. "I don't think anyone knows either of you and, Lily, you don't share the accursed Whitaker last name anymore."

"Oh, Father. Our name is not cursed."

"I'm mostly joking, Dear. But it's true. The two of you could go in our place. Pay our respects. Then come home and share any observations you had with Cedric afterward."

Lily didn't hesitate. "Of course, Father. We'd be honored."

Charles nodded. "Yes. I'd like to see who attends anyway." He didn't say it aloud, but a part of him wondered—would the killers attend? If nothing else, he planned to observe everything very carefully.

A FEW HOURS LATER, Charles was at a little side desk in the parlor, creating a list of questions he'd want to ask Singleton, the missing gym manager, if they ever located him. The house telephone rang. Lily answered it in the foyer. "Charles, it's Mr. Keller."

He got up, made his way to her. She handed him the receiver. "Keller, good to hear from you."

"You'll be glad you picked up. Wallace Kane—my detective friend—you're not gonna believe it...he's found Singleton."

Charles straightened up. "You're serious?"

"Yes, sir. Turns out he didn't just quit, he moved out of the city entirely. He's living in an apartment in Rockville Centre. That's in Nassau County, well out on Long Island."

"That's impressive work. How did Kane track him down so quickly?"

"He started with the hotel staff. Kane found out Singleton was sweet on a young female clerk. Apparently, she's the only one he told where he was going—but he made her promise not to say anything."

"So why did she talk?"

"She wasn't interested in him," Keller said. "In fact, she'd been trying to get him to stop pestering her for a date. So, when Kane asked, she was happy to cooperate."

Charles smiled. "This is a very good development for us."

"Apparently, Singleton came into some serious money right before he disappeared. That's what allowed him to make the move."

Charles's voice sharpened. "Think it was some kind of payoff?"

"That's Kane's hunch. I'm inclined to agree."

"Did Kane talk to him?"

"No, he wasn't sure if you might want to handle it personally. If you do want him to make contact, he asked if you'd let him know what questions you want answered."

"That's a coincidence," Charles said. "I was just sitting here working on some good questions we could ask Singleton if we ever find him. Here's what I'm thinking—after the funeral tomorrow, you and I go out there together. Pay him a visit."

"I like the sound of that," Keller replied. "I'll be ready."

"Tell Kane he's earned every dollar. Whatever he charges for this, we'll make sure he gets it."

"He'll like that. One more thing," Keller added. "Kane says he's available Friday morning for that experiment we talked about—the silencer test?"

"Excellent," Charles said. "I'll bring Cedric down to the gym. If the sound he hears matches what he described, it could be a crucial piece of the puzzle."

"Agreed."

They said their goodbyes, and Charles returned the receiver to its cradle. As he stood there, he felt something shift inside—just the tiniest stirring, like the wheels were finally turning after being totally stuck in the mud.

26

Thursday 10am,
Woodlawn Cemetery - The Bronx

It was a warm July morning.

A procession of sleek black motorcars lined the gravel loop just inside the Woodlawn gate. About two-hundred mourners had gathered. The men in black morning coats and top hats, the women wearing long, flowing dresses of muted tones, most with draped lace or crepe veils over their faces. All stood quietly on the grass, holding the printed funeral programs distributed by uniformed ushers as they walked into the cemetery.

A white canvas awning had been raised near the family plot, offering shade and chairs for the inner circle. Overhead, summer clouds drifted low and slow. The priest's solemn voice echoed faintly over the hush of the crowd. Journalists stood just outside the service area, notepads discreetly in hand. The whole event was saturated in formal restraint. Everyone seemed to be watching everyone else.

And Charles was watching all of them.

Lily, in a black lace veil and matching gloves, held Charles's arm as they stood quietly, several rows back. He guessed the funeral had to be nearly over by now, as yet one more hymn Charles didn't recognize drifted through the trees. A light breeze also rustled through the leaves like whispering mourners.

The Ashcroft family were seated at the front, closest to the gleaming casket draped in white roses and lilies. Standing closely behind them, Charles recognized numerous prominent businessmen, clergy figures, and several well-known dignitaries including District Attorney Tilford, Police Commissioner Mallory, the mayor, and a handful of aldermen and judges.

Charles leaned slightly toward Lily and whispered, "Quite the turnout."

She nodded but said nothing, her eyes fixed on the priest.

The Episcopalian minister, a dignified man in his sixties wearing a long black cassock, lifted his voice for what sounded like the final words of the service. "Into thy hands, O merciful Savior, we commend thy servant Reginald. Acknowledge, we humbly beseech thee, a sheep of thine own fold, a lamb of thine own flock...a sinner of thine own redeeming."

Charles listened but found his attention drifting. He studied the faces of the Ashcroft family. Most were visibly shaken. A woman who appeared to be Reggie's mother clutched a handkerchief to her face, her shoulders trembling. One of the younger siblings, perhaps a sister, sobbed softly into her gloves.

Then Charles's gaze fell on Herbert Ashcroft, Reggie's father.

The head alderman sat ramrod straight, staring past the casket. His face showed no grief—no glistening eyes, no downward tilt of the mouth. If anything, he appeared detached, preoccupied. Charles had seen many forms of sorrow before, but this wholesale absence of emotion struck him as unnatural. If it had been his son, Charles knew he'd be an absolute mess. They say each grieves in his own way, but he couldn't help but wonder what thoughts might be running through Ashcroft's mind?

The priest continued, "Receive Reginald into the arms of thy mercy, into the blessed rest of everlasting peace."

Charles lowered his head respectfully as the prayer ended. A faint shuffle of feet followed. The casket would soon be lowered. The hush of finality hung in the air.

During the service, that group of newspapermen had kept a respectful distance. But once or twice, Charles noticed one bold photographer inching too close, taking pictures. At one such moment, the man lifted his camera to snap a picture of the grieving family from the side.

That's when Charles saw him—a towering figure moving silently and swiftly toward the photographer. He was a thick-shouldered brute with slicked-back hair and arms like iron girders beneath his coat. One glare from him was enough. The photographer immediately retreated to the safety of the press cluster.

Charles then noticed another man standing on the other side just behind Ashcroft. This one was shorter, wiry but muscular, with a long, narrow face and a pair of piercing eyes that darted everywhere at once. Both wore identical suits and matching derby hats, and both projected an air of menace.

Charles nudged Lily slightly and murmured, "Those two men behind Ashcroft, do they look like bodyguards to you?"

She followed his line of sight, focused a moment, and offered a soft nod. "Could be."

Once the priest had finished, after a few moments, the crowd began to disperse, most toward the exit, a smaller number toward the family. But Ashcroft quickly stood. Without so much as a glance toward the casket or his grieving family, he turned and walked directly to where DA Tilford and Commissioner Mallory were standing. The two men greeted him with appropriate deference, extending hands and offering condolences. Ashcroft shook them, but his face remained unchanged, as though nothing had been said.

He pulled them a few feet away from the other prominent men, leaned in, and began speaking in hushed tones.

Charles watched with growing interest. Whatever Ashcroft was saying caused both men to stiffen, their faces instantly utterly serious. From where Charles stood, it almost looked as though Ashcroft were scolding them—like a military officer quietly reprimanding subordinates.

All the while, the two bodyguards hovered just behind him, their heads on a swivel, scanning the crowd like guard dogs alert to every sound. They seemed entirely out of place at such an event. Then Charles thought, a man like Ashcroft, who virtually controlled the city's zoning commission, perhaps he'd made a lot of enemies in his work and felt the need for protection. He'd read about Ashcroft being involved in numerous clashes with angry residents, suddenly made homeless by his decisions "serving the cause of progress" for the city.

He glanced back at the casket. The rest of Reggie's family and several college-age friends had quietly gathered around it, touching it as if to say a last goodbye, comforting each other with hugs. None of the family members seemed the least bit disturbed that Reggie's father was off doing his own thing.

Lily noticed it, too. "What's with Reggie's father?" she whispered. "He's just mingling with all those city bigwigs. He should be comforting his wife and family."

"Yeah, it seems odd to me," Charles said. "But none of them seem to care." He was about to mention the bodyguards again but changed his mind. He noticed all these handsome, well-dressed young men now comforting the family. "I wonder if that's Cedric and Reggie's basketball teammates."

"It probably is," she said. "It's so wrong that Cedric isn't right there with them, instead of stuck at home."

27

Charles pulled up in front of The Belmont Hotel just after lunchtime. Keller was waiting out front in his usual dark suit, a small leather portfolio in hand. He climbed into the passenger seat with a nod and a brief smile.

"Thanks for picking me up," he said. "You're going to like this drive. Not a traffic jam in sight once we get out of the city."

"I've actually been to Long Island a couple of times," Charles said, "right after I bought the car. Wanted a chance to see how well it performed riding at top speed."

"How fast did you get it up to?"

"Forty-five miles an hour," Charles said. "Smooth as silk." He pulled the motorcar out into the street and headed east. Soon they were driving beneath a ceiling of smoke-stained sky. As they left midtown, Charles threaded his car past delivery carts, trolley lines, and the chorus of barking newsboys. Along Third Avenue, elevated trains clattered above them, casting flickering shadows on the motorcars below. Tenements gave way to brownstones, then to quieter, leafier streets as they left the island's center behind.

As they crossed the Queensboro Bridge, the afternoon sun glinted off the steel girders. Charles noticed scaffolding and half-finished towers rising in the distance. "Haven't been out this way in a while. Is that another bridge going up?"

"Two, actually," Keller said. "The Hell Gate Bridge and the Triborough are both in the works. That one's the Hell Gate—it'll carry trains once it's done. Still a few years off."

Once they crossed into Queens, the city structures began to thin. The tall buildings gave way to modest brick homes and scattered shops. By the time they passed through the borough's edge and out into Nassau County, the skyline had flattened out completely. There were stretches where nothing lined the roads but grassy fields and small patches of forest.

"Hard to fathom," Charles said, gesturing out the window, "how different the scenery gets just a short ways past the city. Just like that we've got clean air, no buildings in sight, just fields and trees stretching out to the horizon. I doubt one New Yorker in ten has ever seen this with their own eyes."

"Probably right," Keller said. "I've only been out a few times with the wife. Well, ex-wife now. Before she left, I was hoping to get her thinking when I retired from the force we could leave the big city and move out here."

"Guess it didn't work," Charles said.

"Nope, had her mind made up, I think. Kind of a too-little-too-late thing on my part. I should've left the force years before I did."

They passed through a few small towns—Floral Park, then Lynbrook—each with quiet streets and tidy shops. Just beyond Lynbrook lay their destination: Rockville Centre. Charles noted the British spelling of the town's name on the train station sign. "That's odd," he said. "Centre spelled with an *re*."

"Guess they'll fix that eventually."

They pulled onto a street lined with shady sycamore trees and parked in front of a small garage apartment tucked behind a modest two-story home. A wooden staircase on the left side led up to a private entrance.

Keller nodded toward the stairs. "Let me do most of the talking, at least at first. Singleton knows me. Less likely to spook him."

They climbed the steps and knocked. After a moment, the door creaked open, and a thin, nervous-looking man in his thirties peered out. He blinked in shock when he recognized Keller.

"Mr. Keller? What—what are you doing here?"

Keller smiled. "Hey Mickey. Isn't it obvious? We came to see you. A lot of folks at the hotel been wondering why you vanished without a word."

Singleton hesitated, then Keller asked, "Mind letting us in?"

The man stepped back. Inside, the apartment was modest but well furnished, with new curtains, a small sofa, and a set of polished side tables that looked recently purchased. Charles noticed the shine on the hardwood floors and the newness of everything.

Keller gestured to the sofa. "Mind if we sit?"

Singleton nodded and sank into a nearby armchair.

"So," Keller said, "you gonna tell us why you left without giving notice? You been there over three years, Mickey. That wasn't very nice. I happen to know Mr. Whitaker treated you pretty good. You got raises at least once every year, got to run that gym with very little supervision."

Singleton hesitated. "How...how did you even find me?"

Keller chuckled. "Remember that young lady typist you wouldn't stop pestering for a date? Didn't take much to get her to talk. Guess you can figure out, she had no interest in returning your affections."

Singleton looked rattled. Charles decided to jump in.

"I'm Charles Bennington, Mickey," he said. "Son-in-law to Nigel Whitaker, your former boss. I'll ask again—why did you vanish Friday night, the night before Reggie Ashcroft was murdered?"

Singleton's eyes widened. "Murdered?" he repeated. "What are you talking about?"

"You mean you haven't heard?" Keller said. "It's been in the papers every day since it happened."

"I haven't picked up a paper since I left," Singleton said. "I've been busy settling in here, buying stuff for the apartment. Trying to enjoy a little peace and quiet for a change."

Charles took a few minutes to update him about Reggie's death, the arrest of Cedric, and shared a summary of Cedric's version of events—the argument he heard between Reggie and two men, the quick exit of the real killers out the back door.

Singleton's face went pale. He gripped the arms of his chair. "Two men came to the gym Friday morning," he said slowly. "They offered me a... a deal. Told me to get it I had to leave that day, no exceptions. Not just leave the hotel, but leave the city. Said if I did, they'd pay me more money than I'd make in three years." He looked down at the floor. "I didn't ask any questions. Just saw the money. I never liked that job much anyways, and I didn't have anyone to answer to in the city. So, I said yes and left."

Charles leaned in. "And it never occurred to you that people don't give away that kind of money without a good reason? They needed you gone, Mickey, to pull off a murder the following day with no witnesses. And now Cedric stands accused of killing his best friend."

Singleton looked stunned. He didn't say anything for several moments. "So you think...they're the ones who killed Reggie?" He sat back in his chair. "My gosh. I guess if I hadn't taken their deal, they would've killed me too."

"Describe them," Charles said.

Singleton closed his eyes a moment, gathering the memory. "One was tall, thick like a football player. Slicked-back hair. Big hands. The other was shorter, thinner, sharp face, beady eyes, always looking around, had a flattened nose like an ex-boxer."

Charles couldn't believe what he heard. If asked, he

might have used similar words to describe the two bodyguards he'd seen beside Ashcroft at the funeral. He didn't say what he thought aloud.

"You understand," Keller said, "you're part of this now, Mickey. You helped these guys, even if you didn't mean to. You have to come forward, tell what you know to the cops. The boss's son is gonna take the rap for this if you don't. They've already indicted him. He's facing the electric chair, Mickey, for something he definitely didn't do."

Singleton leapt to his feet and paced. "No. I can't. They told me never to come back. Said they'd find me if I did. You should've seen these guys, Mr. Keller. They're not the kind of guys you mess with. If I come back and testify, they'll kill me. You said it yourself, you think they killed Reggie."

"We can protect you," Charles said. "I'll talk to my father-in-law. He'll put you up at the hotel until after the trial. We can do it in a way that no one even knows you're there. Mr. Keller will make sure you're safe. If we have to, we'll put an armed guard outside your door, day and night."

Singleton stopped pacing but didn't speak.

"Do you know who they are?" Charles asked. By now, he was sure he did. At least, who they worked for.

Singleton shook his head. "Never seen 'em before."

Charles looked at Keller. They both knew...Singleton wasn't ready for this. They wouldn't get anything more from him today. "You think about what we said," Charles said. "Could you really live with yourself if they found Cedric guilty of Reggie's murder?" He waited a moment, but Singleton just stared at the wall. "At the very least, don't tell anyone about this," Charles said. "No one."

"I won't," Singleton said. "Why would I? And you guys don't tell anyone where I am. Unless you want me dead."

As Charles and Keller got back into the car and started the return drive home, Charles said, "The two men he described? This morning, my wife and I went to the funeral. I saw two men who matched that description to the letter."

"Really," Keller said. "At the funeral?"

"They were Ashcroft's bodyguards. At least that's what they looked like, stayed on either side of him the whole time."

"What?"

Charles nodded. "Can't be 100% sure, but...it can't be a coincidence. I mean, if I described them to you right now, I'd use just about the same words as Singleton did.

Keller let out a low whistle. "Then that means—"

Charles nodded. "The men who killed Reggie might very well work for his father."

They drove in silence, both men lost in the staggering implications of what this could mean.

28

By the time Charles returned to the Whitaker mansion, the shadows from the buildings and trees were beginning to darken Gramercy Park. The drive from Singleton's apartment had taken just under an hour. And after dropping Keller at The Belmont, Charles couldn't wait to get with Lily and share with her these new developments. He found her on the veranda, a book in her lap but clearly not reading. Her eyes seemed focused on a small flower garden, but he wasn't even sure she was seeing it.

As he approached, she seemed to snap out of it, set her book on the table, and stood. "You're back." She gave him a big hug and kiss. "How did things go with Mr. Singleton?"

Charles sat in the chair beside her. "We found him right where that detective, Kane, said he'd be. He lives in a garage apartment out in Rockville Centre."

"Bet he was surprised to see you two?"

"Surprised to see Keller mostly. Don't think he'd ever met me. But yeah, he was a little more than surprised. I'd say he was kind of spooked by us being there."

Lily leaned in, eyes wide. "What did Singleton say, about why he disappeared that way?"

Charles exhaled. "Well, it's a pretty crazy story. We certainly found out about the money he'd come into. That's what he told that girl. It must've been a sizeable amount. Pretty much every stick of furniture I saw in that apartment was brand-new."

"So, where did he get it?"

"He said two men came to the gym Friday morning, the day before the murder, and paid him a small fortune to leave town immediately. That was the deal. Leave your job, leave town, and don't tell anyone."

"What in the world? Why would they do something like that? I've never heard of such a thing." She took a sip of her coffee. "The coffee in the carafe is probably still hot. Want some?"

"Sure, that would be nice." She began to pour it, and he continued. "Like I said, it's a crazy story. He didn't even know about Reggie's murder, or about Cedric being arrested for it. He hadn't read the newspaper since he left town on Friday."

"Bet that was a shock."

"He was more terrified than shocked, I'd say."

"Terrified? Why?" she said.

"Because he realized as we shared Cedric's version of

what happened that these two guys who paid him to leave town were probably the killers."

Now, she was the shocked one. "Oh my gosh."

"It's the only thing that made sense. They needed the gym empty, so there'd be no witnesses when they shot Reggie."

"Wait a minute, you just said *when they shot Reggie*. I thought this was a robbery. You sound like they went there to shoot Reggie on purpose. Like they went there to shoot him."

Charles nodded. "That's because now I believe that's what happened. You remember those two tough-looking guys standing behind Reggie's father at the funeral this morning? I thought maybe they were bodyguards."

She nodded.

"Well, this isn't proof positive yet, but when we asked Singleton to describe what the two men looked like, the ones who made him that deal, it's like he was there with us at the funeral describing those two guys. Ashcroft's bodyguards."

Now, her mouth opened wide.

"Right now, I have no idea why these men would kill their boss's son. But that's starting to look like what happened here. Like it wasn't a robbery at all. Like they staged it to look like that, but they really went there to kill him, to kill Reggie. Then set things up to frame Cedric."

"Charles, you have to know how crazy this sounds," she said.

"I told you...it's a crazy story. But it seems like that's where the facts are pointing."

"But you said you need proof," she said.

"Yes. Keller used to be a cop. He thinks we somehow need to get Singleton to see these guys in person, see if they really are the ones who paid him off. Or, if somehow we could get their fingerprints and match them to the ones his detective got. Either one of those could flip this case on its head."

Lily's face lit up with hope. "Oh, Lord. Let this be true. You've got to go speak to Father and Cedric. Right away. He came home early from work. He's down in his study."

Charles stood. "Are you coming?"

She shook her head. "No. Cedric's in his room. I'll get him, tell him to meet you and Father in the study. I'll sit with Mother in the parlor, keep her company. I think Father will want the chance to decide how much to share with her."

CHARLES KNOCKED GENTLY and stepped into the study. Nigel was seated at his desk, gazing out the window with a vacant stare. He looked up slowly as Charles entered.

"Charles. Please, sit."

"There's something important you need to hear. Lily's getting Cedric now. It's actually some pretty positive news about this case."

Nigel ran a hand over his face. "I could use some good news right about now. My banker called earlier, said the loan for the ballroom expansion's off the table. Besides the dentists, two other business conventions have canceled. He feels like it's too risky to do something like this as long as the scandal about the hotel, and about Cedric, keeps dragging on in the newspapers."

Just then, Cedric entered the study and sat down. "Lily said you had some positive news to share with me, with us, about the case."

Charles didn't waste any time. "I believe we now know who killed Reggie—and we're closing in on the proof."

Both men leaned forward, the same look on their face Lily had a short while ago. He gave them a full account of his visit to Long Island with Keller, the meeting with Singleton, and the stunning realization that the two men who paid him off fit the description of Ashcroft's bodyguards exactly. He included how Singleton had never seen them before but had accepted the money without asking questions. That's why Singleton had disappeared. That's why he wasn't there in the gym that morning. When Charles explained how Singleton reacted upon learning Reggie had been murdered, and Cedric arrested, both Nigel and Cedric sat in stunned silence.

"His father's own bodyguards?" Cedric said slowly. "Killed Reggie? That can't be true. Why would...why would they do that? "

Charles shook his head. "We don't know any of the reasons yet. But it adds up with facts. They needed Singleton gone, so there'd be no witnesses. I think they went there to kill Reggie and frame Cedric, planting the gun in Cedric's gym bag. Maybe they didn't expect Cedric walking in when he did, and they rushed things and fled out the back door."

Nigel leaned forward, a new urgency lighting his eyes. "Is there any way to prove any of this?"

"I think so," Charles said. "Not sure exactly how just yet. We need to prove they were the ones in the gym. If we can somehow get a copy of their fingerprints, we could match them to the ones our detective found. Or, if we could somehow get Singleton to come back and see these men, he could tell us if they're the ones who paid him off."

"And Singleton won't come back?" Cedric said.

"He's too afraid right now. He's pretty sure those guys are killers."

"And they might kill him?" Nigel said.

Charles nodded, then mentioned the idea of trying to get Singleton at the Belmont. Nigel liked the idea and said he'd definitely be open to that.

Nigel tapped his fingers on the desk. "Why not give the fingerprint assignment to your detective. Have him follow the two bodyguards—discreetly. If he can retrieve something they touch—a coffee cup, a cigarette case, for example—maybe he can get their prints."

Charles nodded. "That's a good idea. I'll talk to Keller about it right away. He's got Kane lined up to do some silencer testing with Cedric tomorrow anyway." He turned to Cedric. "You still open to doing that?"

Cedric nodded. "Sure."

"You've been quiet about all this," Nigel said.

Cedric looked up, his expression haunted. "Just...trying to process it. Reggie's own father's bodyguards? Charles, I know his father is a hard man, but I can't wrap my mind around this. It's...it's horrible."

Charles reached over, put a hand on his shoulder. "I know. I've been thinking the same thing since the drive home. But that's why we need to keep digging. Find all the missing pieces."

"Do you think you should go to the police with this new information?" Nigel said.

"I don't think so yet," Charles said. "Maybe when I've got a little more proof behind us."

Charles stood and walked slowly to the fireplace. "There's a few other things I've been thinking about."

"Such as?"

"I'm not ready to talk about them just yet. But Cedric? Can we talk again? Maybe tonight, after dinner. Just the two of us. I want to hear more about Reggie—what he said, what he might have been dealing with at home. Maybe there's a clue in something you heard."

Cedric nodded. "Sure, anything I can do to clear my name."

Charles turned back to face them. "We're getting closer, gentlemen. What's that old saying about seeing a light at the end of the tunnel? Not seeing any bright lights just yet, but hey, before today, I wasn't even sure we had a tunnel."

Just before Charles left, Nigel got up and came over, close enough to whisper. "Charles, you're doing a great job digging out these things. But I must tell you. You really need to tread carefully from here on out. These people you're dealing with are ruthless, and they are killers. And I'm sure they won't like the idea of someone working hard to uncover something they worked so hard to conceal."

29

Later that evening, after a quiet dinner, Charles stepped out onto the veranda to find Cedric already seated. The last of the sunlight had drained from the sky, leaving only the soft glow of the gas lamps in the street, and the first twinkling stars. Cedric sat still, a cup of coffee in his hand, his gaze fixed on the sky as if searching it for answers.

Charles approached gently. “Mind if I join you?”

Cedric gave a tired smile. “Not at all. You said back in the study you wanted to talk. I was kind of expecting you.”

Charles settled into the wicker chair beside him, pondering how to introduce what he wanted to discuss. “I’ve been thinking a great deal about what happened today...with Singleton and what came out about the bodyguards.”

Cedric gave a slight nod. “It’s hard to believe, isn’t it?

Reggie's father's own men. But as I've thought more about it, it's not that hard for me to see these men doing something so ruthless. I've never actually met them. I've seen them plenty of times when I've been over there. But Reggie and I never really hung out at his place for very long. He loved coming here, but whenever we were at his house, we just stayed long enough to do whatever he had to do, or get whatever he had to get, and then he'd want to leave. I think those guys made him nervous, too. They didn't seem like the kind of men you'd typically see in a suit. More like the kind of guys you'd meet in some back alley."

Charles had thought something similar.

"Even so," Cedric continued, "why would they kill their boss's son?"

"I've asked myself the same question," Charles said. "But the pieces are starting to form a picture. The more I think about it, the more I wonder—if those two did it, they didn't act on their own. They're not vigilante types. More like men who take orders. I think maybe they were sent."

"You're saying Reggie's father gave the order?" Cedric asked, in disbelief. "For them to kill Reggie?"

"I'm saying it's possible," Charles said. "I mean think about it...what would a man like Ashcroft do if two guys he hired to protect him took it upon themselves to kill his only son? I just can't see that happening. And if Ashcroft did this, it must have been to stop something. Something Reggie knew, something he might have seen...or was about to do."

"You mean like silence him? Kill him to shut him up?"

Charles nodded. "Hard as it is to imagine, yeah."

Cedric was silent for a moment, then said, "I've been going over some things, too, sitting out here. Little things Reggie said lately in our conversations. He was growing more agitated, more disgusted with his father. More so than usual."

Charles leaned in. "What kinds of things?"

Cedric set his cup down. "One time, he said he'd seen his father take bribes. He also heard him on conversations on the telephone, talking about zoning permits and construction projects. Laying out things, amounts he wanted in exchange for political favors and campaign support. One time Reggie said this poorly dressed group of people came over to the house, uninvited. He found out later they were tenants who lived in some low-rent apartments. Their building was about to be torn down to make room for some big office building. Some of them were crying, saying if he did this, they had nowhere to go, no money to live anywhere else. His father just ordered his men to throw them all out off the property." Cedric looked at Charles. "Reggie was so upset he had tears in his eyes as he's telling me this."

Charles sighed. "That actually adds up. Those are the kinds of things—at least the bribery and political favors bit—that could land his father in prison. Let's say Reggie was thinking about exposing his father—like threatening to talk to the press, or maybe even going to the Curran Commission—that could easily be a big enough motive to provoke a violent response."

Cedric's voice dropped. "You know, he didn't come right out and say it. But the night before we were supposed to meet at the gym, he told me he had something serious to talk about. Something important. We never got to it."

"Do you think that's what it was?" Charles asked. "That he was going to blow the whistle on his father?"

Cedric stared into the garden. "I'm starting to wonder now."

They sat in silence a while, as the implications settled. Then Charles asked, "The problem with all of this is that it's just speculation right now. You and I talking out loud. We don't have any proof. Do you think it's possible that he might have ever confided in anyone else about this? Besides you, I mean. Maybe someone in the house? A servant or someone on staff he trusted?"

"The chauffeur," Cedric said at once. "They were pretty close. He is about our age. Reggie told me he confided in him sometimes—said he was the only person over there he felt he could trust. He said the chauffeur overheard a lot of the same types of things Reggie talked about while driving his father around."

Charles's eyes narrowed. "If the chauffeur heard these kinds of things and he and Reggie were close, then maybe he'd be someone we could talk to."

Cedric added, "I just remember one more thing. Reggie had started keeping a journal. He told me he wasn't planning to show it to anyone. Just that writing things down helped him deal with his frustration and clear his head."

Charles sat upright. "Any idea where he kept it?"

"No. But if it's still in his room, maybe the chauffeur could find it."

Charles ran a hand along the armrest of the chair. "That journal could break open this whole case. It could contain everything. To have in writing the kinds of things Reggie said with you, or even better, the kinds of things he heard about his father, maybe even said to his father...it would totally exonerate you."

Cedric nodded solemnly. "That would be amazing if we could get hold of it."

Charles stood. "You think you might be open to chatting with him, see if he'd help us."

"I'd be open, but the courts wouldn't be okay with that. I'm not supposed to have anything to do with the Ashcroft family. Do you think you could talk to him for me?"

"Me?" Charles said, "Well, I guess I could."

A long pause followed. Cedric looked up at Charles. "If Reggie's father had something to do with his death... what does that make him?"

Charles stared into the night sky. "A man who values his power more than his own son's life. Which also makes him a very dangerous man."

Neither of them spoke for a few moments then Charles looked back at Cedric. "Let's keep this part just between us for right now. You can talk it over with your father, certainly. But no reason to worry Lily or your mom about this."

"Right," Cedric said.

"I mean about the danger part."

"I know. And Charles, you be very careful out there. You're the one sticking your neck out with these things. I couldn't live with myself—or face my sister—if anything ever happened to you."

30

It was Friday morning.

Last night, Charles had a difficult time falling asleep. It was more than just the myriad of details about the case whirling around in his mind. At one point, he'd gotten up and moved out to the parlor in their spacious apartment at The Dakota. A few moments later, Lily had come out to see if he was okay. He realized immediately that his disquiet was rooted mostly in the things he had been keeping from her.

All for the good cause of sparing her from anxiety. But they had talked about this a few times in their young marriage. That is, how common it was for the men of that day to virtually keep everything from their wives. Either under the banner of protecting them from fear and worry or, as Lily abruptly put it, because they genuinely believed women to be inferior and incapable of dealing with the complexities of life. These weightier matters, of course, were better left in the hands of men.

Which, by necessity, meant that they rarely ever confided in their wives when they were struggling, and certainly wouldn't seek out any wisdom their wife might offer on a matter.

Charles didn't believe any of this and one of the things he loved most about Lily was...neither did she. She had quite a good head on her shoulders and on more than one occasion had given him excellent advice on handling situations in his business, especially when dealing with difficult people.

So last night, Charles took the courageous step and brought Lily fully up to date on all the things he had uncovered about the case. Of course, she very quickly arrived at the same conclusion her father and Cedric had, which was that Charles was now moving in some very treacherous waters. If it proved true that Herbert Ashcroft had his own son killed to keep him from exposing his corrupt business affairs, clearly he'd have no misgivings about doing the same thing to Charles.

Charles should not have been surprised by this, but Lily's immediate reaction to this information was not to cower in fear or insist Charles remove himself from anything that even hinted at danger. She reached for his hands and suggested they pray together for God to protect him from evildoers and any harm they might seek to do to Charles. And also to give him the victory, as he sought to vindicate her brother from all these lies.

No wonder he loved her so.

. . .

He thought about all these things as he and Cedric pulled up to the service entrance of The Belmont. Charles didn't want to draw any attention to what they were doing by walking through the front doors and the reservation desk. They still had to spend a few brief moments in the lobby to get to the gym door that led downstairs. But fortunately, no one seemed to notice them.

When they opened the door into the gym, Charles saw Keller and someone else standing near the murder scene by the lockers. Keller motioned them over. Beside him stood a man neither Charles nor Cedric had met before.

"Glad you could make it," Keller said, clasping Charles's shoulder. "Charles, Cedric...this is Wallace Kane. He's the private detective who's been working for us lately, and my former partner from my days on the force."

Charles extended a hand. "Mr. Kane. I've heard good things."

Kane gave a modest nod and returned the handshake with a firm, no-nonsense grip. There was a quiet edge to him, like a man totally at ease in difficult situations.

"Likewise," Kane said. "Glad to help. Keller tells me you're trying to make sense of the noise this young man heard the morning Reggie Ashcroft was killed."

"That's right," Charles said. "We're hoping this little experiment clears up one part of the mystery."

Kane gestured to a bench where a leather bag lay zipped. "Let's give it a go."

He unzipped it and pulled out a small pistol. "Cedric,

does this look like the weapon you found in your gym bag?"

Cedric grimaced. "You mean the one I picked up like an idiot?"

Charles spoke gently. "Don't keep flogging yourself over that. It was a natural reaction."

Cedric nodded, looked back at Kane. "Yes, this looks almost exactly like it. I can't be a hundred percent sure—I'd never seen it before—but the shape, the size...it's pretty close."

Kane gave a grunt of approval. "This model is one of only a few that could accommodate a silencer. They have to be able to screw onto the end of the barrel. Watch." He pulled a cylindrical object from the bag and attached it to the muzzle of the gun with a few practiced twists.

Cedric stared. "I've never seen one of those before."

"Most folks haven't," Kane said. "They're not common. And they've only been on the market a few years. A man named Maxim patented it about five years back. Real name for it is a suppressor, but 'silencer' caught on."

"How well does it work?" Charles asked. "Does it really make the gun silent?"

Kane shook his head. "Not silent, just quieter. Cuts the sound way down—enough so most people nearby wouldn't recognize it as a gunshot."

Keller chimed in. "Which is why I always wondered how no one heard the shot upstairs. This gym echoes like a cathedral. A gunshot should've gotten the attention of everyone in the lobby. But none of us heard a thing."

Cedric tilted his head. "What's it sound like?"

"I'd rather not say," Kane replied. "Better if you hear it like you did that morning. I even moved a punching bag over to take the place of Reggie. I'll shoot into it. Let's get you where you were then. Stand in the exact spot."

Cedric moved to the doorway, then down the short hall to where he had stood that fateful morning. From that vantage point, the locker area was just out of sight.

"I'm ready," he called.

Kane raised his voice. "On the count of three, I'll shout a bit—like the argument you heard—then fire one shot. Ready?"

"Go ahead."

Kane shouted some nonsense phrases, then squeezed the trigger. The suppressor released a soft, compressed *pop*. Charles flinched slightly—he could hear it clearly, but it was strange, muted. The echo was all but absent.

Cedric called out from the hallway. "That's it. That's the sound I heard. Exactly."

Kane lowered the gun and called for Cedric to come back.

Charles said, "To me, it kinda sounded like a champagne cork at the far end of a drawing room."

"That's a good description," Kane said. "I've heard it compared to a cork before."

Cedric nodded as he joined them. "That is most definitely the sound I couldn't place."

Charles turned to the others. "This confirms Cedric's version of events again. How could he describe a sound like that—something he'd never heard before—unless he really did hear it? The fact that no one else reported a loud bang that morning makes sense now. That alone should count for something."

Kane nodded. "And very few people own these suppressors. They're not illegal yet, but they are rare. Not something an amateur would just happen to have."

"If the police ever search those two bodyguards," Charles said, "I'd wager one of them still has one." He pulled out an envelope and handed it to Kane. "Your payment—for this and for finding Singleton. You've been invaluable."

Kane accepted it with a small nod. Just then, Charles's eye caught the edge of a newspaper sticking out of Kane's leather bag. The headline was upside down, but part of a photograph drew his attention.

"What's this?" Charles pulled the folded edition free.

"It's the paper from this morning," Kane said. "Haven't had time to read it yet."

Charles opened it to a front-page story covering the funeral, about mid-page. The photograph showed the Ashcroft family standing behind Reggie's casket beneath the white funeral canopy. That's when he saw it, saw THEM—two men standing just behind Herbert Ashcroft, one on either side.

The bodyguards.

Charles couldn't believe his eyes. He tilted the paper toward Keller.

Keller leaned in. "That them? That looks almost exactly like the guys Singleton described."

Kane and Cedric looked puzzled.

Charles held out the newspaper, so they could see the photograph. "Gentlemen...meet your two killers."

Kane took the paper from Charles, and he and Cedric studied the front page.

"Mr. Kane, think I'd like to hire you for at least one more assignment, in light of this development. I'm going to drive out to Long Island right now with a copy of this front page to show to Singleton. Cedric and I were discussing last night that the chauffer who works for Ashcroft was a good friend to Reggie, and that the two of them compared notes about the corruption they both heard or witnessed from Reggie's father."

"You want me to contact the chauffer?" Kane said.

"Yes, very discreetly. Has to be in a way where there's no chance Ashcroft, his two goons, or anyone else who works for Ashcroft sees you. Tell him you're working for Cedric, trying to clear his name."

Cedric stepped in and updated Kane on all the things he shared with Charles. "This guy knows Reggie and I were very good friends. Several times he picked us both up after games last year." Cedric explained to Kane about Reggie's journal."

"So, that's the goal" Kane said, "see if we can get this chauffer to find that journal and get it to us?"

"Ideally," Charles said, "but again, you've got to make sure he doesn't let anyone at that house see him. I don't know how else to stress this..."

"How about if he's caught snagging that journal, these bodyguards'll likely kill him?" Kane said.

Charles smiled. 'Yeah, that would probably do it."

"But what's this kid's incentive to help us?" Keller said. "We're asking him to risk his life."

Everyone seemed to pause and think this over.

"I'm going to take a guess," Charles said, "that if he was bothered enough about hearing Ashcroft's corruption that he felt the need to confide in Reggie about it, the kid has a healthy conscience. I'd appeal to that first."

"He's gotta know," Cedric said, "that I had nothing to do with Reggie's death. And he probably knows who did. Ask him...does he really want Reggie's killers to get away with it, and for me to get the chair?"

"If that doesn't work," Keller said. "We could always offer him money."

31

The sun had just begun its steady climb toward mid-afternoon as Charles waited in his car for Keller in the Hotel Belmont's parking lot. One of the hotel drivers had brought Cedric home. Keller said he needed to get a few things together. Before getting in the car, Charles had called Lily from the lobby to brief her on what was happening.

She was over at her parents' house. Her father had definitely seen the article about the funeral, she'd said, but she was almost certain he had no idea about the bodyguard development. The only thing he'd remarked on was his relief that the hotel was only named once in the article, and that in passing. He was on his way to the hotel now. She'd make sure to call him and let him know what Charles had said, and what he and Keller were doing.

A few moments later, Keller climbed into the passenger seat holding two items. A paper bag filled with cheese danishes from the hotel bakery, and two cups of strong, hot coffee. "Thought we'd need these," he said, handing one to Charles.

"Good thinking." Charles began to merge into light traffic.

They drove east once again across the Queensboro Bridge, retracing yesterday's route. But the mood in the car was decidedly different. Yesterday, they'd been grasping for leads. Today, they carried a weapon more powerful than a gun—a photograph of Ashcroft's bodyguards, splashed right across the front page of *The Times*.

As farmland and scattered houses began to appear past the edge of Queens, Charles glanced toward Keller. "He'll know, won't he? As soon as he sees it."

"If he doesn't," Keller said, "I'll eat my hat."

Just shy of an hour later, they pulled up in front of the same modest garage apartment, parked along the street, and walked the short gravel path. Charles knocked. Moments later, Mickey Singleton opened the door with a cautious expression.

"You again," he said, looking around then stepping back. "Come in, quick."

Once inside, the door clicked shut behind them. Singleton looked even more jittery than before. The curtains were drawn. "Thought I told you guys I needed some time. What are you doing back here so quick?"

"Something came up," Charles said. "We brought something we thought you ought to see."

Keller unfolded the newspaper and laid it out on the coffee table. "Front page. From this morning."

Singleton's eyes were instantly drawn to the photo. For a few seconds, he said nothing. Then his brow furrowed, and his mouth parted. "That's them," he whispered. Then almost shouting, "That's them, right there." He jabbed a finger at the image. "Those are the two guys. The ones who paid me to leave the city."

His hand began to tremble.

Keller gently pulled the paper back and folded it again. "Are you absolutely sure?"

"As sure as I'm sitting here." Singleton dropped onto the couch. "But they didn't just pay me off, did they? They're the ones who killed that poor kid, aren't they?"

Charles nodded. "We believe so, Mickey. And your testimony could be the thing that finally brings them to justice. Makes them pay for what they did to that fine young man."

Singleton shook his head violently. "No. No way. They find out I'm back in the city, I'm dead. I told you that."

"That's not going to happen," Keller said firmly. "I'm going to arrange for you to get a private suite back at The Belmont. We'll slip you in through the service entrance. Move you up to your room. No one will know you're there but a handful of trusted people. You can call room service for all your meals. We'll get one guy to be your waiter, and only one. Somebody we can trust."

For a moment, Singleton seemed open to the idea. Then his face returned to the same mask of fear. "What if someone does find out? Could be a month or more until this trial."

Keller leaned in. "Mickey, no one's going to find out

where you are. Besides, I won't be using my hotel security guys. We'll hire two Pinkertons posted outside your door, day and night. Armed. Best in the business. These men guarded railroad barons during the labor riots. Protected gold shipments out west. You'll be safer in that suite than anywhere else in the state."

Singleton hesitated. His fingers drummed anxiously on his knees.

"I don't know..."

Charles added, "You said it yourself, Mickey —Reggie was a decent kid. He didn't deserve what happened. This could clear Cedric's name and make sure the guys who did this pay for it."

"And Mickey," Keller said, "you know they'll get the chair. Once they do, you'll be free as a bird. You can live here, come back into town, anytime you want. Won't have to look over your shoulder anymore."

Singleton finally looked up, released a pent-up sigh. "Alright. I'll do it. When do we gotta leave?"

"Stay here for one more day," Keller said. "I'll set everything up and come back personally to bring you in. Sometime tomorrow afternoon."

WALLACE KANE TUGGED his cap low and leaned against the corner lamppost, across the street from the upscale row of brownstones, not far from the Ashcroft residence. They owned a big end unit that had access to a separate garage on the side. It had formerly been an old carriage house. Kane could see the chauffeur standing outside the car, leaning on a fender, smoking a cigarette, enjoying the shade from a large elm.

The car was a beauty. A Pierce-Arrow Model 48 Touring Car, looked brand new. Kane knew cars. This one would set a fellow back over $4,500. More than twice Kane would make in a good year. It was the preferred ride for elites, including bank presidents, tycoons and, apparently, Head Aldermen of the Big City.

He'd been tailing the young man all day now. Found out from Cedric his name was Calvin Marsh. Quite tall, with broad-shoulders, in his mid-twenties. Kane could never work a job like this. He'd die from boredom. Marsh had only made two short trips all day, both less than a half-hour long. Kane had quickly jumped into his car and kept his distance. But both times Marsh had someone in the backseat, so there was no chance to talk to him.

Just then, Kane saw a middle-aged woman come out a back entrance, dressed like someone who worked in the kitchen. Marsh straightened up when she came over, put out his cigarette. They talked a few moments. Marsh nodded several times. The woman went back into the house. Marsh walked around the front of the car and hopped inside.

He was alone. He started the car and slowly eased toward the street. Kane saw his moment. He hurried and got into his car. He followed Marsh for about fifteen blocks, until he pulled into a small parking area next to a butcher shop.

Kane quickly got out to intercept the young man

before he went inside. Kane approached from behind. "Excuse me, you Calvin Marsh?"

Marsh turned, defensive until he saw who was talking to him. Kane always wore a decent suit. "Yeah, who wants to know?"

"Name's Kane. I'm a private investigator working on behalf of the Whitaker family. Specifically, Cedric Whitaker."

Marsh frowned. "Cedric? Yeah, I've been reading about him in the papers. It's a shame what they're doing to him. He alright?"

"He's okay, considering the situation. But the truth is, he needs help. Actually, yours."

"Mine? How could I possibly help Cedric?"

Kane kept his voice low and calm. "He told us you and Reggie Ashcroft were friends. You probably know, Cedric and Reggie were real good friends. In the weeks before he died, Reggie confided some things to Cedric." Instinctively, Kane looked around even though no one could possibly hear what he was saying. "Reggie told Cedric all kinds of disturbing things he heard and witnessed first-hand going on with his father. Illegal things. Corrupt things. I think you know what I mean. Reggie told Cedric that you and he had talked, confidentially. And you told Reggie that you heard similar things...in the car. Things about Reggie's father."

Marsh stiffened. Now he looked around to make sure no one was close by. "Mister, I haven't told that stuff to anyone but Reggie. So, if Cedric knows about it, then I guess Reggie felt he could trust him. What's this all about anyway?"

"We believe Reggie's death wasn't what it seems," Kane said. "Definitely not what you read about in the newspapers. Cedric's been accused, but the truth is now pointing elsewhere. We've found a witness. One who knows beyond a doubt who the real killers are — Ashcroft's bodyguards."

Marsh's eyes opened wide. "His bodyguards? How do you know that?"

"I can't go into detail right now, but this guy is absolutely sure. Dead sure it's them. And we've gotten several other significant pieces of evidence that all point to them. But we're missing one thing." Kane paused. "Cedric said Reggie kept a journal. Notes about what he saw and heard around the house. We think that journal might help prove Ashcroft's corruption, and more importantly, help clear Cedric."

Marsh looked away. "I know about Reggie's journal. I saw him writing in it in the backseat one time when I was driving him somewhere. He'd just had an argument with his father. Well, another argument. I asked him what it was, and he told me. That was one of the times I told him about a pretty awful thing I'd just heard his father say in the car that morning. Something he'd told those bodyguards to do for him. I don't know, Mister. I have no trouble believing what you're saying about those two guys. They scare the living daylights out of me, just being around them. The thing is...if I got caught going through

Reggie's room, those bodyguards'll come down on me hard. Good chance I'll lose more than just my job."

Kane nodded, as if expecting the objection. "So, you need a reason to be in Reggie's room. A cover story. I get it. How about this? You do everything you can to not get caught, but anyone sees you, you say you're just in there getting a book Reggie borrowed."

Marsh thought. "I could say it was collection of poems that belonged to my father. I loaned it to Reggie a few months ago. Everyone knows Reggie liked good poetry."

"There you go," Kane said. "There's your excuse."

Marsh hesitated. "You're asking me to risk a lot."

"I'm asking you to do what's right," Kane said. "You know I am. Reggie was trying to, and it might've gotten him killed. You could be the one who gives Reggie a voice."

Marsh looked down. Then he nodded. "Alright. I'll look. No promises. But if I find it...how do I get in touch with you?"

Kane handed him his calling card. "If you can't get me there, get word to Cedric at the Whitaker place. Or ask for Charles Bennington, Cedric's brother-in-law."

"All right," Marsh said. "I'll do my best to find that journal." As he turned to walk toward the butcher shop, Marsh said, "Reggie was the only one in that house who treated me decent. More like a friend than a servant. If I can help put those jerks away who killed him...I will."

32

It was Saturday morning. To try and recoup some normalcy in their lives, Charles and Lily had driven over to her parents' house for breakfast, like they used to before this whole ordeal began.

Nigel had suggested they try to avoid talking about the case during the meal, but there were so many long periods of awkward silence, he soon realized it was an impossible goal. This case was the one thing that consumed every one of their waking moments since the whole thing began.

Charles asked if he could update them all on the positive developments he'd uncovered with Keller and Kane, their private detective. Of course, everyone was eager to hear anything positive, so Nigel told Charles, by all means, proceed.

Charles was happy to oblige but, with all the time spent answering their questions, it had taken over twenty minutes. His food had gotten cold. No matter, he didn't typically eat that much for breakfast, so he simply put some raspberry jam on his toast and drank his coffee.

When he had finished summarizing all the details of their investigation, he could tell that everyone in the family seemed happier and more hopeful than they'd been in quite a while. Everyone, that is, except Lily's father.

Charles wasn't the only one who noticed it. Millicent did, too. And she spoke up. "Nigel, Charles has just finished telling us a number of things we should all be grateful for, yet you still seem so gloomy. Why is that? What is wrong?"

The surprising thing after this was...Nigel answered her. Charles suspected the likely culprit for his melancholy and, once Nigel began talking, his suspicions were proved right. But it wasn't like Nigel to ever talk about hotel business at the table. Particularly, when all he had to share was bad news.

"I'm sure this is only a temporary setback for us. What I mean is, for the hotel. Once Cedric is cleared of these false accusations, and the real killers are exposed, the newspapers will finally leave us alone and, hopefully, economically things will go back to the way they were."

"Father, is it all that bad?" Cedric said.

Nigel sighed. Charles knew whatever he said next would be somewhat guarded and measured, and that the real situation at The Belmont would likely be multiple times worse.

"All of the business conventions we had booked for

the summer have canceled. That's a loss of several hundreds of rooms, not to mention all the guests who won't be eating at the hotel restaurant or ordering room service. Or needing maid service, for that matter. And this week, for the first time in over a decade, our weekly revenue fell short of our weekly expenses. I had to actually authorize dipping into our reserves."

"Oh, my," Millicent said, her jovial expression replaced by instant dread.

No one said anything for a few moments. Charles felt the need to say something. "Well, Father, you're right. That is terribly distressing news. But I am convinced now, that it's only a matter of time before we are able to prove these things during the trial, and when we do, that will result not only in Cedric's acquittal, but also in a vindication for the hotel's reputation. The newspapers will have to print the truth once it comes out."

"Yes, Father," Lily said. "Like you said, this will only be a temporary setback. You'll see. I was just reading in one of the Psalms this morning where David was saying, '*Lord, let not my enemies triumph over me.*' I don't believe God will let all that you've built be destroyed by lies."

Nigel smiled. "Thank you, Dear. And thank you, Charles. That's very helpful."

Just then, the telephone in the foyer rang. Quentin answered it, and a few moments later stood in the doorway of the dining room. "It is a young man named Calvin, asking to speak with either Master Cedric or Charles."

"Calvin, Calvin," Cedric repeated. "Charles, that's the

chauffeur. The Ashcroft's driver. You should probably take the call."

"Right. You're right, Cedric." Charles stood and walked toward the foyer. "Thank you, Quentin."

"You're welcome, sir." Quentin walked the other way down the hall. Charles picked up the receiver.

"Mr. Charles Bennington?" came a breathless voice. "Is this Cedric's brother-in-law?"

"Yes, that's me. Cedric's actually sitting about twenty feet away from me."

"I tried calling that detective, Mr. Kane, the one who asked me about finding Reggie's journal. But I couldn't get hold of him. He said I could call you or Cedric, if that happened."

"That's fine. I know all about the journal," Charles said. "I'm the one who hired Kane and asked him to contact you."

"Okay, then. Good. This is Calvin Marsh. Reggie Ashcroft's driver. Well, for the Ashcroft family."

"Yes, I know who you are. Go ahead."

"I—I got it," Calvin said, his voice shaking. "The journal. I found it. Just this morning."

Charles leaned in, pressing the receiver more firmly to his ear. "How can you tell what you found is Reggie's journal?"

"Because it says so on the very first page. Reggie actually titles it, *The Journal of Reggie Ashcroft*. And I recognize Reggie's handwriting. He used to give me notes when he wanted me to take him somewhere or pick him up. I found it under his mattress. I had a few close calls, but thankfully no one saw me. I swear it."

"You did well, Calvin. This is incredible news. So, you've taken a look at it. Is there anything in it... anything you think might help Cedric?"

There was a pause. "You'll have to read it to believe it, Mr. Bennington. Especially the last entry. Reggie...it's clear to me, he knew what was coming. I really think he did."

"Where are you now?"

"A little diner about half a mile from the Ashcroft place. I walked. It's my day off, so I don't have access to a car. I'm at a pay phone in the back. But Detective Kane... he told me everything you guys have uncovered yesterday. About the bodyguards, and about what really happened to Reggie. When I found the journal this morning, especially after reading the last few pages, I knew I had to get it outta there quick."

"You did the right thing," Charles said. "Can you wait there for me? I'll leave right away."

"Yes, sir. I'll be outside in the parking lot on the opposite side of the front door. You'll see me. I'm pretty tall."

Charles thanked him again, then hung up the receiver. He turned back toward the dining room, where the others looked up expectantly as he entered.

"That was the young man I mentioned—Reggie's driver," Charles said, already reaching for his coat. "He found Reggie's journal. He has it. And he thinks it's going to help us. I'm going to get it right now." He hurried over and gave Lily a kiss.

"Be careful," Nigel said quietly. "Make sure no one sees you."

Charles nodded and headed for the front door.

About thirty minutes later, Charles pulled into the parking lot of a quiet little diner on the edge of a commercial block. The morning sun had risen just high enough to cast crisp shadows across the pavement. Calvin Marsh stood near the far end, pacing slightly, hands buried in his pockets. He turned the moment he saw Charles's vehicle and hurried over.

Charles unlocked the passenger door. Calvin climbed in quickly and shut it behind him, glancing around the lot, as if afraid someone had followed him.

"Thank you for coming," he said, pulling a slim, leather-bound volume from inside his coat. "This is it. Reggie's journal."

Charles took it, handled it almost reverently.

"Before you read it...I just—I couldn't help myself. Like I said, I read the last few pages on the walk over. Especially the last entry. I think you ought to hear it now. Do you mind?" He took the journal back gently and flipped through the final entries, stopping at one marked with a small ribbon.

"This was dated the day before he died," Calvin said. "Let me read it to you."

He cleared his throat and began.

. . .

July 30th, 1914

Friday Evening

I haven't been able to write much lately. But tonight I feel I must. If something happens to me... I want there to be a record. Can't believe I'm writing this, but it feels like things are getting that bad.

I've spent the last several days battling with myself. I keep thinking maybe I'm overreacting. Maybe I've misunderstood. But the evidence is too great. Too real. Too sickening.

My father is not the man he pretends to be. Not even close. So many meetings I've overheard, the documents I've glimpsed, the way his men speak when they think I'm not listening—it all points to the same conclusion. For a long time, he's been involved in something massive, something rotten to the core. And it's not just bribes or backroom deals. It's worse. People have been ruined, lives destroyed. I know of entire city blocks of poor New Yorkers he's forced out onto the street. The huge sums he's made giving special favor to contractors. It's happened several times now.

Even though we've never been that close. Still, I used to idolize him. I see now that I've been willfully blind. Maybe I just wanted to believe the best about my own father. But after that night last week when I confronted him, he threatened he would "cut off any limb that betrays the tree," I can't pretend anymore.

I don't think he was just hinting at cutting me off financially. Honestly, I'm afraid. And not just of the two goons he gets to do his bidding. I'm now afraid of him.

He's always been a man who values control above all else.

And I am no longer someone he can control. I think he's starting to get that.

I keep remembering Cedric's words a few weeks ago, during a long talk we had in the gym at his father's hotel. "You don't have to carry his name like a shackle," he said. He told me I wasn't responsible for my father's sins. That I could use my life to a different purpose. Become my own man. Learn how to serve God's will and become someone honorable.

He's right.

Tomorrow morning, Cedric and I are meeting for another workout. I plan to talk with him—really open up. I need his advice. I need to know what he'd do in my place.

I think the only way to fix this now is for me to go to the Curran Commission and tell them everything that's going on. I can't keep living this lie. People have to know. Our family's reputation will be ruined. I know this. But to me, it's a small price to pay to start atoning for all the sins and crimes my father's committed. All the people he's hurt through his schemes.

—Reggie

CALVIN SHUT THE BOOK GENTLY. His hands trembled as he passed it back to Charles. "Now do you see?" he said. "He knew. Reggie knew what his father was capable of. And now...now everyone else needs to know, and they also need to know that Cedric didn't do this thing."

33

Charles remained at the diner where he'd met Calvin Marsh, although Calvin had already departed ten minutes ago. Charles had thanked him profusely for his help and also had asked him if he'd be willing to testify at Cedric's trial. Calvin said most definitely. Even though he'd likely be putting himself out of a job, seeing as his employer would likely be thrown in jail. He said for now he would keep quiet, keep his eyes and ears open, and wait for them to contact him when it came time for the trial.

Charles did not immediately drive home. Instead, he was now standing by the diner's payphone, clutching Reggie Ashcroft's journal to his chest. Two realizations had dawned on him with equal intensity. First, this journal—its contents, especially that final entry—could very well be the keystone of Cedric's entire defense. Second, it had been days since he'd updated their attorney, Henry Beaumont, on any of the significant breakthroughs they'd uncovered. If anyone needed to be in the loop now, it was him.

Charles dropped a coin into the payphone and dialed the Whitaker residence. Quentin answered. Charles asked him to get Nigel and to say it was urgent.

A few moments later.

"Nigel, it's Charles. Sorry to bother you, but I need the private number for Beaumont. I don't think he'd be at the office today, and I've got something urgent to tell him."

"Of course," Nigel said. "Is everything alright?"

"I think it will be," Charles replied. "I've got Reggie's journal. I think it's even bigger than the other things we've uncovered. The last entry especially...it changes everything. I'll explain more later, but please share the news with Lily and Cedric. And tell them not a word of this leaves the house."

"You have my word." Nigel gave him the number. "You'll be calling him at home on the Upper West Side. 213 Riverside Drive."

Charles recognized the address immediately. "I know the area. I'll call him now and probably head straight over after that." He hung up and dialed Beaumont's number. A housemaid answered, and soon, Beaumont's voice came on the line.

"Mr. Beaumont, it's Charles Bennington. I'm sorry to intrude on your Saturday, but I've just come into possession of something I think you need to see."

"What is it?" Beaumont asked.

"Reggie Ashcroft's journal."

There was a brief silence on the other end. "You're serious? Reggie kept a journal?"

"Dead serious."

"Does it say anything relevant to Cedric's case?"

"Most definitely. And I also have several other big developments I need to brief you on. But to cut to the chase a bit, listen to this—here's Reggie's last entry, dated the day before he died." Charles opened the journal and read aloud the final pages, the ones where Reggie hinted at being tormented by what he knew of his father's actions and wrestled with the idea of going to the Curran Commission.

"That could be the breakthrough we've been hoping for," Beaumont said, his voice firm. "Can you bring it to me now?"

"Yes. I'm still in Queens, but I know your address. I can be there in about forty minutes."

"I'll be waiting."

BEAUMONT'S BROWNSTONE on Riverside Drive was stately but not ostentatious. A housemaid opened the door and led Charles down a hallway to the rear study, paneled in dark walnut and lined with shelves of thick law volumes. Beaumont rose from behind a large mahogany desk and gestured to the seat across from him.

Charles set the journal on the desk.

Beaumont picked it up carefully, flipping through the pages with a studied eye. He re-read the entry Charles had read to him over the phone. "You weren't exaggerating. This could turn the tide entirely."

"There's more," Charles said. "Much more. I've uncovered several other developments that further support Cedric's innocence."

"First, we found Mickey Singleton—the hotel gym manager." Charles told him all about this situation, including the startling moment when he'd identified the two bodyguards from the funeral photograph in *The Times*. Beaumont had recalled seeing that photograph and marveled that he was unwittingly looking at the likely killers.

Beaumont leaned back, absorbing all this. "That is almost as powerful as the journal evidence."

"We're keeping Singleton in a secure suite at the Belmont. Keller's arranging Pinkerton protection as we speak."

"Smart," Beaumont nodded. "Go on."

Charles outlined the fingerprint evidence next—the two sets found on the locker and gym exit that didn't match Cedric's—and their strong suspicion they belonged to the bodyguards. Then he described the silencer test, which confirmed Cedric's account of hearing an unrecognizable sound when Reggie was shot.

"We staged a test yesterday morning," Charles said. "It matched Cedric's description exactly and explains why no one heard a gunshot that morning. Kane believes a search of the bodyguards' quarters or vehicles will turn up a suppressor."

Beaumont shook his head. "You've done exceptional work."

"One final thing," Charles added. "Ashcroft's chauffeur —Calvin Marsh, said, if asked, he'd definitely be willing to testify at the trial."

Beaumont tapped the journal thoughtfully. "With all this, Charles, you've practically built our entire defense for us. If we could just get prints from Ashcroft's men that matched the ones we found at the gym, I think that might be the final nail on the coffin."

Charles appreciated the compliment. "I think we can get hold of that sometime soon," he said. "How long until the trial?"

"The pre-trial hearing is in eleven days," Beaumont replied. "After that? Given the court's calendar...I'd say possibly another four to five weeks."

Charles couldn't restrain his disappointment.

"What's wrong?" Beaumont asked.

"Nigel told me this morning how badly the hotel is hemorrhaging since the news broke about this case. All the convention contracts booked for the summer have been canceled. The overall occupancy is less than half what it should be for the summer. For the first time in a decade, Nigel said he had to dip into their reserves to make expenses. And it's only been a week since the story broke. I'm not sure they can survive another month of this scandal dragging through the press."

Beaumont's expression turned grave. "I understand. But unless something drastic changes, I'm afraid we're locked into the process. Not much I can do to alter it on my end. But I seriously think when we do go to trial, you've given us more than enough to cast reasonable doubt on Cedric. And once that shows up in the newspapers, I'm sure the press will be singing a different song."

Charles rose to leave. "I know, but...I'm not sure Nigel or the hotel can wait that long. I've got to think of something."

Beaumont stood and offered his hand. "Well, Charles, if anyone can, it's you."

34

Before leaving the curb outside of Beaumont's home, Charles said a quick prayer. Mainly, for wisdom. He'd done this often in the last week, rooted in a proverb he had memorized from the Bible, shortly after becoming a Christian. Basically, it said whenever you didn't know what to do, ask God, and he will direct your steps. Most of the better things that had happened since he launched this investigation came after similar such prayers.

So, Charles prayed and just waited there for a bit, trying to clear his mind from the myriad of anxious thoughts clamoring for attention. It wasn't long before a handful of things made their way to the surface.

The first was to call Abe, his right-hand man at the ice factory, see how things were going. He hadn't checked in with him all week. He drove a half-mile toward central Manhattan and stopped at a diner to use the pay phone.

Saturday was a busy day at the plant, and he knew Abe would be there. He picked up after a few rings.

"Hey, Abe, it's me. The guy you used to work for."

"Used to? What, you decided to quit? I guess detective work agrees with you."

"No, not really," Charles said. "I'm really looking forward to the day I get to take off this detective hat and get back to the ice business. Sorry, I haven't been checking in with you. Things have been kind of hopping with this case lately."

"Really?" Abe said. "In a good way, I hope. Not seeing anything good in the papers just yet."

"Turns out, in a very good way. In fact, I think we've solved this case and figured out who really killed Reggie. You're not gonna believe it when you hear the truth."

"And when will that be?" Abe said. "Anytime soon?"

"Hoping very soon. I'd fill you in, but it's kind of a long story and I'm short on time. Just making sure everything's running well at the factory. Any problems you want to talk to me about?"

"Thankfully, no. It's actually been running pretty smoothly around here. Without you beating the bushes drumming up new work, we're able to keep up with the current orders. Haven't had any equipment breakdowns. None of the workers called in sick. I've even got caught up on most my paperwork."

"So, you're okay if I take another week?"

"Yeah, I guess so," Abe said. "Think that's all you'll need?"

"Hard to say, definitely depends on some very big

things breaking loose very soon. But so far, a number of things are breaking our way. But I'm not gonna lie, it's getting a little scary. Could really use your prayers."

"Oh, how so?"

"Well, to put a fine point on it, I'm about to expose some violent killers who thought nothing of killing Reggie to shut him up."

"Whoa, really? Not seeing anything like that in the papers. Are you thinking they might come after you next?"

"I hope not. Right now, I don't think they even know about me. But that could change very soon. And if things go according to plan, you should be reading about it in the papers. But look, I better go. You need to reach me, leave word at The Dakota or with Lily at her parents' place. We're not sleeping there, but she's over there most of the time."

They said their goodbyes and hung up.

NEXT, Charles called Wainwright at the newspaper office, happy to find him working on a Saturday. The switchboard operator at *The Times* put Charles through.

"Mr. Bennington, haven't heard anything from you for a few days. Last we talked, you were going to dig up some things that would enable me to write a more *balanced article*—as you put it—about the case. That why you're calling?"

"Well, yes, in a way," Charles said, "but it's much more than that. I'd like to meet with you today to discuss it, right away if possible. I need to update you on some major developments in the case. Really, some major breakthroughs. But I don't want to talk about it on the phone. I'd be happy to come there, to your building."

"Major breakthroughs, eh? Well, if you're not exaggerating, I suppose I can do that."

"Believe me, I'm not. And when you hear what I have to say, I'll accept your apology for even suggesting I might stoop to exaggeration to get an audience with you."

"Okay, don't get so touchy. I'll just apologize now and get it out of the way."

"The only thing I ask, Wainwright, is for you to find somewhere in your building where we can talk in total privacy."

"Oh, why is that?"

"Because, what I have to say could literally put your life and mine in danger if the wrong ears get hold of it."

"You're...you're not joking."

"I'm deadly serious."

"Okay, how long until you can get here?"

"Say, twenty-five minutes?"

"I'll meet you at the front door in the lobby, and then take us to a room where we can talk in private."

CHARLES STEPPED through the revolving door of *The New York Times* building on West 43rd Street. The lobby was quieter than he expected—just a few staffers loitering near the elevators, and the rhythmic click of typewriter keys echoing faintly from somewhere up above.

Wainwright was already waiting near the security desk, hat in hand, sleeves rolled up, a pencil tucked behind one ear. "Charles," he said with a nod and walked toward him.

"Appreciate you making the time," Charles said, shaking his hand. "You always work on Saturdays?"

"When am I not working? Between the Ashcroft funeral coverage, the Curran Commission hearings, and next week's political endorsements, I can't remember what a full day off feels like. Come on, we can talk upstairs. I know just the place."

They took a narrow staircase up one floor to a hallway lined with doors. Wainwright unlocked one marked "Archives—Private," then peered inside to make sure it was empty.

"We can use this. It's soundproof, or close to it," he said. "Now, what's this all about? You sounded like a man with a serious secret."

Charles closed the door behind them. "More than one. What I'm about to tell you, I believe, will shift this case in a totally different direction."

Wainwright raised a brow and pulled out a chair. "Now you've got me."

Charles took a seat opposite him, lowered his voice, and began outlining everything, starting with the photo from *The Times* funeral coverage. He pulled out the front section, showed Wainwright the front page. "This article you all ran yesterday? The one about the Ashcroft family at the cemetery. Your photographer unknowingly captured the two men we now believe killed Reggie." He pointed to the two bodyguards.

Charles then explained the connection to Mickey Singleton, the gym manager who had disappeared. How Charles and Keller had located him on Long Island, showed him the photo, and watched his reaction as he confirmed the two men were the ones who'd paid him to vanish the day before the murder.

"He didn't just recognize them," Charles said. "He was terrified. They're Ashcroft's men. He realized—as did we—they paid him to quit his job and leave town, so that he wouldn't be a witness to them shooting Reggie at the gym the next morning. There's no other reasonable explanation."

Wainwright sat straighter. "That's a bombshell for sure, if true."

"There's more. We've put Singleton in protective custody at the Belmont. He should be there now. He'll testify in court. Then there's Reggie's journal."

"Reggie's journal?"

Charles described how Cedric's friend, the chauffeur, had retrieved Reggie's personal journal—hidden under his mattress—and handed it off earlier that morning. Charles paraphrased several lines from the final entry, written the day before he died, which confirmed Reggie was about to report his father to the Curran Commission and expose all his corrupt business dealings. "It reads like a death sentence," Charles said. "He was genuinely in fear for his life. I'd show you the journal, but our attorney said he needed to keep custody of it until the trial."

Wainwright looked stunned. "So, the kid was going to expose his own father?"

Charles nodded. "It fits. He'd been growing disillusioned. He confided in Cedric, but also the chauffeur. Wrote it all down in his journal. I'm guessing he must have said something he shouldn't have said to his father. Who then made the barbaric decision to have him silenced."

"What makes you believe the father ordered the hit?"

"I don't just believe it," Charles said. "I'm certain of it. It's the only thing that makes sense. What would a man like Ashcroft do to his hired men if they'd killed his son on their own? And why would they ever do such a thing? We still need a little more proof. But we're very close. We took fingerprints on the gym lockers and back exit door that match each other, but there not Cedric's. If we can get prints from the bodyguards, I'd bet my life they'll match. We're working on that now."

Charles then explained about the silencer experiment and what it revealed.

Wainwright let out a long breath. "Well, if what you're saying is true, you've got the ingredients for a history-making piece here. But my editors won't print a story like that unless it's bulletproof. We've already committed publicly to the narrative given by the DA and Ashcroft. Flipping that around now will take some doing. I'll need to verify this evidence. You're talking about a story that will have an earthquake-like impact on local politics. It could take a few days to put this thing together, gotta be some of my best writing."

"I understand," Charles said. "I wasn't expecting this to hit the front page tomorrow. In fact, I was hoping you'd hold off until I've had a chance to confront the police myself. I'm seeing Rafferty and Shipley next."

Wainwright gave a look. "You think they'll cooperate?"

"I don't know," Charles said. "But they should. I'll be bringing them everything I just told you."

The reporter smirked. "I'd say they're pretty dug in on this case. Police don't ever like to admit they're wrong. About anything. You ask me, you may wind up needing the mighty arm of the free press to force their hand."

"That's why I'm here," Charles said. "If they stall or try to sweep this under the rug, I want your article ready to make them regret it."

Wainwright stood and extended a hand. "Then I'll start writing. But if we're going to run this, we'll need a decent quote from Singleton, like a signed affidavit, and a copy of the journal—or at least a photograph of that last entry. And I need your word that, when the time comes, I get the exclusive."

"You have it," Charles said, gripping his hand. "Just don't run it until I say go."

"I'll sit on it," Wainwright said. "For now."

They left the archives room and headed back toward the staircase, both men moving with a shared sense of purpose. The next step would take Charles from the press to the police.

He knew the stakes couldn't be higher.

35

The moment Charles stepped back into the lobby of *The Times* building, he made his way directly to the nearest payphone. He dropped in a nickel, dialed the police station, and asked the operator to connect him with Detective Rafferty or Shipley. After a brief wait, Rafferty's gruff voice came on the line.

"Rafferty here."

"Detective, it's Charles Bennington, Cedric Whitaker's brother-in-law."

"I remember you."

"I need to speak with you and Sergeant Shipley as soon as possible, right away if we can."

"You do, eh? About what?"

"You may recall I said the day you arrested him, that Cedric could not have possibly committed this crime. It goes totally against his character, and besides, he has no motive. He and Reggie were the best of friends."

"I recall you saying something like that."

"Well, I've spent the past week working on this, and I've uncovered evidence that proves Cedric Whitaker is innocent. Not just theories, mind you, actual evidence. But I won't discuss it over the phone. It's urgent. Can we meet...now?"

A pause followed.

"Sure, I guess. You know where to find me."

"No, it has to be somewhere private. Not the station. Too many ears."

Rafferty exhaled heavily. "You don't trust our own house anymore?"

"Would you? With the Curran Commission exposing new corruption every day? Do you believe they've caught all the bad apples? That everyone working there is totally free of any corrupt connections?"

Another pause.

"Fine. There's a church down on East 22nd, corner of Third. Little chapel room in the back, always empty this time of day. We sometimes talk to informants there."

"I know the place," Charles said. "I'll meet you there in thirty minutes."

CHARLES ARRIVED at the chapel first. It was quiet and dimly lit, filtered light pouring in from the stained-glass windows. He waited near the front, seated on a polished wooden bench. When Rafferty and Shipley entered, the noise was almost startling. Their shadows grew on the wooden pew in front of him. He rose, turned, and greeted them with a firm handshake.

"Appreciate you both coming."

"Follow me," Rafferty said, heading down the main aisle. He walked toward a side doorway just before the altar. "In here."

Once inside, Rafferty flicked a switch. A small lamp came on revealing a half-dozen chairs arranged in a semi-circle.

"Let's hear it," Shipley said, glancing around. "You said you have proof?"

Charles gestured for them to sit. "Before we get to that, I need to ask you something. A reminder, really. Do you remember that morning, outside Nigel Whitaker's office, the day Reggie was killed? Nigel said something about being glad the Curran Commission was finally cleaning house, exposing all the corruption both in the police department and city government."

"I remember," Rafferty said, arms folded. "So, what of it?"

"And if I recall, you both agreed with him. Said you were sick of the crooked cops and politicians, too. That you both wanted things to change. Do you still feel that way?"

The detectives exchanged a glance. Then, slowly, both nodded.

"Yes," Shipley said. "We do. Only been a week. Why would we change our minds?"

"Good," Charles replied. "Because that brings me to my next question: Since Cedric was arrested, how much time have the two of you spent investigating Reggie's murder?"

Rafferty frowned. "What do you mean? We investigated it. We gathered witness statements, examined the scene, fingerprinted the gun."

Charles raised a hand. "That's not what I asked. I'm asking: how much time have you spent *since* then investigating other possibilities? Considering other suspects, following up on any *new* leads. Any time at all? One day? Two days?"

A long silence followed.

"That's what I thought," Charles said. "The answer is zero, correct? You just locked onto Cedric and never looked past him. Why would you? You had just enough evidence to make him look guilty, and the DA was satisfied. Case closed, right? You ignored the fact that Cedric had absolutely no motive to kill Reggie, didn't own a gun, had never even fired a gun before. I pointed this out early on and obviously, it didn't even make either of you curious."

"That's unfair," Rafferty muttered. "We followed the facts."

"No," Charles snapped. "You followed assumptions. Meanwhile, someone else followed the facts. *Me*. Knowing Cedric couldn't possibly be the killer, I knew there had to be other evidence that would support he was telling the truth. So, I started digging, and I followed the evidence—and what I've found changes everything. It will rock your world, gentlemen. And I'm not using hyperbole when I say that." He could instantly see neither man knew what that meant. "I'm not exaggerating one bit."

Charles stood and began pacing slowly.

"Let me start with this: the photograph that showed up Friday, on the front page of *The Times*. From the funeral coverage. Did you see it? In case you didn't, here." He presented the front page. "Look closely, and what do you see behind Alderman Ashcroft? Or, I should say *who* do you see? Two men. I've checked. These are his body-guards. Go with him everywhere. Those same men were identified by Mickey Singleton, the gym manager who disappeared the day before the murder. Did either of you write down that fact? Cedric said he was shocked to find the gym manager not there that morning. He's always there whenever the gym is open."

Neither man answered.

Charles continued. "We found him on Long Island, hiding. Know how we found him? Because we were looking. We showed him the photo, and he turned white as a sheet. They're the two men who paid Mickey to leave town, paid him a small fortune to do so. But only if he left town that day."

Rafferty sat forward. "Wait a minute...Singleton? We did check into that. That guy was a dead end."

"No," Charles said. "He was your missing link. You didn't even try to find him. But we did. He's now in protective custody and ready to testify."

Shipley looked skeptical. "Even if that's true, it doesn't clear Cedric."

Charles turned to them, eyes sharp. "It's just the beginning, boys. Turns out, Reggie kept a journal. Ashcroft's chauffeur found it, gave it to us. Why would he do such a thing? The chauffeur and Reggie were friends and were both sick of the Alderman's evil ways. They confided in each other. The final entries show Reggie planned to expose his father's corruption to the Curran Commission. Named names. Timelines. Even admitted he was afraid his father might retaliate, might even take his life to stop him. Sadly, he was right."

Rafferty leaned back, visibly shaken. "You read all this? In the kid's journal?"

"Yes, to Beaumont, the Whitaker's attorney. He has the journal now. And yes, it reads like a confession signed in fear."

Charles pressed on. "There's more. We found fingerprints on the gym locker and exit door that don't match Cedric's. The gym was on lockdown, since the shooting. So, these prints had to come from the two men Cedric said he heard arguing with Reggie. Then, there's this...our private eye ran a silencer test with the same model pistol found at the scene. Remember that little detail? Cedric didn't hear a gunshot. No one did. Why is that? We did this little experiment, and he recognized the sound instantly. You know what that means? The killers used a silencer. That's why no one heard the shot. Cedric not only doesn't own a gun, he never even heard of a silencer before."

Rafferty exhaled slowly. Shipley rubbed the back of his neck.

"This is a lot," Shipley muttered.

"It is. Here's what I think happened: Ashcroft knew Reggie was going to blow the whistle. Couldn't risk it. He had his men pay off Singleton to vanish, then framed Cedric. Gun in his bag, witnesses in place. But it's crumbling now. All that's left is to match the unknown prints to the bodyguards. Then the whole thing collapses."

Silence fell. The detectives sat frozen, faces unreadable.

"Well?" Charles said.

Rafferty looked up. "We...appreciate you coming to talk to us. It's certainly worth considering, all these things."

Charles narrowed his eyes. "That's all you have to say? After everything I just laid out?"

"It's not that simple," Shipley said. "We have superiors. Procedures we gotta follow. People we gotta answer to. We can't just flip a case over on hearsay and speculation."

Charles stood. "This isn't hearsay. It's evidence. Evidence you never bothered to find, because you never cared to look. Because it was easier to do nothing. Easier to believe Cedric was guilty than to admit you were wrong."

Rafferty stood, bristling. "You've made your point. We said we'd look into it."

"No," Charles said, voice rising. "Look into it? What's that even mean? You stopped looking a week ago. And why? Because the DA told you not to. Because your Commissioner told you Cedric was guilty. And you bought it. Like good little soldiers."

He stepped closer.

"Let me tell you something. I've already shown all this to Wainwright at *The Times*. He instantly recognized that he was looking at earth-shattering stuff. He's writing the article as we speak. If the police refuse to act, if they let a killer go free while an innocent man faces the electric chair, the public will know."

He turned for the door, then paused.

"Only three people know all of this right now: Wainwright, and you two. So, if anything happens to me or my family—if Ashcroft gets wind of Singleton's location, for example—I'll know who leaked it. And I will see to it your names are known by every reporter in the city."

Charles left the chapel without another word, the door echoed as it shut behind him.

36

The phone rang just after 8 a.m. in Wallace Kane's modest flat on the Lower East Side. It woke him up. "Who in the world is calling me on Sunday morning? For crying out loud," he muttered. Kane had stayed up late the night before filing notes and polishing a report he planned to give Charles tomorrow, hoping for another payday. He squinted at the telephone on the nightstand and grunted as he reached for the receiver.

"Kane, here."

"Mr. Kane, it's Calvin Marsh. You know, Ashcroft's driver. Really sorry to be calling you so early, especially on a Sunday."

Kane sat up straighter. The voice on the other end sounded tense, but clear.

"I'm listening, Calvin. That's okay. What is it?"

"The last time we talked, you told me to call if I ever

took the bodyguards somewhere to eat. That's why I'm calling. We're parked outside a fancy French place called *La Maison de Lyon*, over on Madison near 62nd."

Kane whistled. Kid even had the accent down. "Fancy French joint, eh?"

"Very. Ashcroft's inside having breakfast with a couple of big shots. Sounds like some kinda construction deal. Couldn't catch the details from the front seat, but the two men came in with him like they always do. He always has them sit at a nearby table."

"That's excellent. What kind of glasses they use for water in there? Do you know?"

"Tall, thin crystal. Definitely glass. He's eaten here before. Sometimes I've waited in the kitchen. That's how I know. You're wanting fingerprints, right?"

Kane was already halfway out of bed, pulling on his trousers. "Yeah, that's right. How long you think they'll be there?"

"Probably an hour. They just ordered their second round of coffee. These places are all about the style and atmosphere. Everything moves slow. It's definitely not about the food, you ask me. Except they got this one thing that's some kinda egg-and-cheese pie. I kinda like —"

"Perfect. I'll be there in twenty minutes. Do me a big favor, kid. If they leave early, see if you can snag two of the glasses used by the bodyguards. But don't get your prints on them."

"Got it. But, if you get here in twenty, you should be fine."

Kane hung up and was out the door in five.

. . .

TWENTY-FIVE MINUTES LATER, Kane stood just inside the kitchen of *La Maison de Lyon*. Calvin had shown him how to get in through a back door. He was still out by the car. Kane watched a waiter he spotted through the porthole window in the kitchen door. The young man stood at the bodyguards' table, carefully slicing a croissant and spreading a generous pat of imported butter across the steaming center. He chuckled softly at something one of the men said, then turned, balancing a silver tray of empty glasses as he made his way toward the kitchen.

Kane stepped into his path just as the door swung open.

"Got a minute?" he asked.

The waiter was surprised to see a stranger in the kitchen but didn't overreact.

Speaking in a low voice, Kane said, "How'd you like to make the easiest five bucks in your life?" He held up the folded bill. "All I need are the two water glasses the men at that table just used." He nodded toward Ashcroft's men seated in the table behind their boss.

"What these?" the waiter pointed at the glasses in his tray.

"You didn't get your fingerprints on them, did you?" The young man looked confused. Kane forgot, most people never thought about their fingerprints. "You didn't touch the glasses with your fingers, did you?"

"No, we're not supposed to. I only touched the bottom."

"Good." He held up the bill. The waiter's eyes widened. Five dollars was more than he made in three days.

"You serious? You're gonna give me five dollars for two glasses?"

"Dead serious."

The waiter looked around nervously then pocketed the bill without another word. He carefully wrapped the two glasses in a linen napkin and handed them to Kane.

Kane unwrapped the napkin just enough to see the two water glasses, still smudged with condensation and, more importantly, fingerprints. He rewrapped them and placed the bundle gently inside a satchel.

Kane looked out through the porthole again at Ashcroft and his two goons. They had no idea how dramatically all of their lives were about to change.

In a modest brownstone in Brooklyn, Sergeant Shipley was tying his youngest daughter's shoes when his wife called from the parlor.

"Say, Hon? You two almost ready? We gotta leave for church pretty soon."

Shipley sighed and got up. "Just about, but say, I need to call Rafferty real quick."

"Can't it wait? You're gonna make us late."

"No, I won't. Besides, we don't have to leave for ten minutes. I'll be done way before then." He didn't wait for her reply, just walked over to the phone.

He dialed the number. "Hey, it's Shipley. Sorry to call you on a Sunday. You got a minute?"

"I do. Just about to head out to church."

"Listen, couldn't sleep last night," Shipley said. "Thinking about what that Bennington fellow said yesterday."

Rafferty exhaled. "I didn't sleep much, either."

"You think maybe he's right? About the whole frame-up thing with the Whitaker kid?"

"I think he might be. It kept playing over and over in my head."

There was a pause.

Shipley leaned on the doorframe. "We did say what Bennington said outside Whitaker's office that first day. After Whitaker talked about the Curran Commission cleaning house."

"Yeah. I said I agreed with what the commission was doing. You did too."

"Do you still?"

A longer pause.

"I do," Rafferty said. "Why I didn't sleep too well last night. It's been bugging me for days, but more like an annoying fly. Feeling like something ain't right. I've been able to ignore it mostly until Bennington said it out loud."

"Then why are we sitting on our hands," Shipley said, "while this Ashcroft mess goes unchecked? If Bennington's right, Cedric Whitaker could go to the chair for something he didn't do. We haven't even tried to consider other options."

Rafferty bristled. "But we had the two guys who saw

him standing over the body, holding the gun. His fingerprints on the gun. Nobody else in the gym but him. What were we supposed to do, ignore all that?"

"No," Shipley said. "We were supposed to dig deeper. It should've bothered us more, the kid having no motive. Only crazy people do violent things for no reason. And the kid's not crazy. We should-a at least asked ourselves, what if the kid isn't lying? That's all Bennington did, and look what he's turned up?"

More silence.

"You think we're just like the rest of 'em?" Rafferty said.

"No," Shipley said. "But...I think we keep going the way we're going, we'll end up there. We ain't taking bribes, but we're letting politicians call our shots. And I know why...I don't wanna lose my job."

Rafferty blew out a slow breath. "So, what do you want to do?"

"I want us to go to the DA first thing tomorrow and lay it all out. All the evidence Charles has uncovered. The journal. The gym witness. The suppressor. And now, the fingerprints. We don't have to say who gathered it. Just show him what they found. Let him draw his own conclusions."

Rafferty didn't respond right away. "You know the fallout this could bring. Not just our jobs, but our pensions."

Both men sighed. Shipley said, "That could happen. But I also know what it'll mean if we don't. I'll feel like a dirty cop. Every day. And I'll feel like maybe I'm the reason why an innocent kid gets fried."

Another pause. Then Rafferty said, "Alright. I'll meet you in front of the DA's office first thing."

"Good. See you there." Shipley hung up the phone, grabbed his coat, and called to his wife. "Okay, now I'm ready. See? We can still get there on time."

But as soon as Shipley got in his car, his thoughts were already fixated on Monday morning, that meeting with the DA.

37

It was a little after 9am Monday morning. Lieutenant Rafferty and Sergeant Shipley sat in a parked Ford along Centre Street, the looming gray stone facade of the District Attorney's office right behind them. A heavy silence hung in the air, broken only by the occasional rumble of passing trolleys.

"I don't know, Jack," Rafferty muttered, tapping the steering wheel with his fingers. "Maybe you should do most of the talking in there. Between us, you're the one with the gift of gab."

Shipley shook his head. "Rank counts for a lot with a man like DA Tilford. You're the lieutenant. If I do the talking, he'll wonder why the junior man is leading the charge. It'll weaken what we're saying."

Rafferty sighed. "Alright, fine. But how do we start? How do you walk into a lion's den without getting your head bit off?"

Shipley thought for a second, then said, "Lead with this...tell him we've uncovered evidence tied to a brand new witness connected to the gym, the manager who left the day before the murder. Then quickly mention someone paid him off to disappear. And this guy's willing to testify under oath who these two men are. It's breakthrough evidence, not speculation. That should get his attention."

Rafferty nodded slowly. "Okay. I start with Singleton, then talk about the journal pages."

"Right. Then move to the fingerprints in the gym not being Cedric's and the silencer bit, and what it means. Keep it clean and tight. Don't head down any rabbit trails."

Rafferty turned off the engine. "Okay, let's get this over with."

They climbed the granite steps to the DA's building and entered the foyer. After navigating through the usual security and red tape, they climbed the central stairs and approached the secretary at the reception desk.

"Hello, we're the two detectives assigned to the Reginald Ashcroft murder investigation. We need to see District Attorney Tilford," Rafferty said.

The secretary barely looked up. "Do you have an appointment?"

"No, but this is urgent. It's about the murder case. We've uncovered new evidence. Breakthrough evidence."

The secretary's eyebrows lifted. "Wait here."

She disappeared through a side door. Less than a minute later, she returned. "He'll see you now."

They followed her into the inner sanctum of the office. District Attorney Tilford's study was large but not ostentatious: mahogany shelves lined with leather-bound legal tomes, heavy drapes drawn halfway open to reveal the morning sun, a globe resting beside a massive desk cluttered with files.

Tilford looked up as they entered. "Gentlemen. I know you're both handling our most high-profile murder case. To what do I owe this surprise visit?"

Rafferty cleared his throat. "Sir, we've recently uncovered new information that could alter the direction of the Ashcroft case. We thought it best to bring it to you immediately."

Tilford leaned back in his chair. "Alter the direction? I wasn't aware the direction needed altering. The case against Cedric Whitaker is, by all accounts, rock solid."

Rafferty hesitated, then continued. "Sir, we've located the manager of the gym where the murder occurred. His name is Mickey Singleton. He fled town the day before the shooting. We now know why. He was paid off—handsomely—by two men to leave the city."

Tilford raised a brow. "And who are these two men?"

Rafferty swallowed. "He's positively identified them as Alderman Ashcroft's personal bodyguards."

The DA shot to his feet. "Is that what this is about? You're coming in here with hearsay evidence that undermines the physical evidence you yourselves helped me present to the grand jury?"

Shipley tried to interject, but the DA held up a hand. "You testified that Whitaker's prints were on the gun. That two witnesses saw him standing over the body moments after the shooting. Now you're offering up a gym manager who says someone else might've paid him off?"

Rafferty tried to explain, "Sir, this man is willing to testify under oath. And we've corroborated his story with a photo from the newspaper and further evidence—"

"I don't have time for this," Tilford snapped. "Unless you've found someone hiding in the gym who actually saw another man pull the trigger, I suggest you stop wasting my time."

Silence.

Tilford jabbed a finger toward them. "You're asking me to throw out a case built on physical evidence and eyewitness testimony for a theory that involves accusing one of the most powerful aldermen in the city? You know Ashcroft's influence. You know where his support comes from."

Shipley stiffened. "Sir, we believe this evidence is strong enough to warrant further investigation. If you could just give us five or ten minutes to fully go—"

Tilford narrowed his eyes. "And I'm telling you, we are maybe four weeks from trial. The whole city is watching. *The Times* is watching. You want to go up against Ashcroft and Tammany Hall? Be my guest. But if you're wrong—" he tapped the side of his desk for emphasis, "—you'll both be out of jobs. Your pensions, gone up in smoke. Out of everything."

Rafferty looked down. "Understood."

"If there's nothing else—"

The men nodded and quietly left the room.

Back in the car, Shipley let out a long breath. "Maybe if we tried—"

Rafferty gripped the steering wheel. "Don't."

TWENTY MINUTES LATER, Detective Wallace Kane sat at the telephone in the Belmont Hotel lobby, spinning the dial for Keller's room.

"Keller here."

"It's Kane. I'm down in the lobby. Got something for you."

"I'm listening."

"I compared the prints from the restaurant glasses with what we found at the gym."

"And?"

"They're a match. One set on the glass matches the prints found on the gym's rear exit door. The other matches what we found on the busted locker doors."

Keller was silent a moment, then exhaled sharply. "You're certain?"

"Positive. This isn't a maybe. This nails them both at the scene."

"I'll pass this to Charles right away. Great work, Kane. This is the icing on the cake."

Kane hung up the phone and leaned back in his chair, a quiet satisfaction settling over him.

38

It was midmorning the following day, a Tuesday.

Charles Bennington pulled his motorcar to the curb outside the police station, a familiar knot of tension forming in his gut. He could have telephoned Detectives Rafferty and Shipley with the fingerprint news — Keller had called him with it last evening — but knew the impact would be far greater if they'd heard it from Charles in person.

The fingerprint analysis was conclusive: the prints found on the gym's exit door and lockers matched those taken from the glasses used by Ashcroft's bodyguards at the French restaurant.

This could only mean one thing.

After getting off the phone with Keller last evening, Charles had given him Beaumont's address and telephone number, insisting the fingerprint evidence be delivered to the attorney immediately. But Charles's visit to the station this morning wasn't just about the fingerprints. He needed to know if the detectives had done what they said they would — if they had gone to the DA personally and presented him with the mountain of evidence Charles had uncovered.

He stepped out of the car and walked past the front desk without so much as a glance at the sergeant stationed there. If someone stopped him, he'd have to somehow justify why he'd come uninvited and without an appointment. But the goal was to reach Rafferty and Shipley before that became necessary.

He headed toward the back of the station where he knew their desks were located. A younger detective paused to ask who he was looking for, but Charles waved him off politely.

"I have a meeting with Detectives Rafferty and Shipley," he said with a polite nod, not slowing his stride. Technically true, he told himself. They just didn't know it yet.

Up ahead, he spotted them. Shipley saw him first, eyebrows lifting in surprise as he nudged Rafferty. Both men stood as Charles approached.

"Gentlemen," Charles said, extending a hand. "I came straight down this morning because I've got the final piece of evidence proving Cedric's innocence—and confirming that Ashcroft's bodyguards are the real killers."

Shipley's eyes widened with alarm. He immediately stood and moved to close the office door behind them.

"Charles, keep your voice down," he said in a hushed tone. "You don't want that said aloud in here. There are still ears in this place we don't trust. Remember, you wouldn't even meet us here last time. We had to meet at that chapel offsite."

Charles winced, catching his mistake. In his excitement, he'd momentarily forgotten how compromised the station could be. Then he realized something else. Rafferty and Shipley must think so, too, or else they wouldn't care how loud Charles talked.

Rafferty gestured toward the chair opposite their desks. "Have a seat. Quietly, tell us what you drove all the way down here to say."

Charles nodded, lowered himself into the chair, and leaned forward.

"The detective we hired, Kane, his fingerprint analysis is back. There's no ambiguity. The prints on the gym exit door and the mangled locker belong to Ashcroft's men. Kane lifted them clean from the water glasses they used at *La Maison de Lyon*. They were a perfect match."

Shipley closed his eyes and sighed. Rafferty glanced down at the surface of his desk, tapping a pencil slowly.

Their reactions were not what Charles expected. "That's it?" Charles asked, incredulous. "We just proved Cedric was telling the truth, and that your real killers were Ashcroft's men. Why do you both look like someone just delivered a eulogy?"

Shipley looked to Rafferty, who gave a reluctant nod.

"We met with the DA yesterday," Rafferty said. "Tried to share what we had. Had it all worked out before I went in. I barely get going, and he shut us down. Fast."

Charles stared. "You didn't even get to the journal? Or Singleton?"

"Barely made it through Singleton before he cut us off," Rafferty said. "When he realized where we were heading with the story, he got angry. Said we were undermining our own case — the one we helped him build, the one he sold to the grand jury."

"Which you now know is a sham," Charles said, his voice sharp.

"We tried, Charles," Shipley offered, weakly. "But he didn't want to hear it. Called it hearsay. Said unless we had an actual eyewitness who saw someone else commit the murder, he wasn't interested."

"Hearsay," Charles said, rising slightly from his chair. He forced himself to sit back down. "Hearsay? Singleton isn't hearsay. He talked to the killers face-to-face when he made the deal. The guys we now know for certain were at the gym when Reggie was shot. And Reggie's journal? That's not hearsay. It's direct evidence! Written by the victim, some of it on the day before he was murdered. You let Tilford brush it all aside like it was nothing?"

Rafferty looked down again, visibly ashamed.

"I don't know what I expected Tilford to say," Charles muttered. "But let me tell you what's coming, for certain. Wainwright at *The Times* has *everything*. Every last detail. He's writing a front-page article that will blow this thing wide open. It'll be the first thing everyone reads when they open their paper tomorrow. I gave you both a chance to be on the right side of it. I even begged you to do your jobs."

He let the words hang in the air.

"And Beaumont," he continued. "If this goes to trial, Beaumont will bury the prosecution with this evidence. The journal. Singleton. The fingerprints. The suppressor. All of it. He'll eviscerate every assumption the DA made. Tilford will be sitting there with egg all over his face. And won't the newspapers have a field day with him. The jury will see the truth, and the Curran Commission will see his sham investigation as a cover-up. One aimed at protecting Ashcroft, who everyone will know is nothing more than a sadistic, greedy killer, who had his own son murdered to keep his corrupt schemes intact."

The two detectives sat silently, the weight of Charles's words settling over them like a shroud.

"What do you think happens then?" Charles asked. "The Commission will demand to know who buried this evidence. And when they find out that you two delivered only part of the story, they'll wonder what else you kept quiet. If you were pressured. If you were complicit."

After a long pause, Shipley turned to Rafferty. "If you won't go back to the DA right now and demand he hears all of this, I will. I can't sit on it anymore, not with this new fingerprint evidence. It removes any doubt."

Rafferty hesitated, then slowly nodded. "No. We'll go back there together. The DA may not listen. But he won't be able to say he wasn't warned."

Charles blinked, a little caught off guard. "You'll go back to him?"

"Yes," Rafferty said. "He may bury it, but we're not going to be part of it anymore."

Shipley nodded in agreement.

"We're sorry, Charles," Rafferty added. "You've done our job for us, and you shouldn't have had to."

They all stood. Charles offered his hand. "Just make sure it counts this time."

They shook hands, and Charles left the room. Behind him, two detectives sat in silence. He thought he heard Rafferty say to Shipley, "God help us, what have we done here?"

39

Tuesday afternoon, just after lunch, Rafferty and Shipley stood outside the front entrance of *The New York Times* building. Shipley folded his arms and looked doubtful. "I still don't see why we're doing this," he muttered. "You think Bennington made the whole thing up? Seems like a pretty straight-shooting guy to me. Besides, what motive would he have to make it up?"

Rafferty shook his head. "Not made up. But maybe exaggerated a bit, just to get us moving on the case. Maybe Wainwright is writing the article, but what if he's not planning on releasing it for a few weeks? We're about to go toe-to-toe with the DA again, and everything we've got hangs on whether Wainwright's article is real—and if it's about to go to print. If we don't verify that, we're walking in there blind."

Shipley nodded reluctantly. "Alright. Let's get this over with."

They stepped into the cool marble foyer of the Times building and quickly found their way up to the newsroom. The clatter of typewriters echoed through the hallway as they approached Wainwright's office.

The reporter was hunched over his desk, fingers flying across the keys, completely absorbed in his work. The door stood partially ajar. Rafferty knocked twice. No response. Shipley pushed the door open and stepped in.

Wainwright turned with a start. "What in—?" He recognized them. "Detectives Rafferty and Shipley, right? What brings you here?"

Rafferty shut the door behind them, spoke quietly but firmly. "We'll keep this brief. We met with Charles Bennington just before lunch. He said you were writing an article—an *explosive* one he said. We're here to verify that's true."

Wainwright gestured to the typewriter. "That's what I'm working on right now. Just got off the phone with Bennington myself about an hour ago. He told me about the fingerprint match. I take it you men know what I'm talking about?"

They both nodded.

"Well, to me that clinches it. I've got Singleton's statement, the journal excerpts in the victim's own hand, and now this. When I shared it with my editors, they told me to drop everything else. This is front page material. Gentlemen...this story is going to rock this town."

Rafferty and Shipley looked at each other, equal parts awed and horrified.

"So, how much time do we have?" Shipley asked.

"I'll likely have the draft finished tonight," Wainwright said. "Editor gets it tomorrow morning. It should hit the streets by tomorrow's evening edition."

Rafferty took a long breath. "Does the article say we —the police and the DA—ignored all the new evidence?"

Wainwright raised an eyebrow. "Why would it say anything else? That's the truth. Unless...are you two here, willing to deny it on the record?"

Shipley held up a hand. "No, not exactly. But how about this instead? If we can get the DA to wake up and do the right thing—we're leaving from here to meet with him shortly—would you be willing to rewrite that part of the story to show the DA and us indicting Ashcroft and his two goons? And not release the other version that shows how things are going now?"

Wainwright thought a few moments. "I would be open to that but only if you get back to me by the end of the day with confirmation that the DA agrees to what you're saying. Better yet, you have him call me personally and give me a statement that I can run in the article. Otherwise, the DA is going down when this ship sinks."

Rafferty nodded grimly. "Understood."

The two detectives turned and left, the urgency of their mission now doubled.

Less than an hour later, Rafferty and Shipley barged into DA Tilford's office, interrupting a meeting with two detectives from another division.

Tilford looked up, startled. "What the devil is this? I'm in the middle of—"

Rafferty marched to his desk, pointed a firm finger at Tilford. "If you know what's good for you, sir, you'll tell these men to leave right now. Then you'll sit down, shut up, and listen to what we came here to say."

Tilford's face paled. He turned to the other men. "We'll reschedule, detectives. Why don't you both come back tomorrow?"

When they were gone, Rafferty closed the door behind them. He and Shipley walked up to the desk. Tilford, now seated, tried to compose himself, but intimidation was still written on his face. "Now," he said weakly, "what is all this about?"

Rafferty didn't waste time. In rapid summary, he laid out everything they now knew. Singleton's positive ID of the bodyguards. Reggie's journal entries with paraphrased quotes. The suppressor test. The timeline. The motive. The frame-up. And now the hammering blow...the fingerprint evidence that positively tied Ashcroft's men to the crime scene.

Tilford sat back in stunned silence.

Before he could speak, Rafferty drove the point home.

"We've just come from *The Times*. Wainwright is finishing a front-page article right now. It runs tomorrow. He will run one of two versions. One version exposes all this evidence, in great detail, highlights the police department's and the DA's negligence and likely cover-up of the truth. The other version could feature the DA and the police leading the way at exposing this scandal, by indicting the mastermind of the murder, which is Ashcroft, and his two hired thugs, whom he ordered to kill his son. And, of course, this version exposes Ashcroft's motives for doing something so sinister, the longstanding corruption and bribery schemes his son was about to share with the Curran Commission."

Tilford swallowed hard, took a deep breath. He was actually trembling. "Is there still time for that second version? If I act now?"

"Depends on what 'act' means," Rafferty said.

Tilford leaned forward, now regaining some composure. "I'll reconvene the grand jury first thing tomorrow morning. Present all this new evidence. Ask for indictments—first-degree murder—against Ashcroft and his two men. And I'll inform the judge that we're dropping all charges against Cedric Whitaker. Immediately."

Rafferty and Shipley exhaled deeply.

"Two things," Rafferty said. "First, can we arrest Ashcroft and the bodyguards this afternoon? I don't want to take a chance of them getting wind of what we're up to."

Tilford nodded. "Do it. Quietly, but swiftly."

"Second, you need to call Wainwright. Today. Personally. Give him a statement on the record, confirming what you just told us."

Tilford nodded again. "I'll do that right after I call the judge."

Rafferty and Shipley rose. "Thank you, sir."

They walked toward the door.

"Gentlemen," Tilford said. "Wait. I want you to know, I realize the risk you men took coming here this afternoon to warn me about all this. Believe me, I won't forget it."

40

The desk sergeant had noticed Charles Bennington storm into the station the day before with a determined stride and a defiant gleam in his eye. But he hadn't said anything—he'd grown used to the man's unannounced appearances. What he didn't know was that another officer, seated just down the hallway from Rafferty and Shipley's office, had taken an unusual interest in the visit.

Patrolman Eddie Fallon was not a particularly distinguished officer. Middle-aged, balding, and usually quiet, he was easily overlooked. Which suited him just fine. What most didn't know was that Fallon had been quietly earning extra income for the past five years as an informant—more accurately, a paid snitch—for Head Alderman Herbert Ashcroft. Until now, Fallon's contributions had been minor: a heads-up about raids, a shift change here, a harmless tip there. Nothing terribly important.

But today, something had changed.

He hadn't caught every word Charles said to Rafferty and Shipley, but he'd heard enough to know something serious was happening—something that could threaten Ashcroft directly. Fallon had begun to ask subtle questions around the precinct, probing for more information. One cop had mentioned fingerprints found at the Belmont. No, not on the gun, something else. Another had let slip something about the Belmont gym manager being found. Fallon knew this was big. Big enough to get him a bonus from the man he reported to.

So, late that afternoon, Fallon slipped out of the precinct and crossed the street to a payphone. He dialed a number he had memorized years ago.

"Yeah?" came a gravelly voice on the other end.

"It's Fallon. Eddie Fallon out of the 15th Precinct. I got something you're gonna want to hear."

BACK AT ASHCROFT'S private office—a lavish suite tucked away inside a municipal building on Centre Street—his main fixer, Frank Lyle, had picked up the phone on the second ring. A former political operative with a law degree and no moral compass, Lyle had managed Ashcroft's dirtiest tasks for more than a decade. As Lyle listened to Fallon's report, it was enough to make his stomach turn.

Fallon wasn't exaggerating. This was a big deal. He'd

hung up saying, "You done good, Fallon. Earned your keep this month."

Within five minutes, Lyle was knocking softly on the door of Ashcroft's wood-paneled conference room, where the alderman was mid-discussion with three contractors. Lyle knew these men were heavy-hitters, talking about rezoning for some big high-rise office building.

Ashcroft glanced at him with irritation. "Not now."

"It's urgent," Lyle said, just loud enough for him to hear. "We've got a problem." And he shot Alderman a look.

Ashcroft gritted his teeth. He turned back to the contractors, forced a smile. "Gentlemen, please excuse me. This won't take long. Help yourselves to the coffee and pastries."

In the adjacent conference room, with the door closed behind them, Ashcroft glared at Lyle. "This better be good."

Lyle didn't waste time. "It's Fallon. From the Fifteenth. That's where Rafferty and Shipley are based."

"I know," Ashcroft said. "What of it?"

"Fallon says there's been all kinds of chatter recently about a gym manager—Singleton. The same guy your boys paid to disappear. Turns out, he's been found. And he's talking. Says he can identify your hired men, as the ones who paid him to be gone when they went there to, well, you know."

Ashcroft's face went white. "Found? Where?"

"He was somewhere on Long Island. Now he's somewhere at The Belmont. Bennington's got him holed up in some room under Pinkerton protection. Fallon says Singleton's agreed to testify. And there's more. Apparently, there's fingerprint evidence, too—linking your guys to the gym."

Ashcroft slammed his palm on the table. "How is this happening now? Why? I told those fools to deal with Singleton."

"Guess they thought they did. They paid him off. Sent him out to Long Island instead of...doing what you wanted. I've told you, you can't be vague with guys like that."

"Unbelievable," Ashcroft muttered. "Get them in here. Now."

Lyle made the call.

TEN MINUTES LATER, the two bodyguards entered the side room and closed the door. The big and tall one with slicked-back hair—his name was Joe Gannon. The shorter one, who looked like an ex-boxer, was Tommy Drake.

Ashcroft didn't wait for pleasantries.

"Why is Singleton still alive?"

Drake looked uncomfortable. He looked at Gannon who was staring at the floor.

"I told you to *get rid* of him."

Drake spoke first. "Boss, we did. You wanted no witnesses at the gym that morning. There were no witnesses. And the police bought the set up. Everything worked. I don't know how—"

"You're supposed to do what you're told," Ashcroft

snapped. "I said get rid of him, not put him up in some nice place on Long Island. Now he's back, and he's saying he's willing to testify. About you two, and what you did. And now they got him holed up at The Belmont, protected by Pinkertons, no less."

"We'll take care of it," Gannon said quickly.

"You bet you will. Go to The Belmont, now. I don't care how you find out what room he's in—pay off a maid, pose as maintenance, I don't care. You find him. And you silence him."

"What about the guards, boss," Drake said. "The Pinkertons."

"Then take them out. Use that silencer thing you showed me. Quiet and clean. And for Pete's sake, *wear gloves* this time. No prints. No mistakes. No witnesses."

"Got it," Gannon said. "We're on it, Mr. Ashcroft."

The two men left in a hurry.

Ashcroft exhaled hard, straightened his cuffs, and returned to the contractors all smiles and geniality—as if nothing had happened.

TEN MINUTES LATER, Gannon and Drake sat in the back of a sedan heading uptown.

Drake lit a cigarette, scowling. "You know what burns me? I *told* you we should've taken out Singleton when we did the kid. That's what *get rid of him* means."

Looking down at Drake, Gannon said, "And I told you, it would've blown the whole frame job. Who's gonna believe this nice young college kid murders two people in cold blood? With no motive? No way anyone would've bought that."

"Yeah, well, now we gotta clean up after your brilliant idea."

"Maybe. But nobody suspected a thing until now. My plan was working. All we gotta do now is finish the job. Then we're back to square one."

Gannon flicked ash out the window. "Let's just get there and get this done."

41

Charles was in the lobby of the Hotel Belmont. He'd gone there intending to update Keller on the new developments in the investigation, when he'd been stopped by the concierge with a note from Rafferty. The note simply said: "*Call as soon as you get this. Great News! – Rafferty.*" Charles had wanted some privacy, so he'd gone to the little alcove to use a public payphone.

He called Rafferty's number, but another detective Charles didn't know picked up the phone. That detective informed him he had just missed Rafferty, who was now on his way to Alderman Ashcroft's house, along with Sergeant Shipley, to arrest him and his two thugs for the murder of his son, Reginald. Charles could hardly believe it. The detective said Rafferty instructed him to give this message to Charles if he called. And also to say, the charges against Cedric would be dropped by the end of the day. The DA had approved it. And he was going to reconvene the grand jury first thing tomorrow to seek an indictment...against all three.

Charles had barely hung up the phone when he felt a wave of joy wash over him. It was happening. Finally, after weeks of uncertainty, the truth was about to prevail.

He stepped away from the phone, all smiles, and glanced toward the concierge desk. The Belmont's lobby, recently such a place of darkness and tension, seemed suddenly brighter. At first, he thought to continue with his plans to see Keller but stopped.

There was only one thing he wanted to do next—call Lily.

He returned to the telephone and asked the operator to connect him to the Whitaker residence in Gramercy Park. After a few rings, Quentin's calm, familiar voice answered.

"Whitaker residence."

"Quentin, it's Charles. I need a favor—an unusual one. Can you gather Lily, Cedric, and Mrs. Whitaker together in the foyer? I want to share some incredible news, and I'd like them all to hear it at the same time. And I want you to hear it, too."

There was a pause, then: "Very good, sir. I will do that right away."

Despite the usual stoicism in Quentin's voice, Charles could hear a spark of eagerness beneath it.

He waited. Almost a minute passed.

Finally, Lily's voice came on the line, breathless with

excitement. "Charles? Quentin says you have something to tell us—something important?"

Charles could barely contain himself. "I do. Are you all there? Cedric and your mother, too?"

"Yes, what is it?"

"I've just spoken to a detective in Lieutenant Rafferty's office. You're not going to believe this. He and Shipley are heading over—right now—to arrest Ashcroft and his two bodyguards for Reggie's murder! The DA now believes all the evidence I gave them."

A chorus of joy erupted on the other end of the line. Charles could hear Lily's gasp, Cedric shouting something in disbelief, and Millicent's voice, unusually high, exclaiming, "Thank God!"

He smiled and continued, "And that's not all—Rafferty said the DA is going to ask the judge to drop all charges against—"

He froze mid-sentence.

Lily's voice cut through the line. "Charles? What is it? What's wrong?"

Charles stood still, eyes wide, staring at the lobby doors. "No... no, no, no. This can't be," he muttered.

Lily's voice rose. "Charles? What's happening?"

"I've got to go," he said abruptly. "Lily, listen—Ashcroft's two bodyguards just walked in. I saw them come through the front doors. They looked furious. They went straight to the front desk and demanded something from the young man there. Then they headed for the stairwell. As they opened the door, I saw them draw pistols—with silencers attached."

"Oh no—Charles, don't go!" she cried.

But he had already hung up.

For a split second, he considered taking the elevator to follow them. But something else mattered more. He ran to the front desk. "Did those men ask for a room number?"

The young clerk looked pale. He nodded. "Y-yes, sir. I'm sorry. They showed me the pistols under their coats. Said they'd kill me if I didn't tell them. I gave them Singleton's room. Tenth floor."

"Call him. Now. Tell him it's life or death."

The clerk fumbled for the phone. As soon as it rang, he handed Charles the receiver. Moments later, Singleton answered.

"I was just thinking of calling room service," Singleton said casually, "to order a ham sandwich—"

"Shut up and listen," Charles snapped. "It's Charles Bennington. I'm in the lobby. You've got no time. I just saw Ashcroft's bodyguards—they're coming for you. Armed. I saw the guns myself. They're on the stairway heading for your room."

There was silence.

"Tell the Pinkertons outside your door. Now. Tell them two armed men are coming, and they'll shoot on sight. Make sure they're ready."

"Oh my God," Singleton whispered. "What do I do after that?"

"Lock yourself in the bathroom. Now go."

Charles slammed the receiver down and turned—just in time to see Keller stepping out of the security office.

"Keller! Over here!" he shouted. "Ashcroft's men—

they're heading upstairs. Guns drawn. I just saw them. They're heading for Singleton's room!"

Keller ran toward him.

"Do you have a gun?" Charles asked.

Keller tapped his chest. "Always. Let's go."

They sprinted to the elevator, urging the guests inside to step out. "Police matter—clear the car!"

Once the doors closed, the elevator groaned to life and began its slow ascent.

Keller pulled out his Colt .45 and cocked the hammer. "When that door opens," he said firmly, "you stay behind me. Understand?"

Charles gave a tense nod, his hands curling into fists. "Understood."

42

Charles glanced at the elevator controls as they rose. "Which is faster, Keller—the elevator or the stairs?"

Keller pointed up to an arrow-shaped needle slowly moving around a half-moon display marked with numbers. "Usually the elevator. But it depends how fast those two are moving. If they're running, they could beat us."

"Guess we'll know soon enough," Charles muttered, watching the needle inch toward the number ten.

The seconds dragged on.

Keller broke the silence. "Elevator's more central. In the hallway, I mean. Stairwell's at the far end. Singleton's room is closer to us than to them."

Charles nodded. "Still, that hallway's wide open. Pinkertons will just be standing there, nothing to hide behind."

Keller pointed at a button on the control panel. "See that? *Emergency Open*. When the doors part, hit it. It'll freeze them open. I can use the elevator for cover."

The elevator rumbled, then stopped.

They heard shouting.

"Must be them," Keller whispered. "The bodyguards, they're here."

A voice closer to them thundered down the hallway. "Drop your weapons unless you want to die. Do it now!"

Another voice—gruff and defiant. "Can't do that, Pinkerton. We got a job to do."

The doors opened. Charles slammed the Emergency Open button. Keller raised his pistol.

Charles peeked out, just a sliver. "They're facing off—guns drawn. About fifty feet apart." That meant Singleton must've warned the Pinkertons in time.

"Stay back," Keller snapped. "Behind me."

One of the Pinkertons said quietly to the other, "When I say drop, hit the ground and start firing."

"Right."

A bodyguard's voice echoed. "I'm giving you to the count of three. One..."

"Drop!"

Both Pinkertons hit the floor. Gunfire erupted.

Muzzle flashes lit the corridor. The noise was deafening.

Keller leaned out, arm extended, and fired twice. One of the bodyguards screamed.

"I'm hit!" one Pinkerton cried. "My shoulder!"

"I got one of them!" the other yelled.

Keller looked again, shouted, "The big one's getting away!"

Charles watched him sprint toward the stairwell.

Smoke filled the hallway. The stink of powder hung thick in the air.

Charles stepped out. One Pinkerton was down, clutching his shoulder, groaning. Blood soaked through his fingers.

"I'll help him," Charles said. "Go check the other guy."

The healthy Pinkerton nodded and ran.

A nearby door opened. Singleton peeked out.

"Is it safe to come out?"

"Yes. But get back in there. Grab some hand towels. Now. And run right back here."

Charles turned back to the injured Pinkerton. "Just your shoulder? You get hit anywhere else?"

The man shook his head. "Once is enough. Feels like I got clubbed with a bat."

Singleton returned. Charles swapped his blood-soaked handkerchief for a towel.

"Press here. Hard." He stood. "I'm calling the police."

Down the hall, the other Pinkerton had subdued the wounded bodyguard. "You're not dying," he barked, slapping on handcuffs. "But keep yapping and you might be."

Charles ducked into Singleton's room, found the phone, and asked the hotel operator for the police. Moments later, the desk sergeant answered.

"Is Rafferty there?" Charles said.

"Still out. But I know he's gotta be near Ashcroft's

place. Said they'd phone from a box before going in for the arrest."

"Tell him the tall bodyguard's on the run. Headed back to Ashcroft. He's armed—and angry."

"Got it. We'll get him. How's about the other one?"

"He's here at the hotel, wounded. And in cuffs," Charles said. He hung up.

Just then, Keller returned using the second elevator.

"Hold on a moment, Sergeant."

"Lost the guy in the parking area," Keller said. "But you know he's gotta be headed back to Ashcroft."

"I'll tell the Sergeant," Charles said. "They'll warn Rafferty."

"You need me anymore?"

Charles shook his head. "No. Thanks. Go. Handle the guests."

Keller nodded and left.

The unwounded Pinkerton dragged the injured bodyguard to the hallway floor, closer to the room.

"Call me a doctor!"

The Pinkerton punched him in the jaw. "There's your doctor." He held up his other fist. "Keep talking, and you'll meet the specialist."

"I'm calling two ambulances," Charles said, heading for the phone again.

Once he accomplished the task, he turned to the Pinkerton. "Help's on the way. Keep an eye on both."

The man nodded.

Charles moved toward the elevator. Time to see Nigel.

Tell him everything that's happened. But first—he hit the lobby button.

He had to call Lily back, let her know he was still alive.

Lily hadn't moved from the telephone table. Her fingers still trembled as she stared at the receiver. The gentle ticking of the grandfather clock keeping time with her fears. The waiting and not knowing was unbearable. After sharing the best of all possible news, Charles had suddenly left them there standing in the foyer, a dark picture created by words of two killers with guns entering the hotel...and Charles running after them...unarmed.

Millicent sat nearby, pressing a handkerchief to her lips. Cedric paced for the first few minutes. Now stood rigid, arms crossed, his eyes fixed on the door as though he might burst through it and sprint to The Belmont himself.

When the phone finally rang again, Lily lunged.

"Charles?" she said, breathless.

"It's me," came his voice—calmer now, but wearied. "I'm all right. It's over."

"What happened? What's over?" she pressed. "You left me...Charles, I thought—"

"I know, I know. I'm so sorry." He drew a breath. "I saw Ashcroft's men come into the lobby with guns drawn. They went straight for the stairs. I had to warn the Pinkertons guarding Singleton."

"And—did they...?"

"They tried. There was a shootout in the hallway."

"A shootout in the hallway," she repeated. Cedric and Mother's eyes popped wide open.

"One of the Pinkertons was wounded, shot in the shoulder, but he'll live. Keller and I got there in the nick of time."

"Keller and you?" she said. "What could you possibly do? You had no gun."

"I stayed back in the elevator, Love. I'm no fool."

She laughed. "One of Ashcroft's men is in handcuffs. The shorter one. The one who looked like a boxer. The taller one ran back down the stairs and got away. But they'll get him. He thinks he's heading back to the safety of Ashcroft's mansion. But Rafferty and Shipley will be there waiting."

Lily exhaled, her voice tight with relief. "Thank God."

"Yes," Charles said, quieter now. "He's been most definitely watching over us, Lily. In all of it, He's kept us safe. Keller and I are both unharmed."

Cedric leaned in. "What's he saying?"

Lily turned, smiling through her tears. "He's safe. They got one of the bodyguards. He's wounded and in handcuffs. The other's on the run, but they know where he's headed."

Millicent dabbed her eyes. "Then it's really over? We can be glad again about the news?"

Lily smiled, nodded, returned the receiver to her ear. "When are you coming home?"

"Soon," Charles said. "But I really need to speak with your father. I don't know if he knows any of what happened today. I also need to call Wainwright, tell him what just happened at the hotel. It would be great to get a positive story about the Hotel, and about Cedric, in the papers. I'll be along as soon as I can."

"We'll be waiting," Lily whispered. "I don't know what we'll do when you and Father get here. Seems like we should celebrate somehow."

"I agree. Love you," he said and hung up.

Yes. A celebration of some magnitude was in order here.

43

Detective Rafferty stood by the call box on the corner, prying it open with a firm twist. He'd parked a block from Ashcroft's mansion with Sergeant Shipley and another squad car containing two uniformed officers, just in case things went sideways. With two killers on the premises, he wasn't taking any chances.

He picked up the receiver inside and cranked the handle. A few seconds later, the police operator answered. "Operator, patch me through to the front desk sergeant."

"Connecting you now."

A click. Then, "Desk sergeant."

"Rafferty here. Just checking in before we go in."

The sergeant's voice was charged. "Glad you called. Big developments at The Belmont. Just got off the phone with Bennington. There was a shootout on the tenth floor. That's where that gym manager had been holed up. Two wounded. One of the Pinkertons took it in the shoulder.

One of Ashcroft's men got it, too. Not sure where. But he's in cuffs. The other—the tall one—got away. Bennington says he's probably headed back to Ashcroft's place."

Rafferty stiffened. "How long ago did this happen?"

"Just got off the phone with Bennington a minutes ago. Wondering how much time you got?"

"Yeah."

"Don't know how far it is from the hotel to Ashcroft's. But with traffic this time of day, might take him longer to get there. You might still surprise him."

"Okay, yeah. Let's hope so."

He hung up, then waved Shipley and the other two officers over. They exited their cars.

"Change of plans," Rafferty said, quickly explaining what he'd just learned. "So, here's the new set up. We leave the cars here. Go in on foot, double-time. But we're gonna circle around from the south. Won't be good, him seeing four cops running down the sidewalk."

They jogged down the sidewalk on the first block, ducking behind hedges and cutting through a neighbor's side yard. When they reached the driveway of Ashcroft's mansion, they spotted Calvin Marsh casually leaning against the fender of Ashcroft's gleaming Packard.

His eyes went wide, stood straight up. "Detectives?"

"It's okay," Rafferty said, lowering his voice. "We know you're one of the good guys. You're the kid who gave us the journal, right?"

"Yeah, that was me."

"Well, we're here to arrest Ashcroft and his men. Well, one of his men, anyway. No time to explain."

Calvin's eyes lit up. "I was about to say, the boss is here but his bodyguards aren't. When they left here earlier, I could tell something was up by the look on their faces. And I saw them screw those gadgets onto their pistols."

"Silencers," Rafferty said. "Okay. Go hide behind the garage. One of them's coming back. Could be any minute. Might get ugly."

Calvin nodded and hurried off.

Rafferty scanned the driveway. Plenty of bushes to hide behind. "Fan out. Stay out of sight. When the car arrives, wait for him to get out. Wait for me to make the first move."

They quickly got into position.

Minutes dragged by. Rafferty checked his watch. Eight minutes. Nine.

Then the sound of a car engine, coming in hard and fast.

A black Ford tore around the corner and skidded into the driveway, halting just short of Ashcroft's Packard.

The taller bodyguard—Joe Gannon, if Rafferty remembered right—sat behind the wheel, breathing hard, eyes scanning the house.

Rafferty waited. As soon as Gannon stepped out of the car, Rafferty emerged from the hedge, pistol aimed at his head. "Hold it right there, Gannon!"

Shipley and the two officers flanked him in an instant, guns drawn.

"Don't even think about reaching for that gun in your waistband," Shipley said. "You'll be full of holes before you blink."

Gannon froze, hands half-raised. Then he forced a grin. "What's this about, officers? You know whose house this is, right? I work for Alderman Ashcroft. Gannon is my name. I'm one of Mr. Ashcroft's trusted associates."

"Yeah, we know," Rafferty said. "He trusted you enough to kill his son, frame that Whitaker kid. And then trusted you on another hit job at The Belmont just now. But that one didn't turn out too well, did it? Hands up, Gannon. Step away from the car."

Gannon's jaw clenched, eyes darting back and forth at the guns all pointing at his head. Slowly, he raised his hands and backed away.

Rafferty nodded to one of the uniforms. "Cuff him."

As the officer moved in, Rafferty turned to Shipley and the other officer. "Run back and get the cars."

"You're not arresting Ashcroft without me, right?"

"I'll wait. But don't stop for any doughnuts."

Shipley grinned. "No promises."

He and the other officer took off.

Rafferty turned back to Gannon, now cuffed and glaring at him. "You have the right to remain silent, Joe. I suggest you use it."

After patting him down, they placed Gannon in the back of one of the squad cars and left an officer to guard him. Rafferty, Shipley, and the remaining officer moved around to the back steps of the house. From there, Rafferty peered into the massive kitchen, confirming no one else was in sight—until a woman stepped in from an interior doorway and jumped at the sight of him.

He put a finger to his lips and motioned her toward the back door. She opened it nervously.

"Ma'am," Rafferty said gently, "we're going to need you to step outside and stay out here until someone tells you it's safe to return."

She hesitated, then complied. At the bottom of the steps, she spotted Gannon in the patrol car. "What on earth...?"

"I'm sorry," Rafferty said, "but after today, you might want to consider looking for another employer. We're here to arrest Mr. Ashcroft."

Now her face turned pale.

Shipley asked, "Want to sneak in through the kitchen?"

Rafferty shook his head. "No need. His goons are in cuffs. Let's go straight in the front door like proper gentlemen."

They circled to the front of the house, walked up the grand steps, and rang the bell.

The butler answered, surprised to see them. Rafferty flashed his badge, and the three men entered.

"May I help you?" the butler asked.

"You can," Rafferty said. "Take us to your employer."

The butler's brows rose. "Is he...expecting you sir?"

"I highly doubt it," Shipley said.

The butler started walking down a wide hallway, turned and said, "He gave instructions not to be disturbed. He's in the study."

"Well," Rafferty said. "I'm sad to say we are about to create quite a significant disturbance."

They continued following. Rafferty took note of the dark walnut paneling, an ornate grandfather clock, and several portraits of Ashcroft's ancestors.

The study door loomed ahead. Rafferty didn't wait. He flung the door open and stepped inside.

Ashcroft sat behind an enormous mahogany desk, puffing a thick cigar, reading from a stack of documents. He looked up in shock.

"Gentlemen, this is most improper. I recognize you. You're the men investigating my son's murder. If you had business with me, you could've called. I would have gladly had my driver—"

"You can save it," Rafferty interrupted. "And you're right, we are investigating your son's murder, and that investigation has led us right here. Herbert L. Ashcroft, I'm placing you under arrest for the murder of your son, Reginald Ashcroft, conspiracy to commit murder, and the attempted murders of Mickey Singleton and a Pinkerton agent at the Hotel Belmont a short while ago."

Ashcroft's face, now drained of color.

"Not the report you were hoping to hear?" Rafferty said. "Let me guess. You were expecting Gannon and your other man— the shorter one, who's been wounded and is now in cuffs—to return with good news that Singleton was dead, and now you have nothing to fear from his testimony. Am I close?"

Ashcroft stood abruptly. "This is preposterous! I demand to know the basis for these ridiculous—"

"Turn around. Hands behind your back," Rafferty said.

Ashcroft refused.

"Glad you resisted," Shipley muttered.

He marched over, grabbed Ashcroft, spun him around, and shoved him against the wall. He leaned in and whispered, "This is how we treat scumbags who murder their own kids. Get used to it."

Shipley spun him back, now properly cuffed and visibly shaken.

Rafferty gave him a grim smile. "Let's go."

They marched Ashcroft toward the front door as various members of the house staff peered on, a mixture of horror and wonder on their faces.

44

Charles had just called Lily and her family when he headed toward the elevator, intending to brief her father in his office about everything that had just transpired. But as he passed through the lobby, something caught his eye. Two uniformed officers had burst through the front doors and were met instantly by Keller who, after an animated exchange, pointed toward the elevators.

It dawned on Charles...his next move really should be to contact Wainwright at *The Times*. He quickly returned to the phone, dropped a nickel in the slot, and asked the operator at *The Times* to urgently patch him through to Wainwright's desk.

The line buzzed twice before he heard the operator's voice announce him. Wainwright picked up. "Is this something important, Charles? I just finished the big story and was about to hand-deliver it to my editor. I even got the statement from DA Wilford, admitting their mistake on this case and plans to immediately seek an indictment for Ashcroft and his bodyguards."

Charles said, "Well, you might want to hold off calling it finished until you hear what I'm about to tell you."

There was a pause. "Okay. I'm listening. What could possibly be big enough to stop me from running the biggest story I've ever written?"

Charles said, "How about a shootout in the hotel tied to the murder case? Happened not twenty-five minutes ago."

Wainwright was stunned. "You're kidding."

"I'm not. Two of Ashcroft's bodyguards showed up at the hotel to kill Mickey Singleton, obviously sent here by Ashcroft. He's the hotel gym manager who ID'd the men."

"I remember," Wainwright said.

"Don't know who snitched, but somehow they found out about him. They came up the stairway to the tenth floor with pistols—silencers attached. Got into a gunfight with two Pinkertons posted outside Singleton's door. One of the Pinkertons got shot in the shoulder, one of the bodyguards went down, and the other ran off. Keller and I were there when it happened. He even joined in the gunfight."

Wainwright could hardly keep up. "Wait, slow down. I'm taking notes."

"Forget notes," Charles said. "You can take notes later. You need to get down here. Bring a photographer if you can. You might still catch the ambulances and police cars out front. They're tending to the wounded on the tenth floor. Even if you miss them, there'll be blood stains and towels in the hallway. And Singleton's still here. Interview him while it's fresh. He might need a little incentive, but he'll talk. The danger for him has passed."

Charles checked his pocket watch. "And there's more. Just before I called you, Rafferty and Shipley were on their way to Ashcroft's place to arrest him and the taller bodyguard, the one who fled the hotel shootout. They should already be in custody by now—likely en route to the station in a squad car. If you have a second photographer, get him over there. You might get a shot of Ashcroft being led into the precinct in cuffs."

Wainwright was speechless for a moment, then said, "You're throwing too many scoops at me, Bennington. I don't know which one to cover."

"My suggestion? Send a photographer to the precinct to catch Ashcroft in handcuffs. You don't need to be there. He won't be giving any statements. You come here with another photographer—if you have one—cover the shootout story."

"Good point. I think I'll do that. I'll be over there in five minutes, photographer in tow. You mind being interviewed when I get there? Sounds like you were an eyewitness."

Charles hesitated, took too long to answer.

"What's the matter?"

"It's just...I've watched how my father-in-law's hotel business has been almost destroyed by the negative publicity in the newspapers. You know, all the *Scandal at the Belmont* angles depicted in these articles. So far, my name has not been mentioned. I didn't think my ice-making factory could stand the financial hit if my name was associated with everything that just happened."

Wainwright paused. "I understand. But you know, Charles, all the mentions of the Hotel Belmont weren't intended to cause your father-in-law, or the hotel, any financial loss. That's just the nature of the news business, how people react to stories they read."

"Maybe so, but still, here Nigel has spent his whole life creating this successful, high-end hotel with a sterling reputation, and in a matter of weeks he's almost ruined by something that happened there, and as it turns out, his own son — whose own reputation has also been greatly damaged — has now been proven completely innocent. Cedric had nothing to do with the murder, and is actually devastated by the loss of his best friend. But how many people in this city who've read all the negative stories will ever know any of this?"

There was a long pause, then Wainwright said, "Well, maybe there is something I can do about that. At the very least, you should know if I were to interview you, you'd be cast more in the role of the hero than a villain, and rightly so, given not just the events that happened today, but your role in breaking open this entire case."

"Okay, I'll think about being interviewed, but for now how about you just interview Keller, the security chief. He not only witnessed everything that happened at the hotel, but he was more of a hero than me, actually took part in the gunfight in the hallway. Keller would probably cherish the idea of his name being in the papers for doing something heroic."

"Well," Wainwright said, "I appreciate all you've done to break this story open. You've given me a chance to really make a name for myself. My editor said I would not only get top billing with this story, but he's giving me the lead role in all the follow-up stories related to the trial."

"You're welcome. I'm just grateful you listened when no one else would."

"Okay, I'll be over there in just a few minutes."

"We might miss each other. I need to go up and brief my father-in-law on today's events."

Charles hung up the phone and went back through the lobby toward the elevators.

45

Charles made his way up to the third floor, opened the elevator doors and walked toward the hotel offices. Barely twenty steps in and his mind flashed back to that moment eleven days ago when he and his father-in-law — beside themselves with anxiety about the shooting that had just happened in the cellar — walked along this same path en route to Nigel's office. Only then, it was to speak with Cedric who they'd learned had just been detained as the primary suspect in Reggie's murder.

Involuntarily, Charles released a deep sigh. That's not what he was facing anymore. Quite the opposite, in fact. He hadn't even allowed himself a moment to dwell on the reality of their sudden and thoroughly changed set of circumstances. It was over. Cedric was safe at home, but even more importantly, safe from an almost certain appointment with the electric chair. God had providentially intervened over these past days, and in almost biblical fashion, delivered them from the hands of their foes.

As Charles walked along the hallway, he observed that half the desks were empty. The employees who occupied them were all standing about in little groups talking in animated ways amongst themselves, no doubt about all the crazy goings-on on the 10th floor a short while ago.

And once again, watching police officers and ambulance drivers roaming the hotel floors and lobby, only this time the bodies being taken out on gurneys were still alive. Everyone paused in their conversations, as they saw Charles walk by.

When he got to Nigel's rich mahogany doors, he knocked briefly, didn't wait to be invited in. He was somewhat surprised to find Nigel not sitting at his desk. Usually at this time of the day, he would be either combing through documents or talking on the phone. Instead, he was standing between the partially opened curtains, staring out the window. Charles cleared his throat to get Nigel's attention.

It worked. Nigel turned and forced a smile on his weary countenance. Charles had gotten somewhat used to this look in recent days, but he wondered why Nigel wasn't smiling this time. Could it be he hadn't heard the news yet?

"Charles, good to see you," he said, and headed toward his desk. "I was expecting a visit from Keller. Like everyone else in the hotel, I heard the gunfire on the 10th floor. Like a dumb fool, I ducked and hid under the desk.

As if bullets could travel through all these multiple floors. Just glad no one out there in the office walked in just then."

"So, Keller briefed you on what took place?"

Nigel sat at his desk, so Charles picked one of the upholstered chairs in front.

"Yes, brief would be the word. We only talked for a few minutes, enough time to let me know no one was killed, and that none of the guests were harmed. Not surprisingly, since then, all the guests on the ninth through the eleventh floors have suddenly felt the urgent need to check out of the hotel. I won't be that surprised if the guests from all the other floors don't soon join them."

"So sorry to hear that," Charles said. "Well, I'm here to give you a more thorough update on things. Not just the shootout, though I was actually there when it happened, so if you have any questions or want anything additional said about it, just let me know. Could you hear the gunshots down here?" Charles said.

"Oh...yes. They were quite startling. Keller said he was told they could even hear them in the lobby, although not quite as loudly as here. Really drives home the point about the silencer situation. Meaning, that no one in the lobby heard the gunshot that killed poor Reggie. Without that silencer, it's obvious Reggie's murder would have gotten everyone's attention."

"Ashcroft's men did come with their silencers attached," Charles said. "I guess expecting to catch the Pinkertons by surprise. It was quite fascinating to hear them in the hallway, right up against the return fire from the Pinkerton's and Keller's guns."

"How did you and Keller avoid getting shot?"

"We stayed in the elevator the whole time...well, *whole time*. The thing was over in a matter of seconds. I was surprised no one was killed, between the Pinkertons and the bodyguards. So many bullets flying down that hall."

"Oh, Charles," Nigel started massaging his temples. "I can't believe this just happened. Right here in my hotel again. A full-fledge shootout on the tenth floor. Like something out of the old West. I can just imagine what the newspapers will be saying about the hotel now. First it was, *Scandal at the Belmont*, now it's: *Shootout at the Belmont*." He released a deep sigh. Shook his head slowly back and forth. He looked up and said, "This just might finish us off, Charles. After this, I don't know what it will take to start getting people to come back here."

"Well, Father, I don't think that's going to happen. Not after everything I've heard and seen in the last twenty-four hours."

"You don't?" An incredulous expression on his face.

"No, I don't. I have so many things to tell you. And for the first time in a good many days, all of them good."

Charles spent the next twenty-five minutes walking Nigel through all the events of the past few days. Not just the events before the shootout but after, including the likelihood that Ashcroft and his two bodyguards have both already been arrested by Rafferty and Shipley. And that the DA had already called the judge to drop all the charges against Cedric, and to reconvene the grand jury tomorrow morning to indict the real killers on first-degree murder charges, as well as a number of others.

He finished with an update on his conversation that day with Wainwright of *The Times*, and the explosive new article Wainwright said would hit the front page of the papers tomorrow. Charles couldn't be sure of all that it would include, but he was convinced that Wainwright was now fully on their side.

For several moments, Nigel didn't say a word in reply. Then fairly quickly his eyes welled up with tears, which he tried in vain to wipe away, because his shoulders now got in the act, as he buried his head in his forearms and began to sob. Charles had never seen him like this, had never imagined seeing him like this, and was not quite sure what to do.

He went with his instincts, got up, came around the desk, lowered his arms around Nigel's back, and hugged him.

Before he knew it, Charles was crying, too. A flood of happy tears. Grateful tears, that such a terrible ordeal was finally behind them.

The nightmare was over.

46

Aug 11th, 1914
Gramercy Park, New York City
Wednesday Morning, The Whitaker Mansion

Last night, for the first time in a long time, the dinner had been a feast.

More than that, a celebration. Rivaling the best Christmas and the best Easter dinners of their lives. After recovering from the emotional scene Charles and Nigel had shared in his office, Nigel decided it was time to leave for the day and head home. He'd asked if Charles could drive him home, thus sparing their driver the need to come collect him at the hotel.

When they had gotten down to the lobby, Nigel seemed like a changed man. He'd asked Charles if the concierge or any of the hotel staff had learned of the good news Charles had shared with him. Charles said he didn't think so, then Nigel suggested Charles stay there a few minutes, brief the concierge fully — with instructions to spread the news liberally to all the staff in the lobby and beyond, then fetch the car and meet him out front.

"They haven't heard any good news for far too long," he'd said. Then Nigel disappeared somewhere, heading in the direction of the hotel restaurant.

Almost as soon as Charles had pulled up to the front doors of the hotel, Nigel came out, all smiles, and sat next to Charles in the passenger seat. He'd said, "That felt very good. Let's go home."

As Charles drove back toward Gramercy Park, Nigel had explained what he'd done. He'd called home, asked for Lily, and gave her a peculiar assignment. Something he'd never done before. But something that felt right for the occasion. He'd asked her to inform the kitchen staff not to prepare dinner. Instead, they were to come upstairs and join the rest of the family in the parlor, awaiting he and Charles arrival.

He informed her that he'd arranged for a massive feast to be delivered to the house and served by the hotel staff. With so many guests who'd left the hotel abruptly because of the shooting, there was a ton of food in the restaurant that was likely to be thrown out. And all the servers there to work the dinner crowd would likely be sent home without pay.

How much better to put at least some of them to work preparing a celebration meal back at the house? And he wanted the house staff not to have to serve them dinner, but to enjoy having the evening off. He knew they'd never feel comfortable eating at the family dining table, but at the very least, they could feast on all this luscious food downstairs, while the Whitaker family served themselves.

Charles could hardly believe his ears when Nigel had said it and could hardly believe his eyes back at the house when it had all come to pass.

But before the food had arrived, with the family and the house staff all gathered together in the parlor, Nigel had asked Charles to update them all on the marvelous news that had taken place in the past twenty-four hours. Really, over the last several days as — one by one — these various puzzle pieces of evidence came together, resulting in the arrest of the actual killers, and the complete exoneration of all charges against Cedric.

The look on all their faces as Charles shared the news was something he'd never forget. Especially with the house staff, most of whom had been living under the terrible weight of anxiety all week, that the beloved little boy they had watched grow up into a fine young man, and who had been accused of this ghastly murder, could potentially face execution. But now he was totally free, and there was no longer anything to fear.

They literally wept for joy. Even Quentin could not restrain his tears, although he quickly reached for a linen napkin in an effort to stop the flow. Everyone then gathered around Cedric, hugging him fiercely, patting him on the back and insisting they always knew he'd be vindicated.

Needless to say, Cedric was overwhelmed with the affection.

After this, Nigel explained the dinner plans to everyone, including the fact that the house staff would not only be free to enjoy all of the high-end restaurant food about to be delivered, but they could consume it as soon as it came and not have to wait until the Whitaker family had eaten. And that the Whitaker family would serve themselves tonight.

Again, the look on their faces at hearing this...priceless.

Nigel then led them all in a prayer of thanksgiving, both for the food they were about to eat, and the amazing mercy God had bestowed upon this family. His final words, which he could not quite finish saying before, once again, being overcome with emotion was: "Thank you, Lord...for giving me back my boy." He walked over and embraced Cedric.

At this, of course, everyone was reaching for linen napkins themselves.

So, here it was the following day, Wednesday morning. After the festivities the night before, Lily had suggested they stay at the house, and not go back to their apartment at The Dakota. Charles was so tired, he readily agreed.

Now, they were all gathering together at the breakfast table. Everybody in their place, dressed appropriately. Quentin was serving coffee, although Charles could see his entire countenance was different, almost as though the task was a genuine delight. That's when Charles saw a copy of *The Times* folded under his arm.

As he watched, Quentin handed the newspaper to Nigel, but this time he did so with genuine enthusiasm. He even said, "Your paper, sir," with a tone as one giving a gift.

"Thank you, Quentin," Nigel said. "Can I take it by your demeanor that you've at least peaked at the headlines?"

Quentin smiled. "I have indeed, sir. This accounts for the smile on my face."

Charles could not wait to see what it said. He watched Nigel's eyes widen, and his smile quickly exceeded Quentin's, as he spread the paper out before him. "Of course, I will read this in its entirety. But you all must see the headline right away."

He turned it around and held it up:

SCANDAL AT CITY HALL

No Scandal At The Belmont After All

By Franklin Wainwright – Staff Writer

The headlines were not the only sensation. There was also a big black-and-white photograph set between the headline and the article showing a guilt-ridden Aldermen Ashcroft, and his bodyguard, walking in handcuffs into the police station.

"Well," Nigel said, "How about that?"

"Read it aloud, Father," Cedric said. "Please."

"Yes, Father," Lily said, "you can't possibly make us wait."

"All right, I suppose I can do that."

And this is what he read:

In a stunning turn of events that promises to send shockwaves through every corridor of political power in New York City, Head Alderman Herbert J. Ashcroft was arrested late yesterday afternoon at his Manhattan residence, along with his two longtime bodyguards, Joseph Gannon and Thomas Drake. All three men now stand accused in connection with the brutal murder of Ashcroft's only son, Reginald Ashcroft, whose lifeless body was discovered in the gymnasium of the Hotel Belmont twelve days ago.

District Attorney Arthur Tilford confirmed the arrest and stated that charges of first-degree murder, conspiracy to commit murder, and attempted murder are being filed. Indictments are expected to be formally handed down later today.

*Just days ago, this very newspaper carried the prevailing narrative that young Cedric Whitaker, son of renowned hotelier Nigel Whitaker, was the prime suspect in the killing. He had been indicted by a grand jury and released on bail pending trial. However, an extraordinary sequence of discoveries this past week—many of them unearthed through the tireless efforts of Charles Bennington, Whitaker's brother-in-law—**has completely exonerated Cedric of all involvement**. In fact, what now appears beyond question is that he was deliberately framed for the crime by the very men arrested yesterday.*

Among the most damning pieces of evidence now in the hands of authorities is a personal journal belonging to the deceased, Reggie Ashcroft. The final entry in that journal clearly names his father as the man he feared would take his life one day soon. The young Ashcroft had apparently been gathering evidence and preparing to testify before the Curran Commission, which has been investigating widespread political corruption in the city—corruption that now appears to reach deeper and higher than many dared imagine.

Additional evidence, including recovered fingerprints, eyewitness testimony, and forensic weapon testing, is now in the possession of the District Attorney's office. These and other details are expected to be made public as formal proceedings move forward.

To our reading public, a frank admission must now be made. We got it wrong.

In our pursuit of what appeared to be an open-and-shut case, we relied too heavily on early statements and unverified assumptions. In doing so, we misrepresented the truth and wrongly cast suspicion on an innocent young man. For this, we offer a sincere and unreserved apology—not only to Cedric Whitaker, but to his family and to the staff and proprietors of the Hotel Belmont, whose reputation suffered unfairly as a result.

In truth, the Whitakers are also victims themselves, caught up in the destructive crossfire of a father's greed and a city's political rot.

If these revelations were not shocking enough, the violence did not end with the arrests. Just hours before Ashcroft was taken into custody, his two bodyguards—acting on his orders

—stormed the tenth floor of the Hotel Belmont in an attempt to silence one of the key witnesses now prepared to testify against them. That witness, fortunately, was unharmed.

According to a statement released by DA Tilford, the wounded bodyguard has already agreed to testify in exchange for leniency, a development that will seal the case against Alderman Ashcroft and his surviving accomplice.

This newspaper will continue to follow this rapidly evolving story and provide further updates as new evidence emerges and formal proceedings begin.

For the longest time, no one said a word. Finally, Lily walked over, picked up the newspaper, and said, "I want to take just a moment to re-read one little section of this story." She found it and read this aloud: *However, an extraordinary sequence of discoveries this past week—many of them unearthed through the tireless efforts of Charles Bennington, Whitaker's brother-in-law—has completely exonerated Cedric of all involvement.*

"Charles," she said, now putting her arms around him from behind, "although at times you scared me half to death, I couldn't be more proud of you than I am right now."

"Here, here," Nigel said. "Well done, son. This family owes you a great deal."

"Yes, Charles," said Millicent. "We most certainly do." Tears filled her eyes.

Cedric got up and walked over to Charles. "Lily, do you mind?" He was asking her to back off Charles for a minute. "I need to hug my big brother myself. Charles, will you stand?"

He did. Cedric wrapped his arms around him and said through tears, "I owe you my life, Charles. There are no words I could possibly say to express how thankful I am that you're a part of this family. No one else could have—or would have—done what you've done for me."

47

2 ½ Weeks Later
Whitaker Mansion, Gramercy Park
Saturday Mid-Morning

Charles was relaxing out on the veranda by himself. After breakfast, Lily had dashed off somewhere with her mother, said she would be back soon. Charles was enjoying a fresh cup of coffee and some relative peace and quiet. On the table in front of him, sat the Saturday morning edition of *The Times*, the very same newspaper Nigel had read that morning.

The biggest thing Nigel had shared with everyone was not the headline spread across the front page, which Charles could plainly see:

ALL EUROPE NOW AT WAR –
American Tourists Stranded Abroad

And it was not the secondary stories that occupied the bottom half of the front page. All of them had to do with the latest news related to the Reggie Ashcroft murder case. Of course, they had already been indicted. The former Head Alderman, Reggie's father, had been denied bail and, obviously, had been stripped of his title. He along with the bodyguard, Gannon, who'd been arrested at his house had pled not guilty.

But all the evidence laid out in Wainwright's earlier stories convinced everyone of their guilt, especially now that the second bodyguard had agreed to testify against them to escape the chair. The newest story was that the Curran Commission had agreed to investigate all of the claims made in Reggie's journal about his father's crimes, sending many of Ashcroft former Associates heading for the hills.

But none of these things rated as the *biggest* thing Lily's father had shared with the family that morning at breakfast. That was reserved for something that was NOT in the newspaper that day. There was absolutely no mention of the Hotel Belmont anywhere to be found. He had the biggest smile on his face as he declared this, followed by an energetic, "Thank you, Lord."

Some other tidbits Nigel had shared about the hotel — all of them good — were that the crowds were returning to stay at the hotel in numbers similar to last summer. In fact, a large percentage of those who came requested a tour of the hotel gym. Not in consideration of their health or well-being but to see for themselves the infamous "*scene of the crime.*"

And already half of the conventions that had previously canceled had already rebooked their events, which had allowed Nigel to once again meet with the bank to reopen talks about expanding his conference facilities.

Cedric's life had mostly returned back to normal. The basketball coach had personally called him three days after Wainwright's article appeared, conveying to Cedric how that he and the team never believed for an instant that Cedric would ever have hurt Reggie, and he wanted to make sure Cedric planned to re-sign up for the team. As much as it blessed Cedric to hear this, the happier telephone call Cedric had received came from Amelia's father. She was the young lady Cedric had been smitten with before all this ugly business began.

Her father had apologized for his earlier request that Cedric stop courting his daughter. At the time, it was the only prudent thing to do, but now he was glad to rescind that request and personally invited Cedric to continue seeing Amelia at his earliest convenience. Cedric quickly asked if it might be convenient for him to come see her now. Which is where he was at the moment, taking her for a walk through Central Park.

Charles sipped his coffee and smiled as he reflected on his ice business. Fortunately, his name did not appear in any of the negative newspaper articles about the Belmont, so none of his clients canceled their service contracts. But since Wainwright had seen fit to mention Charles as the hero who broke open the murder investigation, Charles could trace back two new restaurants and one hotel who'd signed on as clients when they'd recognized Charles's name this past week, after he'd paid them a sales call.

Just then, Charles heard a slight commotion by the front door, then he heard Lily and her mother's voice talking excitedly about something. Lily said to Quentin, "Where's Charles? I need to see him right away."

He yelled out to her, as he stepped in her direction. "I'm out on the veranda, Love."

She all but ran toward him, threw her arms around him, and kissed him like she hadn't seen him in weeks.

"My, my, what is all this about?" he said.

"Oh, Charles, I have the best of news. I thought it was so for some time but didn't want to say anything until I was absolutely sure."

"The best of news? I like the sound of that." They had more than their fair share of late. "What is it?"

"Oh, Charles. I've just come home from seeing Mother's doctor, and he said it's definitely true. We're going to have a baby, Charles. Isn't it wonderful?" She hugged and kissed him again.

Without thinking he swung her around the room. "That *is* the best of news." He quickly and gently set her down. "I probably shouldn't have done that...in your condition, I mean."

Millicent walked up.

"Did you hear that, Mother?" Lily said. "He said *in my condition*. Isn't that wonderful?"

"Yes, Dear. It is." Turning to Charles. "Congratulations,

my boy. Your father-in-law is going to be over the moon when he hears of this. And we might as well hug, seeing as you're about to give me my first grandchild."

She reached out her arms and he gave her a hug. A wholly unfamiliar experience thus far.

"Thank you," he said as they parted. He was about to say "Millicent" but it didn't seem fitting. He wanted to say *Thank you, Mother*, but they apparently weren't quite there yet. For now, he'd content himself that they had hugged.

But maybe someday soon that, too, would change.

THANK you for reading ***Scandal At The Belmont***.

Hope you really enjoyed it. If you're not aware, *Scandal At The Belmont* is the Sequel to *The Perfect Stranger.* If you haven't read it, I'm sure you'd enjoy it. If you have, I've written another Novel I think you'd enjoy, called *What Follows After*. It's been a major bestseller with over 1,700 Amazon Reviews (4.7 Star Avg), and it won the prestigious Selah Award for "Best Historical Fiction" and was a Carol Award Finalist.

If you did enjoy ***Scandal At The Belmont***, please be a friend and leave a review on Amazon. When you leave even a short review, it goes a long way to help me pay my bills, because Amazon will show the book to more readers. I'd really appreciate your help with this.

If you liked the book but don't have time to write a short review, please consider leaving a 5-star rating. It's quick and easy and—believe it or not—Reader Ratings and Reviews help me to be able to keep writing new books. If you'd like to stay in touch, hear about movie updates of my books, new releases, special deals, and even book giveaways, join my Reader List. Just go to my website www.danwalshbooks.com, and scroll down a little. You'll be able to sign up right there on my Homepage (and even get to choose one of my Books for Free, as a Thank You).

Again, thanks again for reading, and I hope you'll keep reading more of my novels in the days ahead.

Dan Walsh

ACKNOWLEDGMENTS

There is really one person I absolutely must thank for helping to get *Scandal At The Belmont* into print. That's my wife, Cindi. Her editorial advice and input on this book--as with my other novels--was indispensable.

But I also need to thank my great proofreading team. They help to catch any of the typos or other little distracting errors in the manuscript before the book goes to print: Debbie Mahle, Jann Martin, Betty Vallery, Rachel Savage, and Terri Smith.

Dan Walsh

ABOUT THE AUTHOR

Dan was born in Philadelphia in 1957. His family moved down to Daytona Beach, Florida in 1965, when his father began to work with GE on the Apollo space program. That's where Dan grew up.

He married Cindi, the love of his life in 1976. They have 2 grown children and 6 grandchildren. After serving as a pastor for many years, Dan began writing fiction full-time in 2010. His bestselling novels have won numerous awards, including 3 ACFW Carol Awards (he was a finalist 6 times) and 5 Selah Awards. Four of Dan's novels were finalists for RT Reviews' Inspirational Book of the Year.

One of his novels, *The Unfinished Gift*, is being made into a full-length faith-based film. The rights to another, *The Reunion*, have been bought by the production company who made the hit movie "Reagan." They plan to turn it into a major, faith-based motion picture.

Follow him or contact him at www.danwalsh-books.com

www.ingramcontent.com/pod-product-compliance
Lightning Source LLC
Chambersburg PA
CBHW011514240626
47154CB00010B/3030

* 9 7 9 8 2 1 8 7 7 6 3 9 8 *